Scoot

by Christine Morgan

Published by:

Sabledrake Enterprises
2401 Chestnut St.
Everett, WA 98201
http://www.sabledrake.com
sabledrake@sabledrake.com

For everyone who rejects that "but GIRLS can't _____" crap.

Chapter 1

It really was a shame nobody would pay her to kill the skateboard kids.

They were everywhere, the grubby little bastards. To Jeanette, they were all skateboard kids whether they actually rode skateboards or not. In-line skates, those fancy little scooters, bikes, boards . . . if they were doing stunts and tricks with any of their wheeled toys, they were skateboard kids.

She would have done it happily, too, if there had been any money in it. Not much money, either. A pittance, really. If the city – or maybe a collection taken up by the local business owners – established something like a bounty, five bucks apiece even, it'd be worthwhile. Like they did for rat-catchers in certain third-world nations.

And, tell the truth and shame the devil, she was tempted even without any cash compensation. It'd be a public service. If she had a weapon, something rapid-fire and high-caliber, she could make the world a much better place in a matter of seconds.

That, though, would be messy, noisy, and attract all the wrong sort of attention. Even today's self-absorbed, oblivious pedestrians would be bound to remember a pixie-petite platinum blonde with a machine gun. Not that she'd hit any innocent bystanders. She wouldn't go *nuts* or anything. She'd choose her targets with the same caution and care as always, and she was naturally a superb shot.

Still, some things generally just were not done by decent people. Shooting up the general population was one of them. The police would insist on

getting involved. There would be some witnesses who might feel all civic-minded. It would be a hassle and a risk.

Yet, as she walked out of the Jensen Building in a crowd of business-suited lunch-lemmings, she saw the faces around her tighten in sneers of distaste at the rolling-clattering-whooping adolescent parade that met their eyes.

Maybe she was wrong in thinking they'd turn her in. Maybe they'd give her a round of applause. Hoist her up on their Armani-clad shoulders for a victory lap around Century Plaza. Give her the key to the city.

Wishful thinking.

In its original design conception, Century Plaza had been intended as a financial center, a place of influential movers and shakers. The buildings fronting on it were all towering edifices of the steel-and-glass variety, each trying to outdo its neighbor as a stunning example of modern architecture. The sun bouncing off all those windows turned the structures into glittering pillars of silver, gold, or smoked obsidian. The resulting sun-dazzle was blinding and the ambient temperature felt ten degrees higher than anyplace else in the city.

The Plaza itself, a square block of space closed to vehicle traffic, was an exciting arrangement of multi-level terraces, fountains, staircases, planters and large dynamic abstract sculptures of metal and stone. It would have been the perfect place for all those lunch-lemmings to brown-bag it, or scurry back from one of the surrounding bistros with take-away.

Would have been.

Trouble was, the skateboard kids had discovered Century Plaza almost as soon as it was completed. Never mind that there were no less than four skate parks in the greater downtown area. Skate parks apparently required safety gear like pads and helmets, which made them the domain of the helplessly uncool.

So here they were, caroming around, flipping their boards up onto the marble edges of fountains, leaping down flights of stairs. The ratcheting din of their various wheeled toys was nowhere near enough to drown out their conflicting music. Clearly, they believed in headphones about as much as they believed in helmets.

How they could be so quick and agile in those clothes boggled the mind. Most of them wore pants that looked three sizes too large, sagging and bagging down over enormous Frankenstein shoes. Oversized sports jerseys billowed like sails in a fickle wind, often exposing bare arms covered with homemade ink-pen tattoos of rock band logos or pot leaves.

A machine gun and thirty seconds. That was all she'd need.

Or would a sniper rifle be better? Up from one of the high windows, picking them off one by one.

No . . . both! That was the ticket.

She could take out a dozen with the sniper rifle before the rest realized that the wipe-outs hadn't been caused by a miscalculated stunt, and then switch to the machine gun and mow the rest down in the panic.

Not at lunchtime, though. During the morning or afternoon hours, the Plaza would be emptier. The only witnesses and bystanders she'd have to worry about would be the dwindling population of smoke-break refugees and the occasional deliveryman.

She was midway down the steps from the Jensen Building when a parent's nightmare on skates plunged through a nearby knot of suits. They scattered, losing their dignity in a tie-flapping, briefcase-waving flurry. The kid—a teenage girl with too much figure packed into too skimpy of an outfit—shrieked wild laughter as she zipped through their midst.

A woman in sober charcoal grey almost took a header into the fountain, whirled, and shouted, "Why aren't you in school?" after the skater-chick.

Applause. Victory lap. Key to the city.

Public service.

Jeanette shook her head and hefted her bag higher on her shoulder. She slid through the crowds like she belonged there. Trim and pretty in a forest-green suit and a cream-colored silk blouse.

Upscale. Competent. Professional.

She *was* all of those things. In her chosen field. Her chosen field just didn't happen to be law, business, or politics.

Except, in a certain way, it was all of them.

A tall skinny kid with hair dyed the unrealistic orange of Kraft macaroni and cheese shot past on a bike, aiming for one of the sculptures that was unfortunately in the shape of a large sloping crest like a wave. It was as good as an engraved invitation to these people.

The kid went up the curved side, perhaps meaning to do some tricky maneuver at the top, but blew it and crashed in a tangle of handlebars and long, gawky limbs. He lay there, groaning and bleeding from abraded knees and palms.

"Idiot," grumbled a man in a dark suit, giving the newspaper tucked under his arm a satisfied little rattle.

"Pff," another man agreed, with a downward scornful look as he stepped around the boy without slowing.

Jeanette was beginning to believe that she could draw a gun and start plugging the skateboard kids right here and right now. Then, when she was done, she could pass the hat for donations and walk away with enough for a

luxury cruise to the Caribbean.

Not that she needed the money. She could be on a flight to Bermuda tomorrow if she wanted. She had a nice house, an emerald-green convertible that still smelled showroom-new, and a television so big that it was like watching the Brobdingnagian Network. If it was only about the money, she could have retired long ago.

It was about . . . well, about doing a public service, wasn't it? And keeping busy. A career-minded woman had to keep herself busy.

Every now and then, police officers would swing through Century Plaza and encourage the skateboard kids to move along, but in Jeanette's observation, that was about as effective as waving a hand at flies buzzing over a dirty plate. They might disperse momentarily, but they'd be back a moment later as if nothing had ever happened.

What this situation called for was a fly swatter. Or a bug zapper.

She got through the open space without being run down, waited at a corner for the light to change, and checked her watch. Seven past twelve. She had eight minutes, the restaurant was a block up, and so far she didn't suspect anyone was following her. The fine hairs on the nape of her neck were not prickling with unease, and the adrenaline she felt speeding through her veins was the typical excitement of an impending job.

In a few minutes, she'd be seeing Rayburn.

That thought sent a different sort of prickle along the nape of her neck.

"Cool and professional, Jade," she admonished herself under her breath. "You know better."

No one was following. She was sure of it now. She was getting some looks; she got looks all the time. It was unavoidable. Men looked at women. Especially at small, slim, harmless-seeming blondes with soft white-blond hair and big green eyes. But these weren't the wrong sort of looks. Not the "she fell for it; here's our chance to eliminate her" looks, or the "hey, that could be the lady from the police sketch" ones that could lead to a call to any FBI tip line. They weren't thinking looks. Thinking looks were bad.

Fantasizing looks, on the other hand . . . well, she wasn't overjoyed about the notion that she might be prancing through some sleazy young lawyer's or perverted old banker's daydream, but she could live with it.

The Stag and Hound tried to present itself as an Olde English style pub, with lots of dark wood and fox-hunting prints. The specials included beer-battered fish and chips, bangers-and-mash, and shepherd's pie. The waitresses all wore white blouses, red corsets with black laces, black skirts, and silly little lace-trimmed caps.

Jeanette waited behind a quartet, three men and one woman, who seemed to be together but who were each conducting separate calls on cell phones. When it was her turn, she said, "Table for Dufarge, please."

The hostess picked up a leather-bound menu with a gold tassel dangling down from it, and led her toward the back of the pub. In the bar, where twenty different kinds of ale and lager were available, the TV was turned to a soccer game and the air was low and thick with smoke.

Dufarge. One of Rayburn's jokes, not a particularly funny one. Madame Dufarge had been one of the guillotine-hags of the French Revolution. Off with their heads.

The table was in a booth, tucked in a corner by a window. Jeanette sat down with her back to the wall, under a framed print showing a horse-back mounted hunting party galloping through a foggy meadow. She set her shoulderbag on the windowsill, slipping a hand into it so that she would be ready to switch on her cunning miniature tape recorder.

Paranoia or preparedness . . . toe-may-toe, toe-mah-toe. Either way, it had kept her alive this long.

And here he came. If she'd thought that she blended in well with the crowd, just another lunch-lemming, Rayburn stood out, and he did it on purpose.

Tall and well-built, he had a full head of black hair just beginning to go silver, a toothpaste-commercial smile, and enough of a resemblance to Pierce Brosnan that he turned heads. He knew it, too, and Jeanette was willing to bet that he made the most of it.

The hostess, who had been properly courteous and efficient when dealing with Jeanette, went all fluttery and girlish as she escorted Rayburn to the booth. She stopped short of 'dropping' his menu and having to bend way down to retrieve it, but her interest couldn't have been more apparent if she'd climbed right into his lap.

Rayburn wore a crisp suit the color of pewter, and had chosen to defy business-attire convention by pairing it not with a red power tie, but an iridescent one that seemed to shift from emerald to sapphire to amethyst depending on how the light struck its glossy fabric. He carried a calfskin briefcase that might have cost as much as a car.

A plain gold band glinted on his left hand. A wedding ring, but he had once mentioned to Jeanette that he was a widower for almost twenty years. He had a grown daughter, an Irish Setter, a skewed sense of humor, and that was about all she knew.

Jeanette took a mental deep breath as she pressed the "Record" button. He *was* a handsome son of a bitch. There were times when she thought she

wouldn't mind climbing right into his lap herself, so she couldn't really blame the hostess. Wouldn't do, though, to mix business with pleasure.

Still, it didn't hurt to enjoy the scenery. Rayburn was much more scenic than Fletcher or Christopher, the other men she primarily dealt with in her association with the Company. Fletcher, a florid, beefy older man, would have fit in with the three-martini crowd. Christopher, younger and too twitchy to last long in this line of work, preferred to arrange meetings in more suburban venues like shopping mall food courts or fast-food places.

The hostess took their drink orders – Guinness for him, hot tea with honey and lemon for her – and left, though not without a backward glance or two.

"The fish and chips are very good here," he said. "Hungry?"

"Yes, all right."

His cobalt-blue eyes crinkled at the corners, showing the perfect degree of maturity and amusement. "How've you been, Jade?"

"Keeping out of trouble."

"You must be getting bored with that by now."

"I might," she said.

"Glad to hear it."

"Don't think that because I'm bored, I'll work cheap," Jeanette said.

"I know you better than that."

How well *did* he know her? That was the question. How much did they really know, Rayburn and Fletcher and Christopher and their nameless, faceless bosses? They knew how to contact her, and she wouldn't be surprised to learn that they knew where she lived. Had they gone poking into her past? It didn't much matter if they had; all of that was behind her now.

She had no close friends anymore, no relatives, no significant other. Never been married, never had kids. She didn't own a dog, cat, or goldfish. There was no living being that they could use against her if they decided that they wanted to put some pressure on her.

Besides, why would they? She had never crossed them, never let them down, never given them any reason to want to get rid of her. And if they ever decided that they did, well, 'Jade' had a few secrets stored away herself. Insurance. Like nuts for a long winter.

The hostess must have been reluctantly called back to her duties at the front of the pub, because a waitress brought their beverages, recited the specials, and jotted down two orders of fish and chips. She even performed these duties without slobbering all over Rayburn.

When she was gone, Jeanette turned to him with an expectant look. "So,

10

what do you have for me?"

His eyes crinkled again. "Are we talking work, or play?"

"Work," she said, trying to quell an unprofessional flutter.

"Pity." He snapped open the expensive briefcase and took out a thick manila envelope, the kind padded on the inside with a layer of bubble wrap.

To outward appearances, she knew, this would merely seem to be one of two things, either of which were being repeated hundreds of times over in the vicinity of Century Plaza this very instant. Either a legitimate business lunch, or an affair masquerading as a business lunch.

Well, but it *was* business.

"You'll like this one," Rayburn said, sliding the padded envelope across the table to her. "It's practically an antique, but in beautiful condition."

"Is it loaded?"

Chapter 2

"The man's a collector," Rayburn explained as their lunch arrived. "Ah. See, I told you. Wonderful fish and chips."

The generous slabs of golden, crunchy batter-fried fish rested atop heaps of steak-cut French fries, which had been dusted with a seasoned salt that was perhaps not entirely Olde English. It smelled heavenly and tasted better.

"A collector," Jade prompted when the waitress had moved on.

"History buff. Keeps everything in his collection in perfect working order. If you'd rather, I might be able to get you a sword or a knife instead, but I didn't think that would be your style. You just don't have that hack-and-slash *Kill Bill* air about you."

"You thought right," she said, picking up the envelope and feeling the familiar weight and heft. "How old is it?"

"I'm not entirely sure, but it's museum-quality. Ivory-handled."

"And you're confident it will do the job?" She regarded him from beneath arched brows. "Old guns aren't the most reliable. If I didn't know better, I might think I was being set up."

He looked genuinely wounded, which gave him an even more appealing little-boy quality, the sort of look that could make most women want to simultaneously mother him and seduce him. The flip side of Oedipus . . . was there such a thing as a Jocasta complex?

"We regard you as one of our most valuable associates, Jade," he said. "A set-up? Not hardly. You can bet your lucky charm on that."

She touched her necklace in a habitual gesture. It, as well as her green eyes and cool, hard demeanor, had gotten her the nickname . . . code name . . . working name . . . whatever you wanted to call it. A fine gold chain and a milky-green pendant carved in the shape of a sinuous Oriental dragon.

It wasn't a family heirloom or gift from a lover or anything sentimental like that. Only something she'd bought in a Chinatown gift shop on a trip to San Francisco. For Deirdre's bridal shower, that had been . . . five college girls on a crazy road trip because Deirdre had wanted to see male strippers and female impersonators and drink rainbow-hued rum drinks from tall glasses shaped like naked ladies.

Three years after the wedding, almost to the day, Deirdre had offered Jeanette five thousand dollars to arrange an accident for her husband.

"You don't need to reassure me," she said to Rayburn, putting the envelope into her shoulderbag beside the little tape player. "What else?"

Into the briefcase he went again, this time producing a folder stuffed with photos and sheets of paper. She flipped it open and saw a color 8x10 of a young man with wavy blond hair, the sort of tan that used to be considered healthy but nowadays was a walking ad for skin cancer. His smile couldn't rival Rayburn's in the perfect white and straight department, but it dimpled. A cute smile. A cute guy.

The next photo showed the same cute guy shirtless on a sailboat, and Jeanette took a moment to admire his sculpted, hairless chest and lean, chiseled abs. He looked disgustingly fit and athletic. Like one of the perfect specimens usually seen hawking exercise gear on late-night infomercials.

"What'd he do?" she asked. "Is it personal?"

"Tsk, tsk, Jade," scolded Rayburn. "I thought you didn't care about that."

"You know I generally handle corporate cases," she said, and had to close the folder as the waitress came back to ask if everything was to their satisfaction.

"Very much so, although I wouldn't say no to another Guinness," Rayburn said, tapping the rim of his empty glass.

"And more hot water," Jeanette said.

"What makes you think this isn't corporate?" he asked once the waitress had gone.

"He doesn't look like a businessman."

"He's on a sailboat with his shirt off. Donald Trump wouldn't look like a businessman on a sailboat with his shirt off."

"Spare me the mental image, please."

"Besides, you've bent that rule before."

"But I don't like it," she said. "The personal cases are the ugliest ones, and the ones where someone is most likely to crack. Remorse. You never see any remorse when it's politics, when it's business, when it's all about profit and not about emotion."

"Profound," Rayburn said, sounding unimpressed by her philosophy. "But for you, it *is* all about profit no matter the motive. And speaking of profit . . ."

He set another sealed envelope on the table, this one padded not by bubble wrap but by a thick pile of cash.

"What I meant was," she said, eyeballing the envelope and doing some mental math, "that the risk of the buyer blabbing about the deal goes way up when it's personal."

"That's why the fee goes way up."

"How far up?"

"Double."

She thought again about the athletic blond guy on the sailboat. Someone really must want him dead if they were willing to double her usual fee. What could a guy like that have done to make such an enemy? Did he stand in the way of a fat inheritance? Did some rival for a girlfriend want him out of the way?

"Double," she mused.

"A quarter of it now," Rayburn said, nudging the envelope toward her. "The rest on completion, everybody sing along, you all know the words."

Jeanette blew out a breath that was almost a whistle. She could feel the cables of her resolve giving way one by one. It was a lot of money. Not that she needed it; she could keep herself comfortably for a long time even if she never took another job.

But it was a lot of money.

And the blond guy . . . maybe it wasn't emotional after all. Maybe it was as clinical and detached as the others. Purely business, so sorry, you know how it goes. Nothing personal. No offense. So sorry, old bean, that's the way the cookie crumbles.

The less she knew about that end of things, the better. She didn't *need* to know. All knowing did was clutter up her head. It wasn't her job to decide whether any given person deserved it or not.

Maybe the blond guy was a complete shit. Maybe he liked little kids in the wrong way, and had the bucks to keep it quiet. Maybe he was a contender for some trophy or big expensive endorsement deal and a competitor wanted him eliminated. There were plenty of reasons, plenty of possibilities. None of which concerned her.

"Fine," she said. "I'll take the job."

Rayburn broke into a winning smile that Pierce Brosnan could have used to great effect on every leading lady from Famke to Halle to Selma. "Good," he said.

And the hell of it was, Jeanette realized as she put the money and the folder into her purse alongside the envelope with the gun, that a large part of her reason for accepting was because she didn't want to let him down. Didn't want him to go back and report to his employers that 'Jade' was developing principles, or getting cold feet. That maybe 'Jade' wasn't cut out for this kind of work after all . . . and that if she was weakening, if she was going soft, she might become a risk.

Oh, it was the money and the pride and the self-preservation, all stacked up against the life of one hunky blond guy with a sailboat. Was it her fault that she liked her work?

She and Rayburn ate fish and chips and carried on their pretense of a typical business lunch. She left the tape running because she never knew if something of interest might be said. Something of value, either now or later. Every little nugget of information she could put away about Rayburn or any of the people he worked with might some day come in handy.

Jeanette would wait until she was home to go over all the details in the folder, which would tell her the things about her target she would need to know. His name and his address, yes, but also as much about his routines and habits as Rayburn's sources had been able to gather. Where he was likely to be and when. It would be up to her to choose the exact place and time, though she was also provided with a list of no-no's and particulars.

Shot with a gun from his own collection. A man that young, that seemingly outdoorsy, who also collected old weapons. Interesting. Not her concern, but interesting all the same.

But maybe it could become her concern, if she wasn't careful. He was athletic and collected weapons . . . did he target shoot? Hunt? Practice martial arts? Fence, even?

All that would be in the folder. She'd take her time and do this right. Do this right, like she always did.

Not like that first time.

Sipping her tea, she caught a brief shiver and felt her cheeks turn warm with the memory. What a debacle.

Rayburn noticed. "Jade? Something the matter?"

"No," she said.

That first time, a disaster!

She looked back on it now the way that a successful novelist might look back on a first faltering, hackneyed attempt at a book. With cringing embarrassment and a sort of awful contrary defiance. It had been clumsy, stupid, full of mistakes. But it had put her on this path, had gotten her where she was today, so she couldn't complain all that much.

She'd only been in high school, for crying out loud.

Back then – fifteen years ago, had it been that long? – there hadn't been any questions about whether it was personal or business. It was personal all the way, deeply and intensely personal. She hadn't been hired, she hadn't been paid.

And he had deserved it.

Kenny Murphy. The prick.

When Lisa-Beth Perkins had started dating him, Jeanette and all her other friends had tried to talk her out of it. Kenny was a jerk, a thoughtless selfish creep, a poser. He would try to pressure Lisa-Beth into sex, they told her. Never mind her oft-stated desire to wait for her wedding night. He would hurt her feelings and break her heart if she didn't wise up and dump him, they predicted.

Oh, they'd had no idea. Only later, when a sobbing Lisa-Beth told them the whole story, had they really seen Kenny Murphy for what he was.

He hadn't been content with pressuring her to put out, but had slipped something into her drink at a party – one of the so-called "date-rape" drugs that had been new back then but had lately become almost as common a ploy as "if you really loved me" in the male arsenal.

Lisa-Beth had awakened the next morning sore, groggy and sticky, with no memory of the previous night. Rather than confess to any of her friends what she feared had happened, she kept silent.

Kenny dumped her that very day, claiming he felt 'smothered' and that they 'should see other people' and that he wanted to 'still be friends.' Two months later, the miserable Lisa-Beth had gotten an early and very much unwelcome Christmas present when she found out she was pregnant.

When she told Kenny, clinging to some dim and desperate hope that it might get them back together, he had laughed. He sneeringly informed her that three of his buddies had their fun with her that night, too, so she couldn't be sure which of them was the father. If she accused them all, he'd said, she would look like the biggest tramp in the history of the world.

Only after this shattering revelation had Lisa-Beth finally broken down and told her friends everything. Sherry, being a few months older and the most worldly of the quartet, had taken Lisa-Beth to a clinic for an abortion.

Ashley spun the creative lies they told Lisa-Beth's parents.
And Jeanette killed Kenny Murphy.

Chapter 3

The murder had gone so badly it was a miracle she'd gotten away with it. She hadn't planned, hadn't thought anything beyond how Kenny had hurt Lisa-Beth and was going to pay. She'd never even contemplated killing anyone before and expected it would be like in the movies.

It wasn't anything like the movies.

In the movies, she could have simply walked up behind him as he bent into the engine of his hotrod, punched her cousin's old pocket knife into his back, and Kenny would have arched his spine and gone, "Aargh!" and collapsed and died.

No such luck in real life. The tip skidded off his shoulderblade, snagged in his sweater, and clattered to the oil-stained garage floor. Kenny let out a holler, more of surprise than pain – though it had to have hurt; there was blood – and started to turn and straighten up.

Panicked, Jeanette had done the only thing she could think of. She seized the raised hood of his car and knocked the support away with her elbow. Then, using all of her strength, she'd slammed the hood down on Kenny. The edge cut into the back of his scalp, shedding a spray of blood. He went face-first into the engine with a grunt, trying and failing to get his right hand up in time to defend himself.

She'd raised the hood and slammed it again, totally beyond thought. The underside met the rounded back of Kenny's skull with a hollow *k-ponk!* sound, denting the metal and pile-driving his forehead into the engine block. Dazed, he slumped there with his left hand dangling and twitching.

The knife had been within sight, but Jeanette didn't try to reach for it. The moment she did, she knew that this would turn out to be like the movies after all. No matter how out of it Kenny seemed, he would spring up and lunge at her. She must have looked like a crazywoman trying to . . . to clap him to death as she repeatedly raised and slammed the hood on Kenny's head, shoulders, and upper torso.

Eventually, she stopped, arms aching, chest heaving, and watched him to see if he moved. Kenny only hung there, slack, his knees buckled and his one visible arm as limp as that of a drowning victim.

The noise had been horrendous. Wiping sweat from her brow despite the chill in the air, Jeanette turned, expecting to see the entire neighborhood gathered in the open garage door and staring in at her in openmouthed shock. But the driveway and the street at the end of it had been empty of everything but a few spinning flakes of falling snow.

"Kenny?" she had said, barely recognizing herself in the panting, uncertain voice.

He hadn't stirred. As her ears quit ringing, she heard the slow, syrupy patter of blood draining through the engine. When she crouched – carefully, still thinking he might suddenly revive – she had seen a spreading puddle that was *not* an oil leak.

Jeanette raised the hood one final time, saw what was left of Kenny Murphy's head, and barely made it outside in a stumbling, staggering run before throwing up into Mrs. Murphy's snow-covered flowerbed.

Only then, as she'd been hunched and shaking in the aftermath, had she realized what she had done. He was dead. He was dead and she had killed him.

She'd done it for Lisa-Beth, but some cold and rational inner voice spoke up and told her that she had to think of herself now. Even if one of her best friends was worth going to jail for, Kenny certainly wasn't.

So, though the last thing in the world she had wanted to do was to go back into that garage, she had done it. She'd picked up the knife – the only reason she'd had the forethought to wear gloves had nothing to do with fingerprints and everything to do with it being December – and searched around for a way to cover up her crime.

The garage itself provided the answer. Its ceiling was crisscrossed with old rafters crammed to capacity with generations of Murphy family leftovers. She saw old footlockers, crates that might've held dishes or pots and pans, a metal ice chest that had to date back to the 1960's, the poles and chains of a disassembled porch swing, all kinds of stuff.

All kinds of *heavy* stuff.

19

With the long wooden handle of a snow shovel, Jeanette jabbed and poked up into the rafters. She felt absurdly like someone trying to squish a bug in a high corner.

But at last, she'd found a good spot and given a big push. The piles shifted, started to slide, and then she had leaped backward as the contents of the rafters came down in a crashing avalanche on top of the car, on top of Kenny.

She had seen — she would never forget it, not if she lived to be a hundred and fifty — his legs give one boneless, convulsive flailing kick and his left arm fly upward as if in surprise. Then she couldn't bear to see any more, and had run back down the driveway and all the way home.

Some devil's luck must have been with her that night. The snow had continued falling steadily for hours, so that by the time Kenny's parents and younger brother and sister came home from a holiday party, the smooth white fall had blanketed away her tracks.

The Murphys made an extremely gruesome discovery in the garage that night. The police came and determined that something in the rafters must have shifted and brought the rest down, crushing Kenny as he bent under the hood to work on the car.

He might even, they'd theorized, have been trapped alive in the wreckage for a while, judging by the scrapes on his face from struggling against unyielding metal.

Jeanette had always wondered about the shallow wound in his back, where she had initially stuck him with the knife. Had it been explained away as having been caused by some of the falling debris? A pole from the porch swing, perhaps, striking him in the shoulder? Or had it been overlooked entirely in the face of his other, more overwhelming injuries?

She'd never found out, and of course there was no good way to ask. The ugly incident had been categorized as a terrible accident. It even made the 'tragic irony' section of the local news.

The ones she'd really felt bad for in the whole mess were Kenny's younger brother and sister, who'd had to witness their father hurling aside footlockers like a madman, and heard their mother's screams as she saw what was left of her oldest child.

With a start, Jeanette realized that she had been sitting for several minutes without saying a word, poking at the half-eaten fish and chips that no longer held any temptation to her appetite.

Rayburn was regarding her quizzically across the table. "Jade? Are you all right?"

"Sorry," she said, and cleared her throat. "Sorry. I was . . . thinking."

"Not about anything good, I'm guessing," he said. "You're white as a sheet, and your hands are shaking."

"My hands don't shake," she said, though as she looked down at them she saw they were making a liar of her. She set down her fork and folded her hands together. They felt as icy as they had, gloves or no gloves, on that long-ago December night.

To her astonishment, Rayburn reached across the table and covered her small, cold, trembling hands with one of his. It was the first time he had ever purposefully touched her, and she was startled at how warm and strong his grip felt.

"Why not think about something else?" he suggested in a low voice that had the texture of rough velvet.

"Like what?" she asked.

"Like dinner some time." His gaze, direct and deep blue, held hers.

"Dinner?"

"Not a meeting. Not business. Very personal."

"I . . . I don't think that would be a very good idea."

"Hell," Rayburn said, with a slanted grin more Harrison Ford than Pierce Brosnan, "I *know* it isn't. But think about it anyway."

With that, he got up while she was still trying to shift gears in her startled mind. He left enough cash on the table to cover the check and a generous tip, and then he was gone.

Jeanette gave her head a quick shake, not quite able to believe what had just happened. Had Rayburn touched her? Asked her to have dinner with him? She didn't even know his first name.

Though, she supposed with an inner chuckle, she knew what he did for a living, and what kind of money he made.

A glance at her watch showed her that it was almost one-thirty. The lunch-lemmings would be already back in their offices or headed that way. She smiled at the waitress and the hostess as she left the Stag and Hound, and joined the last few stragglers bound for Century Plaza.

Although she did not have what anyone could call a nine-to-five job, she kept an office in the Jensen Building for days such as this when work and meetings brought her into the heart of the city. It was helpful, too, to have an address and phone number she could put on her bogus business cards – *J. Kurrell, Consulting*, the cards read – along with an e-mail address. Any infrequent phone calls were routed to voice mail.

She liked having the office. It wasn't much, just two rooms, a reception

area and an inner sanctum, but she'd had it nicely decorated and it was comfortable. She enjoyed being in there, knowing that the building all around her was full of workaday drones while she surfed the Internet on her laptop computer, browsing the online auction sites for things she would never buy.

Today, the office might be a good place to sit and think about what Rayburn had said, there at the end of lunch. She could listen to him again on tape, and determine whether or not she had read too much – or too little – into his words and the tone of his voice.

The skateboard kids were still in the Plaza, careening around, risking life and limb with their wheeled acrobatics. One, on a black skateboard with electric-blue wheels, shot past Jeanette so fast she felt the breeze. She jerked back, a sharp retort rising to her lips, but caught herself before she said anything.

The kid sped onward, baggy many-pocketed cargo pants drooping, scarlet nylon windbreaker rippling. Jeanette turned to watch, hoping to see a headlong collision with a raised marble bench around a fountain that cascaded water from three bronze bowls into a basin full of pitched good-luck pennies. In her mind's eye, she saw the kid hit the bench, flip end over end into the hard bronze edges of the bowls, and go splash into the water with a skull fracture or broken neck.

No such luck. The kid, who looked about thirteen in a baseball cap with the brim turned backwards, stuck one foot out almost casually, pivoted on it, hopped the skateboard up onto the marble, slid along it for a good six or seven feet, and dropped back down, now facing in Jeanette's direction again. Propelling along, one leg going push-push-push, the kid rocketed toward her.

Jeanette stepped back, but not far enough. Before she knew it, she was knocked on her butt in the middle of Century Plaza. Her right arm felt yanked out of its socket, and a split second later she realized why.

The skateboard kid had grabbed her purse. Had *snatched* her purse, and was even now speeding away with the prize.

Her purse . . . and everything in it.

Chapter 4

"Hey, lady, you okay?"

"He stole her purse, did you see that?"

"Anybody get which way he went?"

"I'll call the police."

"No!" Jeanette was on her feet in a flash.

She yanked at the hem of her skirt, which had ridden up most of the way to her waist. Her pantyhose were run in long ladders down the backs of both thighs and the heel of her left hand was scraped raw from where she'd instinctively flung it out to try and break her fall.

The people who had come rushing around her moved back, but they still formed a curious gawking ring. Jeanette couldn't see over or past their heads, and cursed her lack of height as she craned her neck trying to see the skateboard kid.

Gone. Gone like a damned mirage.

"Ma'am? Did he hurt you?" This from a kindly-faced older gent with finespun white hair, no doubt in reality the ruthless president of some cutthroat board of directors.

Cell phones had materialized in many hands – had, most likely, already been in hand. Several had fingers poised to dial 911.

"My purse," Jeanette said. Her fists clenched, causing a stinging line of pain across the scrape. "Which way did he go?"

"That way," a severe black woman in a burgundy linen suit said. "Went

right past me and almost ran me down."

"Miss, let me call the police," said the man who'd first made the offer. He was tall and youngish and prematurely balding, bespectacled. He held out his phone to her with the air of a knight pledging his sword and honor to a damsel in distress.

A cluster of other skateboard kids had gathered a short distance away, observing developments. Some were snickering. Others had the sullen, wary look of those ready to be blamed for everything.

Jeanette shoved through her protective circle of lunch-lemmings and stormed toward them. They saw her coming, and for an instant their snickers and sulks were replaced by alarmed surprise.

"Who was that kid?" she demanded of the nearest.

Up close, he was not a kid at all but a hulking hairy twenty-something Bigfoot with long stringy dark-red hair, unshaven bristles on his chin and rusty tufts bursting from the collar of his old faded Guns & Roses tee shirt. A bike leaned against the hip of his chain-draped black faux-leather pants. A hand that was all scabbed knuckles and clunky silver death's head rings rested on the handlebars. The smells of sweat, B.O., stale pot smoke and McDonald's grease seemed to hang around him in a cloud.

Bigfoot topped Jeanette by over a foot and was more than double her weight, but the furious, fearless way she got right up in his face caught him totally off guard. "Fuck'f I know," he mumbled.

"What about the rest of you?" She scanned them, feeling like green sparks must be snapping from her eyes.

A skinny black kid, whose pants hung down so far that his plaid boxer-briefs were exposed, scratched the undershelf of his chin. A porky Goth chick with hair dyed the black and pink of a box of Good-n-Plenty was suddenly fascinated with her fingernails – blood red, and painted with tiny silver ankhs. A dark-haired teenager who might've been good-looking if his complexion had not been in revolt glared down at his unlaced sneakers and said something under his breath that Jeanette thought might have been the C-word.

It was as if the line of battle had been drawn in Century Plaza. Finally, for once, the opposing forces were clearly defined and facing each other down.

On one side, the lunch-lemmings stood together in their suits, with their briefcases and cell phones and power ties, haughty with righteous indignation.

On the other side were the skateboard kids, in their defensive, angry cluster. They shot venomous looks at the older crowd.

Jeanette hated them all, and if she'd *had* that machine gun right here and now, she might have chopped every single one of them, lunch-lemming and

24

skateboard kid alike, into mincemeat where they stood.

But she didn't have a machine gun. She didn't have a gun at all.

The purse snatcher had everything.

Call the police? And tell them what, exactly? That her purse had been stolen, and it just happened to contain an envelope of cash, a firearm, and a folder of information that might as well have had "assassination instructions" printed on the cover?

Exhaling a long breath between tight lips, she turned away from the skateboard kids. If she had to look at their willfully stupid, stubborn, drug-using, self-indulgent bratty faces any longer, she would lose it.

She stalked back to the other side. Forced a smile for the benefit of her balding would-be Galahad. "Could I please borrow your phone?"

He gave it to her, now with the air of a knight whose lady-love has conferred upon him a silken scarf or other token of her favor before the big joust.

"Are you sure you're not hurt?" the kindly older gent asked. "I saw that miscreant knock into you."

"A few scratches," she said, showing the heel of her left hand.

"Did you have much in there?" asked the burgundy-suited black lady. "I had mine taken a few months ago. All my credit cards, my phone, everything. Best call the credit card company. And a locksmith while you're at it, because now that no-good punk will have your keys and your address."

"Ah, he'll just grab the cash and plastic, and throw the purse in a trashcan somewhere," another man said.

Past them, Jeanette saw that the skateboard kids had dispersed. Slunk away like the guilty scavenging vermin that they were. Rats and roaches and flies. Scavengers.

Now that the immediate drama had passed, the eager lemmings were reluctant to break up and go away, though it was no doubt high time they were back in their offices and cubicles. It seemed like everybody had a purse-snatching story, and the matter was swiftly turning into a bizarre competition for worst place.

"— wife had all the kids' pictures, the grandkids, too —"

"— been to the bank to withdraw it in cash, twenty-three thousand dollars —"

"— gorgeous suede, the *perfect* match to those boots —"

"Excuse me," Jeanette said with a polite smile, pointing to Galahad's phone. She moved away, turned, and examined the keypad while her mind raced, raced.

She didn't keep her real I.D. in that purse, not when she knew she'd be

going out on a job meeting with Rayburn or one of his associates. That was her working purse, chosen specifically because it was roomy enough to hold the tape recorder as well as large folders and envelopes and whatever sort of weapon her employers decided to provide for each new job.

Her personal keys, thank God, were in the desk drawer of her office. So was her *real* purse, the bag that was really just a fat wallet with a long clip-on strap and delusions of grandeur.

The magnetic key-card to the office itself, thank God again, was in the pocket of her forest green blazer. She had dropped it in there without thinking about it, and was grateful now. She had troubles enough without worrying about that.

What to do, though? Who to call? She couldn't call the cops . . . but if she didn't, Galahad might notice that the police number failed to turn up in his "numbers called" log.

How had she let this happen?

Shit!

Hysteria welled, and Jeanette quashed it.

One thing at a time. One problem at a time.

God, but how could she have been so dumb? She'd gotten thinking about Kenny and Lisa-Beth, and that had rattled her composure badly enough, but then to have Rayburn rattle her even more by asking her to think about dinner with him . . . she hadn't been focused on her surroundings at all on the way back, hadn't gotten that little warning prickle when the skateboard kid had sped by. Her instincts, usually so keen, had been dulled, and now look at this mess!

Jeanette turned back to Galahad, who remained hovering hopefully nearby. Manufacturing a tremulous smile, she handed the phone back to him.

"I'm sorry," she said, and hitched in her breath. "I . . . I'll call them from upstairs. I just need . . . a few minutes. To . . . to . . ."

She hated to do it, hated to make even a pretense of weakness. But as his hazel eyes went all soft and sympathetic, she knew it had been the right move. He'd look at her and see a little ethereal pixie-blonde, small and vulnerable, and forget or dismiss the fearless way she had marched straight up to Bigfoot.

"I'll walk you in," he said. "Where are you going?"

"No, that's all right. You've been more than helpful already. And . . ." she glanced at her watch and winced. "And it's almost two."

"It's really no trouble."

Of course, it wasn't. He might already be far enough along in his fantasy to be telling the grandkids how they'd met, how he'd consoled her after the

purse-snatching and walked her safely back to her office, how he'd asked her to coffee and then dinner and then the ring, the wedding, the house, the children . . .

Somehow, she fended off all his good intentions and the solicitousness of the others, and made her way back to the Jensen Building on her own. People took sidelong looks at her in the lobby and the elevator. She thought it was because of her crumpled skirt, the runs in her pantyhose or her disarranged hair.

But then, with a dull flush mounting in her cheeks, she remembered all that glass. All those windows. Not *everyone* could have been neglecting work to gaze serenely out at the scene in Century Plaza below, but dozens of people might still have witnessed her being sent skidding like a tiddlywink, and the skateboard kid's triumphant exit with her purse.

Her office had never been such a welcome sight. She closed the door, crossed the reception area's dusty-plum carpeting without switching on any lights – more than enough natural light came in to let her avoid the neat arrangement of chairs, coffee table, end tables, and loveseat – and went into the inner room. There was a closet-sized bathroom with a commode and a sink, where Jeanette did flip the light switch, and grimaced as she saw herself in the mirror.

She scrubbed her hands, chewing her bottom lip as antibacterial soap burned into the scrape like a dousing of acid. This made her start bleeding again, so she held a square of folded toilet tissue against the wound until it was only seeping. She kept a supplementary cosmetic bag on the bathroom shelf for emergency touch-ups, and fixed her hair and face.

Stepping out of her shoes, she shed the pantyhose and threw them in the wastepaper basket. She'd look strange without them, but the runs were more noticeable than bare legs would be . . . and at least her legs were shaved. She couldn't do much about the wrinkles in the skirt.

With the worst of the damage repaired, she met her own jade-green gaze and asked herself the question that had been beating in her head like a pulse.

"What am I going to tell Rayburn?"

Chapter 5

Out of Century Plaza, the purse swinging.

Big purse, too, and heavy. Like it was packed with lead weights.

Scoot's luck, it'd be full of books on tax law or binders of corporate policies and procedures.

But you never knew. There might be good stuff. Stuff that was worth some money. Once, Scoot found a velvet ring box in the bottom of a scruffy denim purse, and the diamond-and-onyx baby inside had fetched six hundred bucks.

And even if this buttercream-leather shoulderbag number turned out to be a dud, that wasn't the point. The point was the *taking*. The rush, the thrill, the excitement. The conquest. Taking, not having.

People jumped out of the way, some shouting after Scoot, shouting things like "Watch where you're going, asshole!" as Scoot sped down 10th Street and hung a hard right onto Prewett.

The electric blue wheels hummed, juddering over the grooves in the concrete. Scoot's feet rode firm but easy on the board's fiberglass surface, which was glossy black and airbrushed with blue-white lightning bolts.

Scoot reached into the deep windbreaker pocket and touched the slick, somehow greasy surface of a wadded-up black plastic garbage bag. Tucked in there with it was a bundle the size of a tennis ball, that would unfold into a roomy duffel bag. Collapsible. Space-age.

Out with the garbage bag. Snap-flutter it open, and stuff in the purse.

Little old lady at twelve o'clock!

Scoot's reflexes took over. Swerve and pivot, skimming past with inches to spare, close enough to see the details of the weave in the cardigan stretched over the dowager's hump as the little old lady crept along hunched over her walker.

And then past, into the intersection. Horns blaring. More shouts, and rude gestures jabbed skyward. "Asshole!" again. That was the most common of the unfriendly terms applied to Scoot on any given day. "Jerk" and "Shithead" made the list, too. Once, only once, had Scoot been called a "hooligan." That had been a proud day.

Hooligan.

Kewl.

With the purse hidden in the bag, it looked like nothing more than a bundle of dirty laundry, or maybe scrounged cans and bottles bound for recycling. The one thing it did not look like was a purse, because that of course would be suspicious. A kid like Scoot, with a fancy shoulderbag?

The wail of a siren sent Scoot's pulse rate through the roof, but it was an ambulance and not the cops, an ambulance cutting through traffic.

No cops, no cops yet. And now Century Plaza was three blocks in Scoot's wake, the business high-rises having given way to the seedier urban sprawl.

Prewett was a main thoroughfare, a state highway that still had the number designation. It was a long gaudy row of car lots, motels, fast food joints, gas stations and chain stores. During the morning and afternoon commutes, it was almost as backed up as the freeways that skirted downtown. At night, the scum crawled up from the sewers. Prostitution stings, drug busts, and gang shootings were no strangers to Prewett Avenue.

Scoot decided to take the long way, and swung left onto 7th Street. Here, rundown apartment buildings rubbed shoulders with duplexes. A school crouched behind a wire-topped chain link fence like an ill-tempered bear in a too-small cage at the zoo. The empty playground was a barren asphalt plain where weathered white lines marked out a map of the United States, foursquare grids, and hopscotch. The mangy, peeling tetherballs swaying at the ends of their ropes made Scoot think of gallows and hanged men. The baseball diamond was a weedy dirt-patch.

Deee-pressing. Scoot felt bad for the kids. As bleak as that playground was, they weren't even in it but were instead packed like sardines into too-small classrooms, the troublemakers raising hell and dominating the teachers' time while the few bright students slid lower and lower into apathy.

At 7th and Dunley, after one final glance back to make sure that the cops hadn't made an appearance, Scoot hopped off the skateboard and kicked it up, catching it by one set of wheels. Fiberglass. Nice and light. The wonders of modern technology. In the olden days, it would have been made from wood with steel wheels.

With the board tucked under one arm, and the bulging black garbage bag in the same hand, Scoot strolled casually through a gap in a splintery board fence into the Dunley Street Junkyard.

It took up a quarter of the square block, and consisted of rows and rows of wrecked cars. The lot was hard-packed dirt so poisoned by oil, antifreeze and other automotive fluids that not even the hardiest weeds would stand a chance. Snarls of torn metal and sparkles of broken glass glinted up from the dirt.

The rusty metallic scrape of a long chain heralded the arrival of the proverbial junkyard dog. It ambled into view, a long-legged and floppy-eared mutt that looked like the result of a drunken liaison between a basset hound and a giraffe.

"Hey, Booger," Scoot said.

The dog's drooping jowls rippled as it uttered a low, froggy croak of a woof. His tail, which should have been cropped in puppyhood but had instead been allowed to grow into a long ropy thing, wagged.

Some guard dog. Booger spent most of his time sprawled snoring in the shade, and Scoot had never heard of him biting, or so much as growling, at anyone. An army of stray cats laid insolent claim to the junkyard, stalking and fighting and yowling their eerie love cries. Once, Scoot had looked in a busted-out window and seen a litter of kittens tumbling around on the front seat, tearing at puffs of upholstery, just as cute as could be. And on the plus side, the cats kept the rats at bay.

Most of the cars were mashed flat and stacked half a dozen high, or crunched down into cubes that reminded Scoot of the blocky Borg spaceships from *Star Trek*. Others had accordioned front ends, staved-in sides, sheared-off roofs. Some were outwardly intact, giving no sign of what misfortune had landed them in this unhappy place.

Moving quickly, Scoot set down the skateboard and the garbage bag on a sun-warmed trunk lid and fished out the duffel bag. It was dark red with black straps and a black zipper. Scoot stepped onto a rubber floor mat left here for these very occasions, and kicked off first one sneaker, then the next.

Off came the windbreaker, too, turning inside out as Scoot gripped the cuffs and pulled the sleeves through. It went from scarlet to navy blue with white piping. Left unzipped, it revealed a plain white tank top underneath.

Next were the baggy grey cargo pants. Scoot skinned out of them quickly, not liking the feeling of being exposed even though there was no way this would count as indecent exposure, not when the cargo pants had been worn over black knee-length bike shorts. Still, anybody changing clothes in a junkyard was bound to strike the casual observer as more than a little suspicious.

Scoot put the shoes back on and stuffed the cargo pants into the duffel bag. The bag was long enough to hold the skateboard, too, and the stolen purse.

Booger-the-dog watched with mild interest. Booger had seen this transformation many times before.

Last was the baseball cap, which today Scoot had worn turned around so that the bill was pointing backwards. It, too, went into the duffel.

Scoot undid the redoubled ponytail that the cap had concealed. As long, thick, chestnut-colored hair spilled over her shoulders, the last of Scoot went away.

For now.

Chapter 6

Another gap in the board fence opened onto a rutted gravel alley that ran between Prewett and Dunley.

Allison looked through as she threaded her hair into a single ponytail. She saw a delivery truck parked at one end by the bowling alley and a familiar homeless woman rooting through the Dumpster against the wall of Winnie's Crafts at the other end.

"Hi, Martha," she said, passing the woman.

Nobody knew Martha's real name. The folks who lived and worked around 6th and Dunley called her that after Martha Stewart, because she was always going through Winnie's trash to collect scraps of fabric, yarn, fake flowers and other such fripperies. She lived over in the vacant lot tucked in behind the Dollar Stop, in a corrugated tin lean-to that was tidier and better-decorated than Allison's own apartment.

Winnie threw a lot of perfectly good items into the trash because of Martha. She had tried just giving them to her, had tried inviting Martha to come into the store, but neither of those approaches did the trick. When openly offered anything, even the ultimate homeless-person triple-C of change, cigs or coffee, Martha scurried away.

Martha didn't return Allison's greeting. Her lips were moving, constantly, silently, as she pawed through the Dumpster looking for treasure.

Jamie Tremayne, who had the Readmore Bookstore across the street from the alley entrance, called her silent self-talk 'responding to internal stimuli,'

which was a fancy way of saying that she was in constant conversation with the voices in her head.

Allison popped out of the alley and onto Dunley Street, duffel bag swinging at her side. Now she looked like she'd been out at the gym, nothing more sinister than that. Black spandex bike shorts, open jacket, white tank top over a sports bra, sneakers. Ponytail bobbing at the back of her head.

Jamie himself was out in front of the bookstore, stocking a rolling cart with old paperbacks. A Magic Marker sign announced that they were a quarter apiece, or five for a dollar. The front windows of the store were full of taped-up posters, fliers, and announcements of local events. Between them, the interior could faintly be glimpsed, with its high, dusty shelves of used books.

He saw Allison and paused to wave, resting books in his lap. Like her, Jamie wore his hair in a ponytail, though his was shorter, honey-blond, and tied with a black velvet ribbon like he thought he was Amadeus.

She waved back, and cut diagonally across the street toward him. As always, she felt a pang of guilt as she skipped lithely out of the way of oncoming cars and up onto the curb.

Jamie had told her time and again that she shouldn't feel guilty. "You have two perfectly good legs and you shouldn't be ashamed of using them."

Then, he had cast his gaze downward in a theatrical ogle, though she'd been wearing a calf-length corduroy skirt at the time, about as sexy as a nun's habit.

"Nope," he went on, winking. "You shouldn't be ashamed of them at all!"

Still, whenever she saw him in that wheelchair, there was that pang. It was different when he was in the store, behind the counter, and she could delude herself into thinking that he was sitting in an ordinary chair.

"Milady Allison Montgomery," he said as she reached him.

"Jamie, Lord Tremayne."

He scoffed. "Please! I prefer *Sir* Jamie."

"Sir Jamie it is. What's the catch of the day?"

"Bodice rippers," he said, fanning a bunch of paperbacks so she could see the covers. "Women with their dresses falling off, men with their shirts open. High-spirited heiresses and roguish scoundrels. Throbbing loins. Interested?"

"Are you trying to sell me a book or proposition me?"

"Book? What book?" He tossed them over his shoulder into a cardboard box and showed her his empty hands.

She laughed. So did Jamie. He was twenty-five, three years older than her, and had what he called a not-totally-useless degree in English. "Because I

do work in the field," he'd said, indicating the used bookstore with an expansive gesture.

He also wrote, though as far as Allison knew, she was the only one he'd ever allowed to read any of his stories. And she'd had to pay for that privilege with some honesty of her own. Jamie knew something about Scoot. Uncle Bob had to have some idea, and Eva Cesare might suspect, but Jamie was the only one who knew a part of her secret truth.

"What are you up to tonight?" he asked.

"Nothing much. I'm working from four to seven, covering for Betty so she can go to her grandkid's school play."

"Plans for dinner?"

"There's a can of Chef Boyardee ravioli with my name on it."

Jamie made a face. "What kind of a friend would I be if I let you go home to the Chef? No, no, no, Allison. You're dining *chez* Tremayne this evening. I'm making my mother's meatloaf recipe, with mashed potatoes and gravy."

"*Real* mashed potatoes?" she asked, shooting him a skeptical eyebrow.

"Good God, no! The instant kind, flakes from a box! What do you take me for?"

"If it's the instant kind, I'm there," she said. "What time?"

"Seven-thirty?"

"Okay, but I'm bringing dessert."

"The last time you volunteered to bring dessert," he said, "you showed up with four packets of iced animal cookies from a vending machine."

"I'll do better, I promise."

"Then it's a date." He grinned up at her, then wheeled his chair around to go back inside and answer the door.

Mrs. Oberdorfer had come up to browse the bodice-rippers while they'd been talking. Now she, too, grinned up at Allison. She was a tiny round lady with two fluffy Princess Leia buns of hair on the sides of her head and a curl hanging down her unlined pink forehead.

"Ah, young love," she said, pronouncing it "luff."

"I didn't know you read this kind of thing, Mrs. O."

"I was meaning you and Jamie."

"Oh, hey, you've got us wrong. We're just friends."

"Hmm. But, yes, I like these books. Maybe they are not so much like real life, with the fiery passions and the fighting, but they are fun to read. Just don't tell Lindie. She would be shocked to know her mother-in-law reads such things."

"What about Maggie?" Allison asked, referring to the other Oberdorfer daughter-in-law.

Mrs. Oberdorfer flapped a hand. "Maggie, she reads them too. Eric told me. She is always either reading these or watching that Dr. Phil. Does that make sense to you?"

"Not really, but I don't watch Dr. Phil."

"I have tried, because he looks a little bit like my Gus. Don't you think so?"

Allison smiled. Gus Oberdorfer was a large, burly man of sixty, and she supposed that he did vaguely resemble the famed television shrink.

"The problem is," Mrs. O. went on, "that what you read in these books and what you hear on his show do not fit together. I should like to see Dr. Phil step into one of these and tell this . . ." she looked at the back cover of a Serenity Townshend, ". . . this Alaric Hawke that he needed to help out around the house. Can you?"

"Not really. I better go. See you, Mrs. O."

"Allie?"

"Yeah?"

"Netta's Bakery. Over on 5th Street. Tell Netta I sent you, and that you want the Dutch apple pie."

Saying that she would, Allison continued down Dunley, past the locksmith and the pet groomer. She crossed the street to the imaginatively-named Dunley Apartments and let herself into the entryway.

Her mail always smelled like burnt dryer lint because the laundry room with its three finicky machines was on the other side of the wall from the row of mailboxes. A dark hallway led to the first-floor apartments, including the unit belonging to the landlady. To reach her own, Allison had a choice between a claustrophobic stairwell and an elevator that was as slow and jittery as a palsied old man.

She chose the stairs, thinking that her mother would have a heart attack if she could see the peeling paint, water stains, and worn-through spots in the durable mustard-yellow carpet. But Marian Sherwood Montgomery had never clapped eyes to her middle child's current digs, and if Allison had her way, that was how it was going to stay.

Her apartment wasn't technically an apartment. It was technically a studio, a single bed-slash-living room that shared a kitchenette with the unit next door. The carpet was mustard-yellow in here, too, and the paneling a cheap knotty pine that made the small space feel even smaller. But the bathroom had an amusing old clawfoot tub, the shower curtain suspended above it on a metal ring, and there was a balcony just barely big enough for a white resin lawn chair and a cute little tripod barbecue.

Allison unpacked, dropping the garbage bag with the purse in it onto her thrift-store recliner and stowing her duffel bag on the single closet's top shelf. Next she unlatched the sliding door that led into the kitchen.

Eva Cesare, her neighbor, was a med school student who also worked as a waitress and was trying to help her only surviving brother break away from drugs and gangs and get into community college. As a result, Allison hardly ever saw her.

They got along fairly well and had yet to have any big arguments over the kitchen, though sometimes Eva's brother Hector would come over and help himself to Allison's stash of Mountain Dew in the fridge.

Speaking of which . . .

She "did the Dew," popping open a can and slurping down the bile-green fizzy liquid. The caffeine percolated through her system and the bubbles inspired a hiccup that was not quite a burp.

Supplementing the soda with a package crackers, cheese-flavored and sandwiched with peanut butter, she went back into her room and thumbed through the dryer-lint scented mail.

K-Mart ad . . . Val-U-Pak coupons . . . postcard reminding her of a dental appointment . . . letter from her kid sister . . . travel agency brochure . . . credit card application.

The ad, the coupons, and the application went into the trash. She flipped through the brochure long enough to admire the crystal-blue tropical waters and think that maybe someday she would like to take one of those all-inclusive vacations. The dentist's reminder went up on the corkboard by the phone.

The letter from Missy, she opened and read. It was printed on lined paper in careful sticklike letters. Missy was ten, the youngest of the brood and the only one that Allison really regretted leaving when she moved out on her own.

Dear Allie, I miss you, when are you coming home? David is going to tennis camp this summer and Steven to music camp so it will be boring here. Mom says it won't because I will have Danny to play with but Danny is a baby and he bites me. I drew you a picture so you remember who I am. Love, Missy. The signature, unlike the body of the letter, was an elaborate cursive scrawl with the tail of the 'y' swooping into a long curlicue.

Allison sighed as she set the letter down and picked up the folded sheet of drawing paper. Missy was better at art than she was at putting her thoughts into words, so the picture was quite good. Sad, but good. It showed the big house in the background, with various stick-people on the porch. Even as stick-people, Allison could guess who most of them were.

There were the twins, David with his tennis racquet, Steven with his flute.

There was Daniel Jr., the eldest, with his wife Susan — Susan was depicted with her mouth wide open as if yelling — and their fat baby son, Daniel III. There was Hilary, four years older than Allison, in a ballerina's tutu. And there were Mom and Dad, Marian and Daniel Montgomery.

And, larger in the foreground looking alone and apart from the house and the family on the porch, was a girl-figure with long red hair and enormous sorrowful grey eyes.

It tore her heart to see Missy's picture. How she wished she could have brought her baby sister with her. No one else in the family had time for Missy, or understood her. But it was impossible. Allison knew she couldn't take care of a ten-year-old girl, couldn't provide a good home, structure, guidance, discipline and balanced meals for her.

"Hell, I can't even provide those for myself," she said to the empty room. "I was going to eat canned ravioli for dinner."

No, what it all boiled down to was that Missy would have to learn the hard way what Allison herself had learned. That if you were a Montgomery and a misfit, you could forget hoping that the family would adapt and embrace your differences. You could only wait it out until you were old enough to escape on your own.

It wasn't as if Missy were being abused, starved or even neglected. Overlooked, yes, and misunderstood, but those things did not warrant a Child Protective Services caseworker.

Reading the letter and seeing the picture had left her so down in the dumps that Allison almost forgot about Scoot's prize until her glance happened upon the garbage bag, still sitting in the recliner. She checked the time — not yet three in the afternoon, which meant she had a full hour before she had to leave for work. Plenty of time to change clothes and examine the purse.

She took a quick shower. The building's water heater was old and balky, so a quick shower was the only way to make sure of a *hot* shower. And as charming as the clawfoot tub was, she had yet to satisfactorily fill it with steaming hot water.

Dressed in comfortable old jeans and a man's white shirt, she left her hair loose and dashed on a bit of blusher and eyeshadow. This, too, would have horrified her mother if Marian had been here. Allison could only recall once in her life when she had seen her mother without a perfectly made-up face and perfectly styled hair, and that had been in the hospital after Missy was born.

Sitting on the floor in front of the little table that held her television, Allison unzipped the roomy buttercream-leather purse and reached inside.

Chapter 7

Allison had first become Scoot when she was about fifteen and already feeling stifled.

They had such *expectations*, the Montgomerys. Private schools and country clubs, tennis and ballet. Charity balls and political dinners. French lessons. Old money. Good manners.

No freedom. Nothing wild, nothing fun.

So, she'd started shoplifting. Out of boredom. Knowing it was wrong but having to do *something* to relieve the monotony. The Montgomery monotony.

It had been little stuff, mostly. Stupid stuff. A lipstick here, a pack of gum there, a piece of fake jewelry, a bottle of cheap perfume. The items didn't matter and the price certainly didn't; in those days, she got fifty bucks a week allowance and if she needed more, all she had to do was ask Daddy.

What mattered was the rush, the tremendous walloping thrill of risk and excitement that she got whenever she slipped something into her pocket. Her heart would hammer at a furious pace as she walked toward the door, trying to look calm, cool, aloof. Each time, as she approached the exit, she'd wonder . . . would an alarm go off? Would a security guard chase her?

But it was too easy, so she soon graduated to stealing packs of cigarettes, bottles of alcohol, boxes of condoms. Allison herself didn't smoke, drink, or screw, so she ended up giving these ill-gotten gains to the 'bad girls' at her school.

And, always . . . would she get caught? Would they call the cops? What would her parents say if they had to come to the police station and bail her out? Would the other girls rat on her? Would she get expelled?

She never skipped classes, aware in some subconscious way that she'd only be hurting herself by doing that, but she did start lying to her parents about after-school activities. They thought she was in French Club, Drama Club, Glee Club, when really, she was downtown hanging out at the malls and the arcades.

And then she had gotten involved with the skaters. They were the ultimate in coolness and attitude. They had the freedom she craved, and casually indulged in crazy stunts and death-defying risks.

Of course, they were none too interested in welcoming her into their fold. Not a rich private school girl. They'd think she was stuck up and snotty, even if she wasn't. Here, at last, was a group into which she couldn't buy her way with stolen smokes or impress her way with her parents' money and connections. She had to earn her way in by doing what they did.

Then providence, in the form of Uncle Bob, brought the answer. He got the twins skateboards for their birthday. Black with red wheels and flames for David, black with electric-blue wheels and lightning bolts for Steven. And complete gear – helmets, knee pads, elbow pads, the works.

Mom had pressed the flawlessly manicured tips of her fingers to her temples in a futile attempt to forestall one of her migraines. She had conveniently forgotten her own rather humble upbringing when she'd landed Daniel Montgomery, and now acted like her working-class brother was a mortal embarrassment.

"They're all the rage with the kids these days," Uncle Bob had said. "Davey will be a natural, you just watch. And Steve, it'd do him good to get out in the fresh air and exercise."

Uncle Bob didn't know his nephews very well.

A month later, neither board had ever been used, so Allison had figured her brothers wouldn't notice if she happened to requisition them. She taught herself to ride, having to sneak around because if her parents ever got wind of her new hobby, she was sure there'd be hell to pay.

It wasn't ladylike, and worse, it wasn't classy. It was low. Right down there with dirt-bike racing and monster truck rallies. A bare step above cockfighting, competitive eating or spitting for distance.

Allison loved it. She'd started thinking of those secret training sessions as "scoot time." And of the wild inner Allison unleashed as "scoot Allison."

Her biggest challenge in those early days was keeping her battle scars

hidden from her family. Despite the pads, her knees and elbows were soon scabbed over, and she was no stranger to road-rash on her palms.

When she'd finally felt skilled enough to debut at the skate park, she discovered one final problem that she hadn't considered. Most of the skaters were guys. Most of the girls who hung around with them were not that interested in the sport for its own sake, but were girlfriends or groupies. The few that *did* skate seemed only to do so in hopes of attracting the notice of one cute skater boy or another.

So, when Allison showed up with her board, she found herself the object of a lot of unwanted attention. The guys hit on her or did a lot of adolescent hooting and sniggering. The girls despised her for trying to horn in on their turf. No one seemed to care that she knew how to ride.

The answer? Scoot.

Like her sister the ballerina, Allison was tall for her age and had what Hilary liked to call a 'willowy' build. In other words, narrow hips and barely any tits whatsoever. While this had its downside, it was a definite bonus when it came to dressing like a boy. Frumpy, slouchy, baggy clothes being the fashion helped, too. All she had to do was tuck up her long hair under her cap, and she could readily pass for a slim teenage boy, at least as long as no one came within a few feet.

Then, once she'd mastered the skateboard and the art of disguise, she started snatching purses.

Shoplifting had become dull. She had never been caught, not once. Even the time she'd set off an alarm by carrying a stolen CD past the sensor, the store manager had not questioned her glib excuse. She'd gone into fitting rooms and put garments on under her street clothes and walked out with them. She'd lifted a diamond tennis bracelet, by far the most valuable of her thefts thus far, and gotten away with it.

Somewhere along the line, though, the fun had gone out of it. She hadn't been getting the same thrill anymore, not even when she tried to kick it up a notch with the more expensive items.

It was, she'd gradually come to realize, impersonal. Flat, and faceless. Oh, they said shoplifting was not a victimless crime, because it caused prices to go up so that the average consumer took it in the shorts, but really, all she was doing was hurting the big anonymous corporations. Hurting? That was a laugh . . . even if she took ten CDs a day, she doubted it would be more than a ripple in the profits.

The purses, though . . . !

Her first purse hadn't been a snatch, but a finders-keepers kind of thing.

She had been Scoot that day, pleasantly exhausted from an afternoon of wheeled stunts, pushing along in a mellow, lackadaisical sort of manner.

Push . . . and coast . . . push . . . and coast . . . headed for the parking garage where she'd stowed the Corvette her parents had given her for her Sweet Sixteen. It had been waiting outside the house, cherry-red with a big white bow. They'd all gotten cars for their sixteenth birthdays. A silver Porsche here, a turquoise-blue Beemer there . . . it was just the way the Montgomerys did things.

She'd been coming up on a bus stop, and saw a chubby middle-aged lady heave herself onto the city bus, leaving her purse sitting on the bench.

"Hey!" Allison, still disguised as Scoot that day, had called. "Hey, lady!"

The woman had looked around, seen Scoot, and gone wide-eyed with alarm. Probably mistaking Scoot for a junkie, gang member, or generic punk, she had nearly *leaped* up the bus steps, mouthing frantically at the driver. The door wheezed shut.

"No! Lady, you forgot your purse!" Scoot had shouted, but the bus pulled away from the curb with a gassy exhalation of exhaust.

Grabbing up the purse, she had gone flying down the street on her skateboard, after the departing bus. But pedestrian traffic on the sidewalks slowed her and drew a lot of dirty looks and some swearing, and the bus kept going.

Scoot had not known what to do, so she'd taken the purse with her back to the car. There, her Scoot-clothes in the trunk with the board, she had opened it and started going through it.

And oh, how the excitement had coursed through her! Not because of the contents; the most exotic things in there had been a metal box of cinnamon Altoids and a ticket stub from a matinee showing of an extended director's cut of *Titanic*. It was the thrill of going through someone else's stuff.

This was not faceless and impersonal. This was as personal as it got. She'd gone through every compartment and pocket of that purse. She read the woman's shopping lists and receipts, criticized her choice in cosmetics, ate some of the curiously strong mints, looked at pictures of the kids.

It was, she'd found, even more exciting than the shoplifting. Lasted longer, too, because the rush she got from swiping a bracelet had usually faded by the time she was out of the store. Exploring a stranger's purse, really taking her time with it and being thorough, could entertain her for quite a while.

A woman's purse was such a trove of secrets, too.

She remembered visiting her Sherwood grandparents, a few duty-visits to their retirement community in Arizona, and when Grandpa Art had needed

a pen, Granny Helen had not told him to get one from her purse.

"Bring me my purse," she had said.

And he had done it. Had carried that purse – a big, black, heavy old-lady purse with the gold clasps – all the way into the kitchen and waited beside her, humble as a church-mouse, while she had rooted around to find a pen.

A man wouldn't willingly look in a purse, Allison had determined.

Part of it might be some deep-rooted homophobia, him thinking that if he opened a purse or even held it in the wrong way, some inner switch would get thrown and the next thing he knew he'd be wearing ladies' dresses and singing show tunes.

But most of it was fear, a man's plain and simple fear of what he might find in there. What if there were tampons? Or feminine hygiene spray or some other dubious, icky product? What if there was proof of an affair in there, love letters or motel room keys or pressed flowers?

She even suspected that some men thought they might open their wife's purse and find a voodoo doll, or a vial of poison, or a fat insurance policy with his name on it. They harbored some hidden belief that there was death inside, just like they had that deeply buried superstitious fear of women themselves.

Women, who bled in monthly cycles and had incomprehensible mood swings. Women, who may or may not have *teeth* down there . . . they didn't, of course, everybody knew that . . . but didn't all rumors have some basis in fact? Would *you* want to be the one to stick the most important part of your anatomy into that strange darkness and find out for sure?

And just as a man's car was an extension of his you-know, to be shown off and compared and bragged about, a woman's purse was an extension of hers. Dark, mysterious, containing sought-after treasure.

Finding that first purse, mundane though its contents had turned out to be, had been like a brilliant bright light going on inside her. She was hooked, as hooked as anyone had ever been by a drug.

She tried to control it. Not *quit*, no, not give it up . . . but control it. Not go nuts with it or anything. Taking purses was a lot more dangerous than shoplifting. It required that up-close-and-personal contact. The victims tended to notice right away, and scream or shout or chase after.

A couple of times, they had thrown things. Scoot had been beaned in the back of the head and damn near knocked in front of a taxicab by a lady who had chucked a plastic water bottle. She had been smacked in the face once by a furled umbrella, and bombarded with oranges from a shopping bag held by a stout woman who was a fearsome shot.

Others on the street reacted, too. When a hue-and-cry went up, some lady shrieking, "Thief! Thief!", people turned to look. Sometimes they'd try to be heroes. Scoot lost her favorite baseball cap three years ago to a newspaper vendor who'd tried to grab her as she whizzed on by, and once a clean-cut Eagle Scout type had tackled her clean off her board. As they'd struggled, he got a good feel of what little tits she had through her quilted flannel shirt. He had yanked his hands away so fast he'd nearly given himself a whiplash, and sputtered an apology as his face went brick-red, thus giving her the opportunity to make her getaway.

The skateboard helped with all that. Usually, she could strike and be half a block down the street before the victim realized what had happened. A running person looked guilty, but everyone was accustomed to seeing kids on wheels slalom recklessly through pedestrians or plunge into traffic. And if she had to, all she needed was to get around a couple of corners or into a semi-private spot long enough to do a quick-change.

Over the years, she had honed her routine, adding little touches like the duffel, and the plastic garbage bag to hide the purses in. If she did it right, by the time anyone came charging along in pursuit of Scoot, all they'd see would be innocent Allison.

She still smiled at the memory of the first time a sweating, panting man had puffed to a stop and looked past her, then asked if she had seen a kid on a skateboard go by. "Scuzzy little prick, about so tall, skinny, had a ball cap and a jacket and his pants three sizes too big. Snatched a purse off a woman back there. Did you see him?"

Allison, who had reversed the jacket, hidden the hat, and whipped a long wraparound denim skirt over the pants, told him that yes, she had. "He went that way," she'd said, pointing with one hand while the other held the stolen purse at her side, making no effort whatsoever to hide or conceal it.

The man had thanked her and jogged on, and once he was out of sight she had retrieved her board from where she'd kicked it under a mailbox, and been on her merry way.

That had been a good purse, too. Small, but nice things came in small packages, wasn't that what they said? She'd found a lovely scuffed-suede wallet in there, a silver filigree heart-shaped pendant on a silver chain, an unopened bar of Toblerone white chocolate, and a fancy gold pen.

It was the infinite variety, the infinite possibility that appealed to her. She'd taken tiny beaded evening bags from elegant ladies on their way to the theater, and she'd taken funky patchwork-quilted satchels from hippie women in shapeless dresses and Birkenstocks. Old-lady purses like the one Granny Helen had, black and clunky and full of laxatives, prescription medicines and reading glasses. Teenager purses with Flirty Boys pins stuck to the strap. A stitched leather purse made to look like a decorated horse-saddle. All kinds of purses with all kinds of contents.

Like Christmas every time. A *real* Christmas, a fun Christmas. Like how she imagined Christmas might be if Mom's personal shopper hadn't gone out with lists from each kid so that they all knew exactly what they'd find under the tree.

She'd lost count a long time ago of how many purses there had been. Maybe a hundred and fifty, spread over the past six years.

Now, this one.

This supple buttercream-leather number with the long strap.

Chapter 8

She unzipped it slowly, thinking about the woman from whom she'd snatched it, playing a mental guessing-game. That added to the fun, seeing if she could predict what sort of objects might be in the purse based on what its owner had looked like.

Most of the time, she got it right. People were fairly predictable. But there had been a few startling exceptions.

Like the hard-faced woman with the rigid posture, who had reminded Scoot of nobody so much as the scary Englishwoman who ran that *Weakest Link* game show. Her purse had been iron-grey and square, but inside of it Scoot had found a high-tech vibrator, a pair of wispy hot-pink panties, and a knobby circular thing that she later learned was a cock ring.

Or the harried, overweight mother of three whose purse Scoot had relieved her of in a grocery store parking lot. There amid the half-eaten cookies, Happy Meal toys, moist towelettes and broken crayons, had been an honest-to-god switchblade with an onyx handle . . . and when Scoot popped the blade, it was crusted with dark stuff that sure *looked* like blood.

Or, her favorite, the stylish handbag that had belonged to a leggy, model-beautiful redhead in a seafoam green sheath, gold heels and a patterned seafoam and gold silk scarf. Inside, amid the usual make-up and hair spray, had been a black leather trifold wallet with a driver's license and business cards identifying the model-beautiful redhead as Adam Villiers, veterinarian.

The woman who'd owned this buttercream bag had been petite, Scoot

45

remembered. Petite with platinum-blonde hair in a pixie cut, fair skin, aquiline features. Very pretty in a fragile, elfin way. She'd worn a jade pendant on a gold chain, and a dark green business suit.

Scoot hadn't meant to bowl her over. The bag had been heavier than she'd anticipated, and it had jerked on the blonde's arm and thrown her off her feet. But if Scoot had stopped to check on her, she would have been caught. The only thing to do was keep right on going.

A little blonde in Century Plaza. That meant a businesswoman, maybe a lawyer. She'd kind of had that *Sex in the City* air about her, a deceptively delicate-looking creature who could be a real ball-buster in the courtroom and kittenishly playful in bed with the defense attorney.

So, the purse would have a cell phone, maybe a Palm Pilot. Not much cash but a ton of credit cards . . .

The first thing she took out was a tape recorder. A mini-corder, the kind used for dictating memos. It had a tape inside. Scoot rewound it, pressed "Play."

Just as she'd thought . . . it was a tape of two people at a business lunch. Ordering drinks, ordering food. Something about a job. She pushed "Stop," planning to listen to the rest later. It would be boring, legal talk always was, but there might be something interesting in there too. The two people – a woman who had to be the blonde, and a man with a sexy voice – sounded like they might have something else going on.

Next was a manila folder, which probably pertained to whatever case they had met to discuss. Scoot flipped it open, saw a few photos of a handsome blond man with a great tan. Could this be Mr. Sexy-Voice on the tape, perhaps?

The papers didn't look like what she thought legal briefs should look like, but then, her only experience was derived from shows like *Law and Order*. She set the folder aside and delved into the purse again.

A sealed 5x7 envelope, thick and full. She took it out, turned it over.

Blank. No address, no return address, no stamp, no postmark. It had not been mailed.

She slit it open, and her jaw hit somewhere in the vicinity of her collarbones.

The envelope was stuffed with cash.

A lot of cash.

Scoot's breath escaped in a *whoof*. She riffled the edges of the bills with her thumb. Hundreds. The envelope was full of hundred-dollar-bills, rubber-banded together in stacks.

"That can't be right," she murmured after a quick count and some mental arithmetic. "That'd mean . . . that'd mean there's twenty-five

thousand bucks here."

All at once Scoot felt the back of her neck prickle. She looked around. It occurred to her that she was sitting on the floor of her shabby apartment with the cash cost of a new car in her lap and the balcony drapes wide open. She couldn't think now if she'd locked the hall and kitchen doors or not.

She jumped up, drew the drapes, checked the locks. If someone had pounded on her door that very second, she would have wet her pants and maybe had a heart attack to boot. Never mind that she was twenty-two and in good shape. She would keel over, dead.

Twenty-five thousand dollars!

Was it a bribe? A payoff?

Hell, for all she knew it could be ransom money, lottery winnings, or counterfeit bills.

Who in the hell went around with 25 G's in her purse?

Scoot crammed it all back in the envelope, re-sealed it with strips of masking tape, and then crammed the envelope under the seat cushion of her ratty old recliner. She went to the hall door again and squinted through the peephole. Her nerves were buzzing, and she wouldn't have been surprised to see the petite blonde standing right there.

Or maybe a couple of guys in dark suits and sunglasses, like the FBI agents always looked in movies. The men-in-black, wasn't that what they were called? There were men-in-black, and men-in-white-coats, and if the way she was feeling now meant that she was going crazy, then maybe the men-in-white-coats would turn up, too.

The hall, as far as she could see in the distortion of the fisheye lens, was empty. She opened the door and stuck her head out. Just then, a door at the far end opened and old Mr. Gavins stepped out, shirtless, scratching his hairy potbelly with one hand and lugging a pillowcase full of laundry with the other.

She grimaced and ducked back in, quick. Closed the door. Locked it. And, for the first time since she had moved into the Dunley Apartments, hooked the chain.

The purse still sat on the carpet, its mouth gaping, the zipper-edges like a multitude of tiny teeth. There was another envelope in it. A big manila one, the padded kind used for mailing.

Telling herself that the *smart* thing to do would be to shove everything back in there and ditch the purse in the nearest Dumpster, Scoot nonetheless went back to it and hunkered down.

"Besides," she said into the stillness, which was only broken by the irregular herky-jerky tick of the grotesquely ugly sunburst clock over the television,

"the nearest Dumpster is the one where Martha hangs out. She could use the money, yeah, but it'd get her killed."

With thumb and forefinger tweezing like pincers, she got the corner of the envelope. It was heavy. Scoot prodded the shape through the sides, both hearing and feeling the faint pip-pip-pip of bubble wrap giving way.

Solid. Lumpy.

"I'll probably regret this," she said, and tore open the end so she could peek inside.

A gun.

"Holy crap!" Scoot almost dropped the envelope, had a vision-flash of the gun going off when it hit the floor and maybe putting a bullet through her ankle, and gingerly lowered it into the seat of the recliner. She tipped it, and the gun slid out.

She was no judge; aside from an old skeet-shooting rifle that had belonged to some Montgomery ancestor or another, she had never seen a real gun up close. But it looked like an antique. A revolver, not an automatic. In good shape. Polished, shiny. The handle had the mellow, satiny gleam of ivory.

Scoot stood over the gun, rubbing the heels of her hands up and down the sides of her face. Her hands were cold, but her face was numb, so that was all right. The fine hairs on her arms and the back of her neck were quivering on end and it felt like the ones on her head would have liked to do the same. Despite the stuffy heat of the apartment, she was all-over goosebumps. Glissandos of ice strummed up and down her spine.

"Shit, shit, oh shit," she whispered.

Her mind grasped desperately at straws of explanation.

The petite blonde was . . . um . . . an antiques dealer? In the movie biz, and this was a prop?

Every instinct told her otherwise. This was no prop. This was a real, actual, could-kill-you gun.

Was it loaded?

The goosebumps that had begun to settle now hunched up again.

She didn't know how to tell if it was loaded or not. Short of pulling the trigger, which she was *not* about to do. The neighborhood around Dunley and 6th might not be the best, but it wasn't such an urban wasteland that a gunshot would go unnoticed.

Okay. A gun.

A gun and a pile of money.

Think about this. Think about it rationally.

But Allison didn't *want* to think about this, rationally or otherwise. She

wanted to get out, get away from the problem and let distance and routine help bring it into some sort of perspective.

Thankfully, she had just the excuse she needed. It was time to go to work.

Chapter 9

Mr. Gavins wasn't in the hall when she left. The only person she saw was three-year-old Billy Strevyk, playing with toy cars on the grubby hallway carpet. The door behind him was open, and through it issued the smell of cooking pot roast and the sounds of one of the afternoon shows, something too raucous to be Dr. Phil but not quite trailer-trash enough to be Springer.

The Strevyks had two of the units and the connecting kitchen. Mr. Strevyk had been laid off from his job on an auto assembly line and now minded the house and kids while his wife worked. Whenever their paths crossed, Allison always saw a sort of hurt befuddlement in his eyes, as if he couldn't understand how his life had come to this.

On the stairs, she passed Mr. Gavins after all. He had his now-empty pillowcase slung over one meaty, hairy shoulder and a box of Tide in his hand. There was no need for conversation; his doctor had advised him to take the stairs instead of the elevator as much as possible, and he was wheezing and sweaty-faced as he trudged up the last few steps with the air of a climber finally reaching the peak of Everest.

Her landlady was in the entryway, pushing a vacuum that wheezed almost as badly as Mr. Gavins.

"I'm telling you, Allison," she said without looking up, as if carrying on an earlier conversation, "I finally appreciate the difference between suck-and-spit, and suck-and-swallow."

If asked, Allison might have expected a woman like Teddi Lace to have

a whiskey-roughened voice with a smoker's rasp. Instead, she affected a cooing little-girl voice like the actress Jennifer Tilly, which made the things she said seem even dirtier.

"Uh . . . yeah," Allison said.

"Swallow, you bitch," Teddi said to the vacuum. It rolled back and forth, picking up bits of paper and cat litter and spraying them out from under its undercarriage.

Ex-stripper, possibly ex-porn-star and ex-prostitute as well, she claimed she'd once had the face and figure of a living Barbie doll. Now, though, the living Barbie doll had put on fifty pounds . . . most of it in the chest. Each of her boobs was bigger than Allison's entire head, though considerably less firm.

Teddi had a slight pooch of a gut, a slight sag to her rear, and lots of unconvincing brassy-blonde hair in a Farrah Fawcett 'do. She slathered on too much make-up, but to Teddi's credit, she didn't do herself the further disservice of trying to shoehorn herself into clothes designed with much younger and shapelier women in mind. Instead, she was mostly seen in a succession of drawstring sweat pants and men's triple-X extra-tall flannel shirts that still had a job of it bridging the gap of her canyonesque cleavage.

Allison went around the chugging, grinding, laboring vacuum and let herself out onto the street. The sun was low, golden rays slanting like melted butter between the buildings and lending even this part of town a hazy daydream charm.

The two blocks stretched between Prewett at the top of the hill and Pine at the bottom. Prewett was a sleazy main drag, all fast food and bowling alleys and motels. Pine was quieter, tree-lined, residential.

What Allison liked best about her neighborhood was that, in a weird sort of way, it was a small town unto itself. She wouldn't have thought such a thing was really possible in the bustling but anonymous heart of the city. People still *knew* each other here. They talked to each other . . . even more, they talked *about* each other.

It was like living in the middle of a soap opera, where you quickly got to know all the characters and their problems. Allison hadn't been a resident of Dunley Street for two weeks before she'd learned more about the people around her than she'd ever known about the other 'good' families with whom the Montgomerys associated.

She had heard about Teddi Lace's checkered past. She had heard about Martha. She'd heard how Mike, who ran Mike's Pool Hall, had a drinking problem. And how Samuel "Needles" Jefferson from the tattoo parlor had once broken both the arms of a flasher who'd exposed himself to little

Gretchen Oberdorfer . . . and how that had just been the beginning of the luckless pervert's punishment. She knew that Ralph the barber had lost his wife to cancer, and Al the bartender had lost two wives to divorce and was up to his eyeballs in alimony and child support payments.

Some of the secrets of the neighborhood remained secrets, though. She didn't know, nor did anyone else, exactly how Jamie Tremayne had ended up in that wheelchair. Nobody knew whether Kurt, the middle Oberdorfer son, had officially come out to his parents, or if the family was playing a game of willful ignorance and denial.

And then there were the weird kind of secrets. She didn't know *what* the deal was with Mama Delilah, who some people said was a voodoo queen, and others said was just the requisite crazy old neighborhood cat lady . . . though she *did* know that Mama Delilah's one milky cataract-filmed eye made her skin crawl. It was enough to make a person sympathize with that guy from the Poe story, who had chopped up the old man and buried him under the floor . . . here, you fiends, the beating of his hideous heart.

People said that Nathaniel Caron, who sold crystals and incense and Tarot cards, and charged forty bucks a session as a 'psychic advisor' was really about as psychic as Uncle Bob, and that the only reason he kept a roof over his head was because he bore a striking resemblance to Johnny Depp. A steady clientele of teenage girls and older ladies alike were willing to pay that forty bucks for an excuse to hold his hand and look into those dreamy dark eyes.

They also said that the little house Nate ran his business out of, which huddled between the Dunley Apartments and Red Bowl Teriyaki, had been the site of a murder back in the 1920's and that the ghost of a young woman still turned up in mirrors, window glass, and any other reflective surface.

Allison crossed the intersection on a diagonal, waving to the only car currently moving. The driver, Tina Wendmeyer from the video store up by the 7-Eleven, tooted her horn and raised a hand in return.

Once across the street, she was in the Dog Haus zone, awash in the aromatic goodness that surrounded the corner shop where the Oberdorfers had been fattening up the locals for twenty years. Her mouth watered as helplessly as that of any of Pavlov's test subjects. Hot dogs, bratwursts, salami, pepperoni, corn dogs . . . if it was meat in a tube shape, it was on the menu at the Dog Haus, either served hot and ready to go, or available from the deli counter.

When she had first moved here, Allison had discovered that she could easily eat two meals a day at the Dog Haus. A grilled bratwurst on a bun, served with a heaping side of Mrs. Oberdorfer's German potato salad – tender paper-thin slices of potato melting in sour cream, bacon and cheese – was sheer

heaven. She had also discovered, shortly thereafter, that she didn't dare eat two meals a day there if she wanted to stay trim. Not after putting on four pounds in two weeks.

These days, she allowed herself a trip to the Dog Haus a couple of times a month, usually every other Saturday or on a special occasion.

Two doors up, past the Close Shave, was Sherwood Second-Hand. It was set back from the sidewalk, under a portico roof with a perpetual pigeon problem. Trash cans and squat, columnular ashtrays of pebbled concrete flanked the entrance.

Signs on the glass doors promised *50% Off All Red Tags, 20% Off Seniors Every Day, Early Bird Special – Buy One Get One Free All Clothing Items Before Ten A.M.,* and *Donations Gladly Accepted.*

"Sherwood Second-Hand," she said, reaching for the door. "Robbing the rich to give to the poor since 1992."

Inside, the store was spacious and well-lit by florescent fixtures. The floor was tan-flecked-with-green linoleum, the ceiling off-white. To her immediate left was a large wooden bin for donations, which was a third of the way full of bagged clothes and cardboard boxes of toys and dishes despite the posted hours. To her right, a row of changing room stalls and a rack full of rejected try-ons.

A year ago, Uncle Bob had hired teenage Jake Oberdorfer to paint murals on the interior walls. "Putting the punk's graffiti talent to good use," he had explained, grinning his patented Uncle Bob grin. As a result, the walls were almost entirely covered with images from the Robin Hood legends. Robin and Little John duking it out with quarterstaves. Friar Tuck. Maid Marian. Will Scarlet. Prince John.

Except that Allison thought that somewhere along the line, either Uncle Bob or Jake had gotten Robin Hood mixed up with William Tell and Legolas from the *Lord of the Rings* movies. She certainly didn't remember reading about Robin Hood shooting apples off of anybody's head, or riding a shield down the steps of Nottingham Castle in a smooth skater-move that even Scoot wouldn't be nervy enough to try.

Lyle Kane, a not-too-bright but amiable enough guy a few years older than Allison, was at one of the registers, selling a stack of puzzles to Winnie from the craft store. He bobbed his head in greeting as Allison came in. Winnie smiled cheerily and waved.

A few other people browsed the aisles. Allison saw the Beekers from one of the apartments downstairs from hers arguing over a headboard, and Caroline Dressler digging through a tray of flatware in hopes of finding a matching set.

In the toy section, Needles' girlfriend Tisha was telling their four-year-old son Isaac that he could choose one stuffed animal from the bin or one baggie of action figures – old He-Man toys, with a couple of Happy Meal prizes mixed in.

Seeing Allison, Tisha raised her voice. "You need your nails done, girl!" she said, shaking back long bronze-dyed beaded cornrows. She had gorgeous mocha skin that she refused to let Needles touch with his tattoo inks, and the kind of figure that Teddi Lace might have envied even back in the day.

"What's wrong with my nails?" Allison held out her hands and looked at them.

"They're short, they're uneven, they're bare and they're boring," Tisha said.

"Besides that."

"Besides that? Besides that, you've got a cuticle nightmare going on. Give me one hour, and you won't believe the difference."

"I bet I wouldn't," Allison said, though of course a manicure with the fancy, jazzy polishes that Tisha liked was out of the question. She couldn't very well make her transformation into Scoot with shaped, buffed, sparkling-gold nails and perfect cuticles, now, could she?

"Mama, I have this one, it little, *and* the hero-men?" Isaac asked, holding up a small floppy stuffed tiger and the action figures.

Tisha gazed down at him and blew out a fond sigh, and Allison had the feeling that Isaac was going to get what he wanted. Mama Delilah, the maybe-voodoo-queen, was Tisha's great-grandma. If the bloodline did possess any powers of persuasion, they'd resurfaced in the youngest generation.

"Sounds like you've got some negotiating to do," Allison said. "See you, Tish."

"Don't you forget about those nails," came Tisha's parting shot as Allison continued toward the back of the store. "I hate to have a hex put on you just to get you in my door."

Swinging metal doors opened into the thrift store's back room, which was the great land of Not-Yet. It was a hodgepodge of donated items not yet sorted and priced, broken items not yet hauled off to the dump, and holiday decorations not yet in season. A short hallway led to the staff room, where Betty Tullia was in the process of taking off her smock.

"Allison, thank goodness, I thought you might not remember," Betty said.

Her purse was open on the bench in front of the dented steel row of lockers, and Allison took an automatic peek inside. Grandma-clutter. Half-eaten rolls of Life Savers, crochet hooks, a coupon-saver with frolicking

puppies on the cover, a disposable camera.

"But here I am," Allison said. She opened her own locker.

The staff room was a windowless space that also included a card table, chairs, a coffee maker, a microwave, a small fridge, the old-fashioned time clock that no one ever used, a water cooler and a single swaybacked couch with burnt orange cushions. The walls were hung with posters gleaned from Hank Cotterman's travel agency showing exotic locales like the glaciers in Alaska, Ireland's misty fields, sunny Mexico, the African savanna and that Disneyland castle in Bavaria.

The smocks were really aprons, but Uncle Bob never called them that. Maybe because Lyle Kane and Donny Fielding would balk at wearing anything called an apron. They were a bright shamrock-color, probably intended to be the famed Lincoln green of the Merry Men, with a gold bow and white arrow stitched above the lettering. Deep pockets in the front, suitable for holding a heavy stapler, pens, a bunch of the little cardboard tags used for pricing clothes and bagged toys, and a roll of stickers used for pricing other things.

"Thank you so much for doing this," Betty said. She patted her purse. "I'll take pictures. Penny is *such* a darling. And I'm not just saying that because she's my granddaughter. She'll be the star of the show."

"Hope so. Is Bob in the office?"

"Listening to that music of his," confirmed Betty. "'Bye, Allie."

"Bye." She pinned on her nametag – Hi! My Name is Allison! – and shut her locker.

The short hall continued on to a bathroom, and at the end of it, a flight of stairs climbed to Uncle Bob's office door. Allison could hear Elvis doing "Heartbreak Hotel," the song filled with the scratches, pops and hisses that only came from a record player.

She tapped, heard The King turned down. "C'min!" Uncle Bob said.

Allison did so. The office was even smaller than the staff room, with a tinted window so Bob could survey his domain without being seen except as a smoky shadow behind the glass.

There was not much in the way of a family resemblance between Allison's mother and uncle. Marian Sherwood Montgomery was a small graceful china doll of a woman, with a soft cloud of auburn curls and limpid, expressive sapphire eyes. Her brother Bob was tall and stocky and red-faced, with a comb-over fringe of grey all that remained of a flaming red head of hair. His eyes were a light cornflower blue, twinkling behind spectacles. Put him in a fake white beard and a red suit, and hey, presto! Santa Claus. He did it, too, every year, though no longer at his sister's family's house.

He had a monstrosity of a desk, the flesh-colored paint peeling off gunmetal steel, the top of it hidden beneath piles of papers. His chair was a wooden slat-backed swivel on wheels, which he had rocked back to the point where it was about to tip over, his feet up on a stack of milk crates, one foot bopping in time to the beat.

What had possessed her grandparents, who seemed so normal in all other ways, to name their children Robin and Marian was beyond Allison. Her only guess was that Granny Helen, who had always been hopelessly enamored of Sean Connery, had been inspired by the movie in which Connery played an aging Robin Hood.

"Allie-girl," Uncle Bob hailed.

In here, the walls were not covered with travel agency posters or fanciful murals, but concert posters and album covers. The shelves were full of records, organized in a system that made sense to no living being but Bob himself, and the pride of place in the room was given to a table where the record player sat.

"You know," Allison said, smiling, "you can get a better sound from a CD."

"Heretic." He made as if to swat her, but she was well out of reach and they both knew it.

"Smaller, too," she said. "Better storage. Because, you know, one of the operative words in CD is *compact*."

"Silvery Frisbees," he said. "Saucerian slipped disks. Vinyl, Allison Danielle. As God intended."

And yet, once you dug a little below the surface, there were some similarities between brother and sister. This deep and abiding love of music, for instance. True, in Marian's case it was all classical stuff and opera, while Bob's true loves spanned the big band era right up through disco, but neither could be happy without music in their lives.

"As God intended? God listens to records?"

"If He does, you can bet it's on vinyl."

Instead of going on to tease him about MP-3 players and digital playlists, she heard herself ask, "Uncle Bob, do you know anything about guns?"

Chapter 10

Elvis had gone on to another song, one Allison didn't know. Bob frowned and sat up, taking his feet off the milk crates. "Allie-girl, Allie-girl, what do you need a gun for? Has someone been bothering you?"

"It's nothing like that —"

"Some crazy guy, you just let me know and we can have that taken care of. This is a good neighborhood. We look out for ourselves and we look out for each other. Do you think I would have encouraged you to move here if I thought it was a bad place?"

"No, I —"

"So if you're not feeling safe, we have to fix that, but I'd hate to see you carrying a gun. We'll get you some of that pepper-spray stuff, sign you up for some self-defense courses. I should have thought of it sooner, a pretty young girl like you and all the times you spend out roaming, you should have something like that, just in case. But there's no sense in getting you in trouble with the law, either."

"I'm not!" Allison said, blushing hotly.

"Why do you need a gun?"

"I don't need a gun."

Bob rubbed his pate, disturbing his comb-over. "What are we talking about, then?"

"Never mind."

"Never mind? I think not. If someone's been bugging you, following

you, some stranger or boyfriend who won't take 'dumped' for an answer, I need to hear about it."

"I can take care of myself, Uncle Bob, really. Nobody's bugging me. And, sheesh, the way you're talking it sounds like you'd hire someone to —"

Her thoughts broke off with a snap, or maybe it was the decisive snap of a last puzzle piece fitting into perfect place.

"Allie?"

"Oh, whoa, hey," she murmured.

Uncle Bob, his disorderly office and his Elvis music faded out. She was thinking of the blonde in the forest green business outfit. She looked like the least likely hired killer anybody could imagine.

And yet . . . a gun, twenty-five thousand in cash, and that folder . . .

She wished she had taken a better look at the folder and its contents. Wished she had listened more closely to the tape.

"Allison, are you okay, hon?"

It was nuts. Wasn't it?

Of course it was. She had been listening to Uncle Bob talk about how in this neighborhood, they looked out for each other. How, if some creep was stalking her, she should tell him and he'd have it taken care of. Like Needles took care of the flasher that had shown his version of bratwurst to Gretchen Oberdorfer . . . took care of him to the tune of two broken arms and worse.

All of that floating around in her head, was it any wonder she'd come to such a conclusion about the blonde with the buttercream-leather shoulder bag? When, really, there was probably another explanation, a perfectly logical and perfectly innocent one, for the things that had been in her purse.

She shook herself. "Sorry, Uncle Bob. I got thinking about something else."

He leaned closer, his blue eyes not so much twinkling now as penetrating. "I can tell something's up, Allie-girl, something's on your mind. I promised your mother that I'd keep an eye on you, remember. While I've broken more than a few promises to my baby sister, this is one I'd like to keep."

"I'm fine," she said. "No creeps, no stalkers, no psycho ex-boyfriends. I haven't even dated anybody long enough to qualify as a boyfriend, let alone an ex. What have you been telling Mom about me, anyway?"

Four years ago, at the age of eighteen, Allison had announced to her stunned family that she didn't want to go to college. That, in fact, she wanted to move out on her own, get a job, and be independent. It had not been a speech that received rave reviews from the Montgomerys. They couldn't believe that anyone, least of all one of their own children, could reject their wealth, their influence, their luxurious country-club and high-society lifestyle.

Her father waxed wroth, saying that if she wanted to do such a foolish and irresponsible thing, she'd have to do it without any help from him. The money meant for college would be put away in a trust fund and she would have no access to it until she came to her senses. The car, the cherry-red birthday Corvette, would be taken away. So would the allowance, which by then had gone up to a hundred a week. He had hoped that he could scare her into complying, but all his threats had done was to make Allison more belligerent and determined.

Her mother had been crushingly disappointed. Hilary was too caught up in her ballet career to even think of marrying yet, and Susan's mother got to have all the fun and bask in the glory when Susan and Daniel Jr. married. Marian had been banking on Allison to go to college long enough to find a husband, thereby letting her plan the idyllic storybook society wedding. The fact that Allison had no interest in prospective bridegrooms mattered not one bit in these maternal dreams, which were so brutally trampled underfoot by Allison's uncaring, callous, selfish desire to lead her own life.

Finally, seeing that they could not dissuade her, and perhaps coming to an unwilling understanding that she really did *not* care about the money, the connections, and the privilege, her parents had consented to let her move out. They might even have been glad of it, since clearly, whatever her DNA, she was no true daughter of theirs in spirit.

But they had imposed one condition. A condition that her father perhaps thought of as a dismal fate guaranteed to bring Allison groveling home again. They wanted her to go to work for Uncle Bob at his thrift store. Surely this humiliation would get through to her, would teach her a lesson.

Wrong.

She'd loved the thrift store from the moment she had first set foot inside. It had been like a larger version of the purses, an entire building full of oddball items. Mostly trash, occasionally treasure.

Dealing with the donations, or with the customers, offered Allison the same secret peek into the lives of strangers that she got when rifling through the contents of a stolen purse. Everything, and everyone, had a story to tell.

There was the one woman who had undergone weight-loss surgery and came in every month to drop off the clothes she could no longer fit into, while buying smaller ones. She had told Allison, laughing and shamefaced at the same time, that once she reached her goal, she would go on a huge spending spree at the ritzy downtown department stores and blow a fortune outfitting her sleek new body, but until then she would get by on second-hand.

And there was the guy who came in every week without fail, looking for

board games, which Allison suspected he sold on the Internet for a tidy profit. She had once seen him almost capering with glee when he found a set of old Lawn Darts, the kind that had been discontinued because of their deadly metal tips but which apparently sold for big bucks. Jamie said that the same guy made regular stops at the Readmore, looking for role-playing games.

"I haven't been telling her anything," Uncle Bob said, in response to Allison's question about her mother. "Only that you're fine and well, you're not starving, you're not sleeping in a cardboard box."

"As far as they're concerned, I might as well be," she said. "They'd croak if they ever saw my place."

"Well, it *is* a little run down," he said. "You're always welcome to the rooms above the garage, if you want."

Uncle Bob lived on Pine Street, in a long skinny house that looked tiny from the front and like a railroad car from the inside. He had a detached garage in the back, with a two-room apartment over it. At the moment, the utilities in the apartment weren't hooked up and he used it to store all the spare furnishings and possessions he'd moved out of his house to make room for his ever-growing collection of records and music memorabilia.

"I like my place," Allison said. "Besides, I'm supposed to be independent, aren't I? How could I be independent living over your garage?"

The phone hidden somewhere in the papers on the desk let out a braying buzz. Bob excavated it. "Yes?"

As he talked – to Virginia, by the sound of it – Allison let her thoughts go back to the blonde, the gun and the money. What if the blonde *was* a hired killer? A hit man, or hit woman if you like. Maybe things like that *did* happen in the real world, and not just on the cop shows.

If it was true, how pissed must she be?

How pissed, and how alarmed and scared?

Another chilly glissando ran down Allison's spine, just like the one she'd gotten when she had first seen the gun.

Pretty damn pissed. Pretty damn alarmed. Pretty damn scared.

Suppose that the blonde had just . . . what did they call it? Had just been offered a contract on someone's life.

Whose life?

The guy in the pictures. The muscular guy on the sailboat.

Again, the chill, spreading out through her body. She had only glanced at the photos, but had seen enough to know that the man in them had been handsome, smiling, cheerful.

So, suppose that he was the target. Suppose the blonde had been given

the information, the weapon – wouldn't she have her own weapon? Allison didn't know – and the cash. The payment. Some sort of contingency. Half now, the rest on completion? That'd be fifty thousand dollars.

Fifty thousand dollars to kill someone. To take a human life.

Was that enough?

People did some pretty gross and unbelievable things for that kind of money, if reality TV shows were to be trusted. People ate live spiders and immersed themselves in tubs full of rancid animal parts for that kind of money. People lied, betrayed, and cheated.

Would they kill?

Probably.

The blonde, then. Assume the blonde is the kind of person who would accept money to shoot a guy, to murder him. She gets her preliminary payment, her gun, all the details . . . and then . . .

"And then someone steals her purse," whispered Allison, feeling pale and cold all over. "Some skateboarder knocks her down and makes off with her purse. What's she going to do? What does she *have* to do?"

Uncle Bob was still talking, explaining to Virginia with the aggrieved air of someone repeating himself for the umpteenth time that, no, they didn't buy used items. No, not even for store credit. It was all donations.

"She has to get her stuff back," Allison said, still whispering. "She has to find the purse-snatcher. And . . . and make sure nobody else knows. Ever."

"Tell him to hang on, I'll be right down," Uncle Bob finally said, in a grumpy tone. He got up and turned off Elvis. "Time to get to work, Allie-girl."

"Okay," she said, barely aware of what she was saying.

It was a strange feeling, realizing that someone wanted to kill you.

Chapter 11

Allison didn't want to leave Uncle Bob's office. She was filled with an irrational surety that the moment she set foot back in the store, she'd see the petite blonde with the jade pendant come striding through the front doors like a gunslinger.

Irrational. Yes. It was totally irrational. There was no way for the blonde to have found her. Scoot had been well out of Century Plaza by the time she could have gotten her feet and her bearings back.

Even if someone *had* followed, Scoot would have lost them during the transition back into Allison. Booger might not have been the greatest guard-dog, but he would have given her some kind of indication if a stranger had been nearby.

So, though she was holding her breath in anticipation and dread, she made herself leave the safety of the office.

Betty was long gone, and business was picking up. It usually did in the afternoons, once school got out and more people left work. Weekends were the busiest, except for holiday Mondays when Uncle Bob liked to sell everything at half-off.

The Beekers had evidently decided on the headboard and were now trying to figure out how they were going to get it home. They didn't have a car; Allison knew that Mr. Beeker was a janitor up at Dixie Lanes, the bowling alley on the corner, so he walked to work. And Mrs. Beeker took the bus to the big Shop-N-Go grocery store a mile up Prewett, where she worked

nights as a checker.

Uncle Bob, done dealing with one problem customer, moved on to a young guy who wanted to donate his computer. By the look of him, he was an Atherton College student who must've just upgraded, a dude who'd gotten a Dell. Sadly, the thrift store couldn't take used computers. Something about the tubes or the chemicals. Then Uncle Bob hustled over to the Beekers and offered them the services of Donny Fielding. Donny, who had played high school football before discovering beer and flunking out, was a moose whose main talent was lifting and carrying heavy things.

Allison took up a post by the donations bin, where a long table had been set up for sorting. She dragged a large cardboard box up onto the table and opened it. Clothes. Baby clothes. Though they'd been washed, the ghost-smell of old spit-up wafted out.

She took cute tiny garment after cute tiny garment from the box, inspecting each. A small hole or missing button was okay, but anything with huge rips or broken zippers went into a second bin destined for the dump. As she went, she scribbled prices onto cardstock tags and stapled them to the sleeves, cuffs, necklines or waistlines. Fifty-nine cents, ninety-nine cents, a buck twenty-nine.

Shooting wary looks at the door each time it opened, she told herself not to be so jumpy. All right, maybe she had *reason* to be jumpy. Maybe Scoot had gotten them both in over their heads this time.

But what, really, could the mystery blonde do? It wasn't like she'd go to the police. How would that look? Call up and report a stolen purse . . . one that happened to contain a firearm and a pile of cash? Not likely.

From the baby clothes, she moved on to a box of old magazines. Women's magazines, outdated copies of *Cosmopolitan* and *Glamour* and *Elle*. The smell lingering on these was like some Dickensian spirit, the Ghost of Perfume Samples Past, but it was a far sight better than stale baby-urp.

She bundled the magazines back-to-back and slipped each pair into a clear plastic bag, which she folded over at the top and sealed with a row of staples. Cardstock tag – ninety-nine cents. What a bargain. Double feature.

Next was a purse. Not one of her donations. It had been cleaned out, except for a balled-up gum wrapper caught in the lining. She bent a cardstock tag around the handle, stapled it. Two dollars and forty-nine cents. It could go hang on the rack with the rest of the purses, backpacks, fanny packs and tote bags . . . some of which *were* hers.

That was the trick, one of the perks of her job. Once she had gone through the purses, spying into the lives of the women who'd owned them,

she always brought them here. The purses, maybe the occasional wallet or scarf or pair of gloves. They'd be tagged and put on display, and if anyone should ever happen along who recognized a particular bag, well, Sherwood Second-Hand got donations all the time. Often anonymously. There were mornings when Uncle Bob or Allison showed up to unlock and found the bin so full that the excess had been piled against the front doors.

Oh, but she wished she had gone through the rest of the buttercream-leather purse. She had been so spooked that she'd only wanted to get out, get away. Not wanting to find anything more. Anything *worse*.

What could be worse?

Opening a plastic grocery sack that bulged with someone's unwanted shoes, Allison made a wry noise. She could have found a severed *hand* in there, for gosh sakes . . . *that* would have been worse. Or hard drugs, or kiddie porn.

She had been lucky in her purse-snatching career so far to have run across comparatively few really bad things. A fair amount of pot, either in baggies or in joints, which she had thrown away. A vial that she surmised had been crack cocaine, which she had chucked down a sewer grating. Once, horrible Polaroid photos of a woman and a Doberman, which she had burned and felt unclean for days afterward.

Maybe, she thought as she lined up the individual shoes in hopes of finding their mates, she shouldn't look through the rest of the blonde's purse after all. Maybe she should stuff everything back in there, weight it with a couple of bricks from the vacant lot, and toss the whole thing into the river.

Sneaker . . . pump . . . slipper . . . aha! Another sneaker. Which didn't match. Leopard-print ankle boot with stiletto heel. Snazzy! The matching boot had the heel broken off, though, too bad. Into the reject pile.

Somehow, she got through her shift. She sorted, she hung up clothes, she took a turn on the register when Lyle went on break, she directed traffic as Donny single-handedly moved the sections of a donated sectional sofa into the furniture area.

By quarter to seven, her nerves had calmed. She was no longer sure that the blonde was going to walk in and accuse her, or skip right over the accusations and put a bullet between her eyes. The spent adrenaline left her feeling tired and hungry, and all she wanted was a big meal and then a long sleep with the covers pulled up over her head.

She and Uncle Bob were the last ones to leave. "Plans for tonight, Allie-girl?" he asked as he locked up.

"I told Jamie that I'd come over for dinner."

He smiled and raised an eyebrow. "Oh-ho!"

"Don't *you* start," she said. "We're friends, that's all."

"Nice young man, though," Uncle Bob said. "Smart as a whip."

"I don't think he's my type."

"Sweetie, you don't have a type."

"Gee, thanks. I'll go out with anybody, is that it?"

"I didn't mean it like that." He gave her a thoughtful look. "It's not the wheelchair, is it?"

"No! How shallow do you think I am?"

"Well," he said, drumming his fingers on his chin, "you *are* a Montgomery."

Allison stuck out her tongue. "I'm half Sherwood, aren't I?"

"Don't know," he said. "I think your mother had all her Sherwood blood transfused right out of her when she married your dad."

"*So* true!" Allison said, resisting with effort the urge to roll her eyes.

"Not the chair, then?"

"No, Uncle Bob, it's not the chair! If you must know, it's that I don't think I'm *his* type. We're friends. A guy and a girl are allowed to be friends nowadays without it having to turn into some complicated thing, you know."

"Now, how could a clever, pretty girl like you not be his type?" He regarded her skeptically. "You're not saying that . . . well, that Kurt Oberdorfer might be more of his type?"

"I never said that, and I'm not saying it now."

"All right, all right, your nosy old uncle will keep out of your business. See you in the morning."

He had parked in the lot between his store and Dixie Lanes, an arrangement that the bowling alley managers allowed because Bob Sherwood, along with Gus Oberdorfer, Mike Hartnet, Ralph Wilkowsky and Al Chesterton formed the core of the longest-running bowling teams Dixie Lanes had ever seen. The Sixth Street Strikers, as they called themselves, held a canned food and toy drive every Christmas, sponsored community events like egg hunts on Easter and Halloween trick-or-treating at the local shops, and took turns supervising the Little Strikers junior bowling league. If the neighborhood was a small town unto itself, that bunch comprised its town council . . . old white guys to a man.

Allison watched him go, then turned back down 6th and headed for Jamie's place. He didn't live above his store the way Needles and Tisha, Nathaniel Caron, and several of the other area business owners did. Instead, he had a ground-floor two bedroom unit in the Greenview Apartments, a fancier building than Allison's.

Halfway there, she remembered she had offered to bring dessert, and took a quick detour around the block to the bakery. It was two doors down from a Weight Watchers, which had always struck Allison as fiendishly sadistic.

The bakery was warm, well-lighted and redolent with brown sugar, cinnamon, dough, and chocolate. A man who looked like he had never and would never attend a Weight Watchers meeting if his life depended on it – which in fact it might – was in the process of sliding a sheet of cookies into one of the ovens. More cookies sat cooling on wire racks. They were chocolate-chip-walnut by the lumpy look, each one the size of a hubcap, and Allison's mouth watered.

She bought a Dutch apple pie from Mrs. Oberdorfer's friend Netta, another sweet-faced older lady with a hint of an accent and long pure-white braids that had probably once been as yellow as daffodils. She also caved in and bought a couple of the cookies, and sampled the broken pieces of gingerbread and shortbread piled in shallow bowls atop the glass display cases.

Walking back, she passed the Weight Watchers again just as a group of heavyset women came out. Allison felt them staring at her, at the slim girl carrying what was obviously a pie-box and a white bakery bag. The combination of resentment, envy, raw craving hunger and self-disgust in their expressions made her want to flinch.

Across Dunley from the Weight Watchers, to make matters worse, Lucky Sue's Diner was upwind and giving off powerful grease fumes. Everything at Lucky Sue's was griddle-fried or deep-fried. Burgers, bacon, chicken, onion rings, onion blossoms, fries, curly fries. It was also one of the few places in town that had deep-fried Twinkies on the menu.

A few minutes later, relieved to be away from the baleful glares of the overweight women, Allison and her pie and cookies arrived safely at Jamie's front door.

The Greenview Apartments were not totally inaptly named; it was possible to see some greenery from the windows on the east side of the building, where trees and a small neighborhood park and a parochial elementary school stood on Pine Street. Jamie, however, had a view of the covered parking slots and the alley and the stairs that climbed the side of the Eight Ball Bar to the pool hall.

He had left the door ajar for her, and she nudged it open with her foot. "Hello?"

"In here!"

His apartment was three times as large as hers and much nicer, with all of the furnishings down low and widely spaced to accommodate his chair. She

had only been here a few times, once to help Donny deliver the mammoth roll-top desk, but had been given the grand tour.

The second bedroom had been turned into a study, with even more bookshelves for a guy who already spent his days surrounded by them. Here was where Jamie wrote his stories, and where he fussed over them endlessly, not wanting to send them out to magazines unless they were perfect. He had both a typewriter and a computer, and said he preferred the former for his writing while the latter was primarily used for games and surfing the 'net.

Jamie had goldfish and angelfish and neon tetras in an aquarium with a bubbling sunken ship fixture, and a single irritable Japanese fighting fish named Bruno. Bruno had elaborate scarlet and indigo fins and lived in a glass punchbowl, endlessly cruising its watery home with such menace that you expected to hear the low, thrumming theme from *Jaws*.

Allison found Jamie in the kitchen, aggressively bright with yellow cabinets and white tile. It was full of good cooking smells that reminded her of the kitchen at home, though certainly not of her mother. Marian only ventured into the kitchen to give instructions to the cooks and caterers.

"I brought pie," she said.

"Hostess pies from the 7-Eleven?"

"Real apple pie from the bakery." She set the box on the countertop. "How's the meatloaf?"

"Coming right along." He had potatoes boiling on the stove, a pot of brown gravy simmering, and an orange mound of baby carrots poised to go into a third pot where water steamed.

The question, which had come and gone in her mind all afternoon, popped out before she knew it was going to.

"Hey, Jamie? Would you kill someone for fifty thousand dollars?"

Chapter 12

Putting on yellow quilted mitts to remove the meatloaf pan from the oven, Jamie barely batted an eye. "Depends on who it is, I guess. Why?"

"No reason."

"Hell of a thing to ask a person for no reason. Is there someone you're trying to get rid of?"

"No. I was only wondering."

"You wonder this kind of thing often?"

"Not usually." She couldn't see how to help in the kitchen without getting in the way, and leaned on a counter. "So you would, depending on who it was? Like who, for instance?"

"There've been times when I thought I'd kill for a publishing contract," Jamie said, setting the meatloaf on a trivet to rest before slicing. "Not even a six-figure one; a modest advance would do. Or an agent. I'd kill for an agent. Maybe for fifty thousand, I could publish my own book and promote the heck out of it, but it wouldn't be the same. Of course, that would mean I'd have to let people actually *read* my stuff . . ."

"I'm serious, here."

He spun his chair and studied her with dark, intent eyes that could have given Nathaniel Caron or even Johnny Depp a run for his money. "The question is if I'd kill someone for money. Is it someone I have a personal beef against? Or is it a total stranger?"

"Does it matter?"

"Sure, it does. Want something to drink? I've got that vanilla-flavor Pepsi."

"Thanks." She took one from the fridge and poured it over ice. "Why does it matter?"

"If it's someone I've got a beef against," Jamie said, "someone I really hated and really wanted dead, then, no, I wouldn't do it for the money."

"You wouldn't kill them?"

"For the money." His smile was predatory, like Bruno the Japanese fighting fish. Didn't suit him. "That would take away from the purity of the revenge, wouldn't it?"

"You're weird."

"If it was a total stranger, then no, I wouldn't do it for the money either."

"What, you'd kill a total stranger for fun?"

"I wouldn't do it at all. Not to a stranger. How would I know whether that person deserved it or not? I'd only have the word of whoever hired me."

"Then they'd have to deserve it?"

"They'd have to deserve it. They'd have to have done something against me personally, or against people I cared about. Otherwise, what's it to me whether they live or die? If someone wants to hide a person to kill someone else, I think that's cowardly. It's wanting them dead, but not wanting it badly enough to risk yourself."

"Fifty thousand dollars, though," Allison said. "That's big bucks."

"Not really."

She looked around the apartment, which was nicer than hers but still no high-rent ritzy downtown condo. "No?"

"It wouldn't buy a house in this city," he said. "Wouldn't leave me set for life. Fifty grand doesn't go as far as it used to. A good car would eat up half of that, and a really good car would eat up most of it. On the other hand, if I got caught, I *would* be set for life . . . life behind bars."

"You'd get the same thing for no profit killing the person you hate," she said.

Jamie shook his head. "Not necessarily. Murder-for-hire, or assassination, or whatever you want to call it, is premeditated and in cold blood. They catch you, and they throw the book at you. Killing someone for emotional reasons . . . in a fit of jealous rage, say . . . you could argue it down to a lesser charge. If you could convincingly claim that it was a crime of passion, a heat-of-the-moment thing, and not something you planned to do. Juries are more sympathetic in those cases."

"Do you sit around and think about this stuff?"

"Hey, you're the one who brought up the subject." He dumped the baby carrots into the water and set the timer. With a fork, he speared one of the

potato chunks and tested it. "These are ready. Want to drain and mash them while I slice the meatloaf?"

"Sure." She poured the pot into the colander, clouds of steam billowing into her face. "Let me get this straight . . . it's wrong to kill someone unless you have personal reasons? And that it's cowardly, if you *have* personal reasons, to hire someone else to do the job for you?"

"Basically," Jamie said, maneuvering the meatloaf from the pan onto a cutting board. Clear juice ran from it, collecting in the trench around the edge of the board.

"Interesting."

"What's this all about, anyway? Who do you want dead?"

"Nobody. Sheesh!"

"What, then? Were you offered the job? Fifty thousand dollars to kill someone? Anybody I know? Not me, is it?"

"Jamie, what kind of person do you think I am?" She dumped the potatoes back in the pot, slopped in some milk, salt, pepper and most of a stick of margarine, and plugged the hand mixer into the wall.

"A good one," he said. "But you do have your sinister side."

"Sinister!"

"Maybe not sinister," he amended. "Still, you did tell me about how you like to disguise yourself and terrorize innocent pedestrians on that skateboard of yours."

"Terrorize!"

"I have fish," he said. "My mom has the parrot."

"What?" She was thoroughly confused for a moment, then got it. "Oh. Sorry. But I don't *terrorize* people."

She felt like she was on her skateboard again, whirring close to the edge of a precipice. While Jamie knew that she liked to dress up as a teenage boy and go caroming along on her board, she hadn't told him about her other hobbies. He didn't know about the shoplifting, or the purses.

"You've never been out innocently minding your own business on the sidewalk when a pack of skateboarders come speeding by, have you?" he asked. "Maybe blasting their rap music. Maybe just shouting and laughing, unable to construct a sentence without using an obscenity every other word."

"I think I know those guys."

"Face it, Allison . . . they can be scary. How are the potatoes coming?"

"Good." She stuck the mixer in, and began mashing. Raising her voice, she said, "All right, so maybe boarders do scare regular folks. It doesn't make us killers."

"Point taken," he said, laying slabs of meatloaf on plates. "And I'm sorry for besmirching your reputation. But you did bring it up."

"I did. You like lumpy mashed potatoes, or smooth?"

"Lumpy. Gives them that homemade taste."

"Hey!" Allison cried, suddenly remembering. "You promised me the instant kind! Flakes from a box!"

"I lied," Jamie said, his grin widening. "I wouldn't eat that crap if you paid me. Not even fifty thousand dollars."

"Somehow, I don't think shows like *Fear Factor* would be as much of a hit if they only challenged people to eat instant mashed potatoes," she said, scooping her finger through the pot. She tasted, had to admit that they were pretty good, and flicked a wad at him.

"No food fights in my kitchen." He grabbed a dishtowel and spun it into a rope. "I'm warning you."

"You wouldn't dare," she said, turning away to reach for a large serving spoon.

The towel snapped out and stung her on the butt. She jumped, whirled.

"Wouldn't I?" he asked, still with the grin.

"You want these potatoes on your plate or over your head?"

He let go of the towel and held up blameless hands. "Truce."

"Jerk."

"Meanie."

"And to think I bought pie." She rubbed the sore spot. "That hurt, you know."

"Shall I kiss it and make it better?"

Allison scoffed. "That, I'd like to see."

"You have eyes back there?"

"Ha, ha."

Jamie puckered his lips and made kissy noises. "Bring it on over here, why don't you?"

"Smartass."

"Yours is the ass that's smarting," he said.

She pivoted and cocked her hip so that her butt was thrust jauntily in his direction. "Well?"

To her surprise, he propelled his chair forward with one strong push, curled an arm around her waist to hold her in place, and smacked a loud kiss on the rear pocket of her jeans, right where he'd scored with the towel.

"Jamie!" she yelped. She tried to pull away, he wouldn't let go, and she fell into his lap.

"Most places, it costs thirty bucks for this kind of action," he said.

"Let go of me!" She scrambled out of his lap, her usual agility abandoning her, and stood flustered in the middle of his kitchen. Everything she had said to Uncle Bob not an hour ago came back to her in a tangled, confused rush. And, having no other idea how to handle it, she approached as Scoot might – recklessly and head-on. "Was that a pass? Are you making a pass at me, Jamie Tremayne?"

He eyed her. "Not if it's going to get a pot of mashed potatoes dumped on my head."

"I'm not going to dump potatoes on you."

"Gravy?"

"Not even the carrots. Unless you're planning to throw the meatloaf."

"I wasn't."

"Making a pass?"

"Planning to throw the meatloaf."

"So it *was* a pass?"

"If you want it to be."

She raked her hands through her hair and let out a huff of exasperated breath. "What's that supposed to mean?"

"Nothing," he said. "Let's let it drop, shall we? Our dinner's going to get cold."

"Okay," she said, still looking at him.

Did she want it to be a pass? Was she interested in Jamie? He was a friend, yes, and a good one. They had a lot in common. He lived vicariously through books and she lived vicariously through other people's belongings. Neither of them much liked to talk about their pasts, and they both liked to poke fun at the craziness of the world around them.

And he *was* cute, with his long honey-colored hair tied back in that little black velvet Amadeus ribbon.

They filled their plates and went into the living room. His apartment, while spacious, only had a dining nook with a stout round wooden table, two chairs, a hanging light fixture, and several framed wildlife photographs – grey wolf, black bear, bobcat, mountain lion, bald eagle.

The television was on with the volume down low, and Allison saw that it was tuned to one of those adventure-race shows where teams competed in hideously grueling challenges. They went biking or hiking or kayaking or climbing their way over the world's most unforgiving terrain, driving themselves beyond exhaustion into sheer physical and emotional meltdowns, and claimed to love every minute of it.

"I thought I was an adrenaline junkie," she said, sitting down in one of the chairs, "but even I'm not crazy enough to do that stuff."

"What, you don't want to ride a mountain bike down a sheer cliff face in a thunderstorm?"

"No, not particularly."

"Looks exhilarating. You might like it."

"People get killed doing that. They don't show it on TV, but they do."

"I know. One guy got killed in Washington State not too long ago. The team above his dislodged a boulder while they were on a rock-climbing leg of the race, and it fell on him."

"Was that the guy who had to cut off his own arm with a pocketknife?"

"Different guy." His wheelchair had a lever that raised it to table-height, so that they were at the same level. "The one who cut his arm off was out hiking, not racing. And it was someplace in Utah, I think."

"Brr," Allison said. "The unforgiving wilderness, huh?"

"Yeah." He punched the Off button on the remote.

As they ate, they chatted about neighborhood stuff. She told him about the Beekers and their new headboard, and about Tisha Anthony's insistence that she get her nails done. He told her that Nathaniel Caron had been in to buy a bunch of books on parapsychology and the occult that an Atherton student had traded in for store credit, that he'd had to chase some of Jake Oberdorfer's friends out of the erotica section, and that Mama Delilah had come by to offer him a kitten.

"She thinks every used bookstore needs a resident cat," Jamie explained. "Or she just has a surplus of kittens and is desperate to unload them. I saw that she also had a 'Free Kittens' sign in the window of the pet groomer."

"Should have taken the kitten," Allison said. "You turned her down, and now she might put a curse on you."

"That's just what I'd need, thanks for the cheerful thought."

It was almost nine by the time they had finished their pie, which they heated up in the microwave and served with scoops of the vanilla ice cream Jamie found in his freezer.

All through the dinner conversation and dessert, Allison had been thinking about the incident with the towel. How she'd fallen – or he had pulled her – into his lap. His arm had been very strong. She supposed that she should have realized it . . . of course his arms were strong, from pushing that chair around all day.

Had it really been a pass? Had she blown a chance at something that could have been good by reacting like some skittish virgin? Or, worse, like somebody who was put off by his disability?

She helped him with the dishes over his protests, and then, as she was getting ready to go, leaned over to kiss him on the cheek.

On the corner of the mouth, really, and not just a sisterly peck. She felt the smoothness of his skin and smelled spicy after-shave and understood in that instant that he must have shaved again that afternoon solely for her benefit. She let her lips linger a beat or two longer than she had intended, hearing his quick indrawn gasp.

A fluttering thrill, similar to that she got when riding her skateboard, went through her. She drew back before she could get swept away in the rush. "Thank you for dinner, Jamie."

Jamie sat in his chair gazing solemnly up at her with his dark eyes, a hesitant smile playing about his mouth. "Thank you for dessert."

"You liked the pie?"

"There was pie?"

"Very funny."

"So . . . out of curiosity, what was that for?"

"Maybe it was a pass."

"Was it?"

"If you want it to be."

Chapter 13

Hector Cesare was in the hallway when Allison got there, and for one bad moment she thought that he was trying the door to her apartment.

He was a good-looking eighteen, with a smoldering dark sullen air that the girls who went for bad boys must find irresistibly appealing. Short, compact and fit, he sported an eagle tattoo and a bracelet made of heavy silver and turquoise links.

Allison stopped short, more alarmed by what he would find in there than by the prospect of him breaking in.

She had never exchanged a cross word with Hector, not even over the Mountain Dews he sometimes pilfered from her side of the fridge she shared Eva. She knew that despite his tough-guy image, he was at heart a good guy.

He and Eva had, like phoenixes, risen from the ashes of a disastrous family. They had a father in jail, a stepfather on drugs, a mother who silently accepted regular beatings as part of her wifely due, a sister who was a burnt-out wreck of a prostitute by the time she'd turned twenty, a brother who had been killed in a drive-by shooting, another brother in jail for knifing a rival gang member, a third brother who'd been killed in a middle-school shooting, a half-sister who was pregnant at thirteen by a thirty-year-old man, and two still-younger half-siblings at home.

Eva and Hector had gotten away from all of that as untouched and unscathed as could be hoped for. Or, at least, Eva had, and was trying to save Hector by encouraging him to ignore the ridicule he got from his peers and

the rest of the family, encouraging him to stay clean. He had dropped out of high school but was, with Eva's constant support, working toward getting his G.E.D., and escaped to her place whenever things got too rough at home.

Allison *knew* he was an okay guy, but still the sight of him at her door dumped quarts of adrenaline into her veins. That purse and its contents could tempt even the saintliest of people. The last thing she wanted was to be responsible for Hector's fall from grace after his long struggle to climb above his beginnings. She would never be able to look Eva in the eye again. Never be able to look herself in the mirror again.

Hector must have heard her, because he turned. His dark eyes were hooded and something long and thin glittered in his hand.

A stiletto.

No.

A pen.

A silver pen, and in his other hand he had a notepad. A plain brown grocery sack rested at his feet.

"Allison, hey," he said. The hooded look disappeared as he flashed her a smile. "I was just leaving you a note."

"Me? Why?"

"I owe you some sodas," he said, and nudged the bag with his toe.

Closer now, she saw that it contained two six-packs of Mountain Dew, and that her name was scribbled on the top sheet of paper. She felt ashamed of herself for jumping to conclusions.

"I would have left it in the kitchen," Hector continued, "but Eva's got to work early tomorrow and I didn't want to wake her. They work her to death at that hospital, you know?"

"Yeah," Allison said. "I wonder who ever thought it would be a bright idea to do that to med students? Run them ragged, make them try to get by on pure caffeine and three hours' sleep, and then put other peoples' lives in their hands. It'd make me crazy. I don't know how Eva does it."

"Hey, you want some good news?"

"I could really used some good news."

"Our brother Juan is getting out of jail next week."

"Oh," Allison said, thinking that this did not exactly sound like good news to her.

Juan Cesare's street name was Rattlesnake, for the tattoo on the back of his hand and for his penchant for jabbing people with sharp objects. She had never met him, but Eva had once shown her a picture, and Juan had the flat, dead eyes of something you'd expect to see sunning itself on a rock, coiled

but always alert and ready to strike.

"He's coming back home," Hector said. "And Juan, he won't take any crap from Miguel. Won't let our mom take any crap from him neither. Isn't that great?"

She failed to see how it was great. It was worse and worse all the time. Miguel was the drug-using, wife-beating stepfather. She could only hope that Hector was nowhere in the vicinity when Juan and Miguel started mixing it up.

"How's school going?" she asked.

Hector shrugged and sighed. "I thought it would be easier studying for this G.E.D. test, you know, on my own. School was hard enough with teachers who don't give a shit and everyone else in the class only caring about making it to the weekend so they can get some beers and get laid."

Her high school had not been equipped with metal detectors at all of the entrances, but her fellow students had for the most part not been able to see beyond Friday either. Beers and getting laid. Rich or poor, inner city or country club, deep down everybody was exactly the same.

"Don't you give up, though," she said.

"No way," he said. "And let Eva down, like the rest of our family? No way." He put the pen and notepad back in his pocket and picked up the grocery sack. "Here you go, Allison. Besides, last time I was here you were out, so I figure I should make sure you have some next time I'm thirsty."

She laughed and took the bag. Hector gave her a grin and headed off down the hall, which at this time of the night was quiet except for the television turned up loud in Mr. Kaminski's apartment. It brayed an infomercial about the latest orange-oil cleaning product while Allison unlocked her door and went inside.

The room was not dark, enough light filtering in through the curtains and spilling past her from the hallway to let her recognize the familiar shapes of furniture. Her tension returned as she stood on the threshold, a target in the open rectangle of the door, gaze flicking from one possible hiding place to the next searching for movement.

Nothing. It all looked exactly as she'd left it.

Switching on the lights, she went in and shut and bolted everything behind her. The purse, which she hadn't wanted to touch, sat beside her bed with its zippered mouth gaping. Beside it on the floor rested the miniature tape recorder and the folder. Because Allison knew where to look, she could see the corner of the manila bubble-wrap envelope that contained the gun, sticking out from under the recliner. The money, when she checked, was still under the seat.

On her way home from Jamie's, comfortable and full of meatloaf, mashed potatoes and pie, warmed by the kiss and the flirtatious exchange, she had thought that she'd be able to get into bed and forget about the purse until morning. Seeing Hector in the hallway had changed all that, and seeing the purse right there waiting for her made any thoughts of sleep impossible.

She popped open one of the lukewarm Dews and took a deep, steadying breath. Then she went back to the purse and resumed her investigation through its contents.

Next was a compact with a mirror framed in a ring of battery-operated light, the make-up bed divided into a subtle dusty-pink blusher and powder while a thin tube of lipstick — a sort of pearly cream-red shade that Allison rather liked — fitted into a notch beside an eyeliner pencil. A folding hairbrush and a slim plastic holder for tampons.

Three pens, all garden-variety ballpoints, one with the name of a downtown hotel stamped into its barrel. A matchbook from a bar on 12th Street. A box of mint-flavored Tic-Tacs. A bottle of Purell antibacterial hand gel.

She dug deeper.

A parking stub from a garage near Century Plaza. A toothpick in a paper wrapper. A crumpled receipt for a latte and a croissant from a downtown coffee stand, paid in cash, ninety-three cents in change. The ninety-three cents were loose in the bottom of the purse — three quarters, a dime, a nickel and three pennies. No other money.

No other money . . . no wallet. No credit cards. No identification. No keys. No business cards.

No name for the mystery blonde.

All afternoon and evening, Allison had been trying to think of some other explanation for what she'd found in the purse. Few realistic answers had presented themselves, and she'd hoped that she would find something else in there that would make her slap her head and say, "Oh, of course!"

This didn't. This made her think that maybe she'd been right after all.

The blonde wasn't carrying anything to identify her. While she might not have been thinking of a robbery in particular, there was always the possibility of some sort of accident. So she'd been careful.

"Okay," Allison said, having exhausted the purse and even turned it upside-down to shake out a few bits of lint. "The next question is . . . was she being hired, or doing the hiring?"

Her gut told her that the blonde was the killer. The would-be killer, anyway.

But maybe she was wrong.

Maybe the man in the photographs was the blonde's husband and she'd

decided to have him put out of the way. Maybe for the insurance settlement. Maybe he was about to divorce her for some younger brainless bippy with fake California breasts and a fake California tan, and she wasn't happy with the prospect of alimony. Maybe some prenuptial agreement had come back to bite her in the butt.

Allison knew from observation of her own parents, her parents' friends and her friends' parents that nobody got more worked up about money than the people who had it. A taste of the good life left you hungry for more.

Unless you were a renegade like Scoot, who had a taste for the wild life instead.

She pushed "Play" on the tape recorder and listened to the whole thing.

It opened with the bustling sounds of a crowded restaurant. She heard a woman – the blonde? – and a man ordering drinks, ordering fish and chips. The man had a low, suave, sexy voice. The woman's was a cool contralto.

He called her Jade. Whether it was really a name, or an alias, it fit her and Allison was relieved to finally have an identity for the mystery blonde.

The way they talked suggested that they were on familiar enough terms, and maybe even more than a little bit interested in each other.

And then they were talking about the gun.

"You'll like this one. It's practically an antique, but in beautiful condition. Ivory-handled."

Allison hit "Stop" and peeked at the gun again.

Practically an antique. Beautiful condition. Ivory-handled.

And she'd thought, in listening to the first few exchanges earlier, that this was just a business lunch.

Then again, wasn't it? A kind of business, anyway.

She pushed "Play" again.

The two went on to discuss corporate cases and personal motives, and it was soon obvious that they were discussing the man in the photographs. The shirtless man on the sailboat. The target. The speaker with the suave, sexy voice was hiring Jade to kill him. He, and whoever he worked for, wanted that man dead. Jade was getting double her normal fee . . . a quarter now and the rest on completion . . .

Allison stopped the tape again and rubbed a hand across her brow. Her mind hurt. If what she had found in the envelope was only a quarter of the fee instead of the half she had assumed, that meant a grand total of a hundred thousand dollars. Forget a new car; that was a nice condo, or a small house in an outlying suburb.

A hundred thousand dollars.

And the woman, this Jade, was no stranger to killing-for-hire.

79

The man with the suave, sexy voice invited Jade to contemplate a dinner date with him some time. When she said she didn't think it would be a very good idea, he came right back with, *Hell, I know it isn't. But think about it anyway.*

Then, knowing a good exit line when he got one in, the man with the suave, sexy voice left. Allison listened as Jade finished her meal, listened as Jade moved out of the restaurant and onto the street where traffic noises replaced those of diners.

Listened, with her mouth open in a daffy, unwilling grin, to the familiar growing sound of Scoot's wheels on the pavement, the scuffle and thud as Scoot hooked the purse and knocked Jade down.

She was hearing the purse-snatching, hearing Scoot in action. The whir of wheels and Scoot's light puffs of breath, the blurred sounds as Scoot sped past pedestrians and in front of cars.

The tape reached its end sometime before Scoot got to the junkyard, and the machine turned itself off with a final resolute click.

Chapter 14

Jeanette lay wakeful, not even bothering to toss and turn. She lay flat on her back like a mannequin. Arms straight at her sides. Staring blankly at the dark ceiling.

Finally, when she turned her head and the clock told her it was three in the morning, she gave it up as a lost cause and got out of bed.

In nothing but a shortie satin nightshirt, she padded through the house switching on lights. She was unconcerned about peeping Toms. All of her windows not only had curtains and shades, but the glass was either tinted, frosted, or covered with a layer of pebbly film to make seeing in an eye-straining chore.

She had far more house than she needed. Five bedrooms, three and a half baths, sunken living room, formal dining room, entertainer's kitchen, furnished basement rec room with a full-wall river rock fireplace. Fenced and landscaped backyard with a redwood gazebo and a hot tub. Three-car garage.

What the hell, she could afford it. For a while there, she'd been doing five or six jobs a year, tax-free, at fifty grand a pop.

Her house was sparsely but expensively decorated, with the sleek lines and spare designs of modern furniture. The art on the walls was all abstract except for one Thomas Kinkaide full of pale colors and ethereal light.

A cleaning service came twice a week, as did a landscaper – he refused to be called anything so prosaic as a mere gardener – to keep up the yard. The neighborhood had a homeowner's association to keep everything nice, and a

gate to keep the riffraff out. The lots were large, the houses spaced to provide cherished privacy. All Jeanette usually saw of her neighbors was the occasional upscale car backing out of a driveway, the occasional spoiled brat biking lazily along one of the curving streets.

Five bedrooms, and she only used one for sleeping. The others weren't even guest rooms, as she never had guests. One was a well-equipped home gym, one was an office where she kept her computer and files, the sunniest one in the southeastern corner was devoted to houseplants and herbs.

The last and smallest of the bedrooms was kept vacant. She went in there now, the hardwood floor satiny beneath her feet, and looked around at the eggshell-white walls.

The baby's room.

There was no baby. There never had been a baby. There hadn't been so much as a close call along the lines of a missed period or broken condom.

It wasn't as if she had any plans to start a family, any urge to become a mother. Yet, somehow, whenever she tried to think of doing something else with this room, she got a knot in her stomach.

Her own family life had been fragmentary and unreliable. Her parents had gotten married right out of high school, her father a Navy man who had knocked up his wife every time he came home on leave.

Jeanette's earliest memories were of cardboard boxes. The family had moved three times before she started kindergarten. Then her father had died – killed in a senseless training accident at a base near San Diego – and her mother Diane had been left with four young children, no job, little education and hardly any skills.

She tried getting work, no easy task for a young white woman in a region of the country where immigrants and illegals were willing to work for next to nothing. After paying a babysitter out of what pittance she was able to earn, there was hardly enough money left for to keep Jeanette and her siblings fed and clothed.

Some friends with good intentions set Diane up on dates, but not many men were keen on a widow who had four kids. Except for one. Chuck. He had been *very* keen on Diane . . . not in spite of her kids but because of them.

Even at eight years old, Jeanette had known that there was something wrong with Chuck. That it wasn't right for him to volunteer to give the girls their baths, offering to scrub their backs, wash their hair. He'd often told them what pretty little girls they were, and how much he wanted to be their special friend.

With her, it had never gone beyond talk. She didn't know whether he'd

done more to Carrie and Deena, her sisters. All she knew was that she had been overjoyed when he and Diane broke up and Chuck was out of their lives.

Finally, swallowing her pride, Diane had been forced to fall back on relatives for help. She tried first with her father-in-law, but Hank Kurrell was a no-good drunk who lived in a rundown trailer huddled in the dusty foothills at the edge of a dying town on the wrong side of the San Bernardinos. Hank had shown no interest in the welfare of his grandchildren or daughter-in-law. To get rid of Diane, he had supplied her with an old car, enough cash to fill up the tank with gas, and the address of his sister, Cecilia, up in Oregon.

Aunt Cece, as she insisted she be called, was an enormously fat woman who wore flowered housedresses and kept parakeets. She had agreed to take them in, so Diane had packed them all into the car for the long ride north.

Cece worked in a candy factory which, to the severe disappointment of the Kurrell kids, was nothing like the one they'd seen in the famous movie. No edible gardens, no Oompa-Loompas, no benignly psychotic man in a purple velvet suit. Just ordinary workers, most of them women, most of them fat, packaging candies off of a conveyor belt.

For a while, with Aunt Cece, things had been okay. Not great; the house was small and Jeanette had to share a room with both of her little sisters while Mitchell slept on a cot in the laundry room. The parakeets twittered and cheeped twenty-four hours a day. But, for the first time since their father's death, they'd had enough to eat. *Too* much to eat when it came to candy. Cece got Diane a job at the factory and there was money for new clothes from K-Mart, and weekly trips to McDonalds and the movie theater.

It took almost a whole year of living with Aunt Cece for their bad luck to catch up with them. When it did, it came with a vengeance.

One day, when Jeanette was at the kitchen table doing her homework, her sister Carrie burst in, her face ashen and tear-streaked. Mitchell, their little brother, had been hit by a car.

He'd been playing catch, and Jeffy Ryerson had thrown the ball too hard. Without stopping to look for traffic, Mitchell had dashed into the street after it. The driver of the car had stopped long enough to see what had happened, and then, while Carrie, Deena, the Ryerson kids and Lottie Hessman watched, leapt behind the wheel and roared off.

Then, like dominoes, the rest had begun to fall. The shock of Mitchell's death had most likely contributed to Aunt Cece's stroke. Perhaps while visiting Aunt Cece in the hospital, Deena, always the frailest of the four, had gotten bronchitis that became pneumonia. The medical bills and the cost of the nursing home ate up what little they'd been able to save and Cece's house had

83

to be sold to cover the rest, leaving Diane and the girls homeless again.

Jeanette had never met her maternal grandparents. She got a birthday card each year, with an impersonal signature and a dollar tucked inside. On Christmas, the Barnes grandparents always sent a box addressed to all the kids. It invariably held one of the standard board games – checkers, Chutes and Ladders, Candy Land, Aggravation, Yahtzee – plus a package of store-bought holiday cookies. In return, Diane sent Sears Portrait Studio pictures of the children.

Diane called them when Mitchell died, and even in her own grief, Jeanette had been able to hope that maybe this tragedy would have some good, and bring them together as a family. She'd been wrong. Big Jim and Lucy had not come to the funeral. They had sent a flower arrangement as impersonal as the signatures in the birthday cards and that was all.

The family returned to southern California, where Diane worked two jobs to make ends meet. Jeanette was left in charge, though she found it impossible to discipline her wild sister, Carrie . . . and didn't have the heart to be too strict with poor sickly Deena.

Carrie smoked and drank, and hung around with older boys. It came as no real surprise when, at thirteen, she ran away from home and was never seen again.

Deena's lungs never fully recovered from her bout with pneumonia. On a school field trip, she had suffered an asthma attack and suffocated to death while her horrified classmates had looked on.

Perhaps those final tragedies had used up the last of the bad luck. Things had turned around for Jeanette and her mother after that. Diane got a good job at a ski resort up in the mountains, and there, in that small town that thrived during the winter season and slumbered the rest of the year, Jeanette made her first real friends.

It was also where she had made her first kill.

And somehow, she had ended up here. In this comfortable neighborhood and this wonderful house. With more money than her mother had ever dreamed of.

Jeanette looked again around the empty, unfurnished room.

The baby's room.

If there ever was a baby. If she ever dared try.

What did she want with a family anyway? It would only bring trial and struggle, grief and despair. Her mother had been so glad to be quit of the reminders of that whole ugly mess that Jeanette hadn't heard from her in years. Diane had happily settled into a new life with a new husband and two stepsons.

In her darker hours – like now – Jeanette wondered if there was a curse on the Kurrells. It would explain a lot.

Though she kept the house at a comfortable temperature year round – energy bills be damned – she shivered.

God, she hated these trips down memory lane, but lately she found herself taking them. Hashing over the past, remembering the poverty and the misery and the grinding hopelessness.

As much as she'd tried to put it behind her, it was all still there. The endless tweeting clamor of Aunt Cece's parakeets. Chuck smiling through a haze of whiskey fumes, telling her what a pretty little girl she was. Carrie screaming about the car, about Mitchell. Trying to sleep on the trundle bed, hearing Deena gasping, and waiting, just *waiting* for the time when her sister wouldn't be able to get a breath. Her mother, puffy circles under her eyes, aged into a hag before her time.

Not me, she'd told herself again and again during those long, wretched years. That won't happen to me.

And it hadn't. She had avoided her mother's fate. Rather than have children and watch helplessly as they died, or went bad, or grew away and apart and indifferent, she had this empty room. The baby's room for the baby that wasn't. That would never be.

This was her life, such as it was. A little hollow, maybe. A little empty. But hers, a damn sight better than anything she'd been able to reasonably hope for as a child. Her life, and she liked it.

If that damned skateboard kid didn't ruin everything.

Jeanette couldn't stand the prospect of losing what she had worked so hard to attain. The money was part of it, but her reputation was on the line too.

How could she dial one of the contact numbers that would put her in touch with Rayburn and his associates? How could she tell them what had happened? She would look like a hundred different kinds of fool. Letting her purse get stolen? They would be disgusted at her carelessness.

What was she going to do?

Finish the job, that was what she was going to do. If she was clever enough, she could do it and have Rayburn's people be none the wiser.

It would mean losing a quarter of the money. That hurt, but it wasn't going to kill her, especially when she had been promised double her usual fee. She would still stand to clear seventy-five thousand, no matter how you sliced it.

But how was she going to finish the job? They wanted her to use that specific gun. The one from the collection. The target's own gun.

She could get around that hitch somehow. It might be difficult, but it

wouldn't be impossible.

Jeanette went downstairs to the kitchen. An entertainer's kitchen, the real estate agent had called it. A feature that was lost on her, for she never entertained.

Her large refrigerator and cupboards were kept well stocked. Perhaps excessively so, obsessively so. She supposed it was some holdover from her childhood, when there had so rarely been enough to eat. An overcompensation.

She took out the makings of a ham sandwich, supplemented it with carrot sticks and a glass of milk, and carried her post-midnight meal back up to her bedroom.

It wasn't the money and it wasn't the gun. If either or even both of those things had been the real problem, Jeanette wouldn't have worried.

The target. *He* was the problem.

Whoever he was.

There it was in a nutshell. She had not so much as glanced at the name of the man she was supposed to be killing. She didn't know who he was, or where he lived, or what he did for a living.

All she knew was that the photographs had shown a fit, healthy blond man who looked to be in his mid-twenties, but could really be as old as forty if he was diligent about his health. And that he had a sailboat, or had at least once in his life gone sailing.

Not a lot to go on. Not nearly enough to get her started.

If she contacted Rayburn, he could provide her with copies of the file. But would he? Would he agree to do it without wanting to know why she needed it? Unlikely. He'd want to know. He'd want an explanation.

No, the only thing she could do would be to retrieve the original information. If she got it all back, gun and folder and all, she wouldn't have a problem. She could carry out her assignment and no one would ever have to know.

She needed to get her stuff back.

Which meant finding the skateboard kid.

Somehow. Anyhow.

Come hell or high water, she would find that skateboard kid.

Chapter 15

A muffled but loud hammering noise gradually seeped into her awareness. Once she acknowledged it, she also became aware of a steady drilling beep that drove into her head like someone pushing a long thin nail into her ear.

Allison sat up disoriented, in the grips of a decongestant hangover, and stared stupidly around at the room.

She had made herself go to bed after listening to the tape. Since she hadn't been the least bit sleepy, she'd taken a sinus-relief tablet to help her along. Her sinuses were fine, but the drowsiness side effect dragged her down like an anchor into a thick, dreamless darkness.

The banging came again, accompanied by an unintelligible but irritable voice through the wall.

Her alarm clock was going off. Had been going off for a solid fourteen . . . no, fifteen minutes. The banging on the wall was Mr. Kaminski next door. He kept his television on at full volume until four in the morning most nights, but if anyone made noise before ten on a Saturday, he would raise the goddamn roof.

She turned off the alarm. The pounding continued for another half a minute, then ceased, and blissful quiet descended. Still, she knew she could count on finding a nasty note tacked to her door later, or a complaint made to Teddi Lace. Or both. Why not, Mr. Kaminski? Live a little.

A shower and two cups of coffee helped to clear away the fog. Clad in stretchy leggings and a long sweater, Allison was back in her dilemma about

the blonde's purse.

The smart thing to do would be to turn the purse and everything in it over to the police.

Thinking about the police made a flutter of panic beat in her belly, as if she had swallowed a large moth.

Not that she had anything against them in principle. Police, not moths. Not that she had anything against moths either . . .

She drank a third cup of coffee.

In principle, she believed that a strong police force was a good thing. Mr. Colucci at the locksmith shop had a brother-in-law who was a cop. Officer Tony Rugerro sometimes came into Sherwood Second-Hand. He liked to browse through the old furniture for pieces that could be fixed up, and always carried a box of like-new stuffed animals in the trunk of his patrol car in case he met any distraught kids on the crime scenes.

Allison liked Officer Rugerro, but whenever he was in the store she got clammy all over, just waiting for him to wander past the rack of purses and recognize one from a robbery report.

She could, she supposed, claim that the buttercream leather purse and its contents had shown up in the donation box. That would be the easiest way to get rid of it.

But what about the money? Who, really, who in their right mind would dump a purse containing that kind of cash? Even the most honest of persons would have a hard time passing up such a windfall. You sometimes heard of thrift store employees finding overlooked valuables in coat pockets, but a wad of twenty-five thousand dollars was a hell of a lot harder to overlook than a ring or a folded hundred-dollar bill.

What, then? Hold onto the money, but turn everything else over?

And if she held onto the money, what would she do with it?

Off the top of her head, she could list fifty people in this neighborhood alone who could benefit from a surprise bonus.

Eva, for example, and Hector. With that kind of cash, Eva could afford a bigger place and actually have her brother live with her, to keep him away from the bad influences of his stepfather and soon-to-be-released convict brother.

Or Martha. Even if Martha *wanted* to live in her vacant lot, it couldn't be good for her and she couldn't really be happy.

Or the Strevyks . . . or Needles and Tisha . . . or even Jamie Tremayne. Indeed, practically everyone she knew on Dunley Street could make good and welcome use of twenty-five thousand dollars.

For that matter, if she was being truthful with herself, so could Allison "Scoot" Montgomery. She didn't *need* a nicer apartment or a car . . . but if she *had* those things, she could bring her sister over for visits. Spend weekends with her. Summers, even. It would be a way to erase some of the loneliness and misery from Missy's eyes. A way to get her out of that luxurious, loveless house for a while.

But she couldn't keep the money all for herself and not share with her friends and neighbors . . . and she couldn't realistically share with her friends and neighbors. What would she tell them? That she happened to find twenty-five G's and wanted to share the wealth? That she'd won the lottery? She never played the lottery and they all knew it. Even the most grateful of them would have to be a little suspicious . . . and someone might say the wrong thing to the wrong person.

"For God's sake!" she said into the stillness of the living room. "Forget about the money! The money's the least of your worries right now!"

While that wasn't entirely true, it was true enough for her to push the issue aside and turn her attention to what really mattered.

The gun.

The gun and the folder.

A man was marked for death, as crazy as that sounded. Someone wanted him killed and was willing to pay big bucks to see it done.

Allison wasn't naïve enough to believe that the people who'd hired the woman called Jade would, upon learning of the mishap, shrug and say, "Oh, well, never mind then . . . let him live." There had been steel beneath the smoky sexiness of Jade's lunch date's voice. He wasn't someone to change his mind.

No, whatever else happened, somebody wanted the man in the photographs dead, and would find some other way of accomplishing it.

For all Allison knew, he might be dead already. Was it so far-fetched to think that Jade, alarmed by the loss of her purse, had decided to strike fast before the target could be warned?

She smacked herself in the head. *That* was what she should have done first! If he *was* dead, it was her fault.

When she opened the folder, the photos slid out. Handsome man, blond curls, bronze tan, excellent teeth. Looked a little like the actor Heath Ledger had. Expensive clothes. The watch on his wrist looked like a Rolex. Pricey sailboat.

He appeared to be the kind of guy that might have been buddies with her Montgomery-side relatives. From money. From influence. Tennis, yachting, polo. His nickname was probably Chet, or Chas, or Skip . . . if he had a sister, she was Tiffy, or Muffy, or Babs.

Was it possible that she might even *know* him? Had they been guests at the same parties? If he was local, it wasn't that far-fetched. She'd certainly met plenty of men *like* him. But she didn't recognize this specific one.

On one of the pages of information, she found his name.

"Benedict Westbrook."

She didn't know the name . . . yet felt the nagging, niggling feeling that she *should.*

The address was in Palmyra Hills, which Allison knew to be an area of opulent mansions, waterfront property, and general extravagance.

New money, as her father might say with a sneer. The Montgomerys had made their fortune several generations back. Their particular branch of the family was not associated with the department stores but with canned fruits and vegetables, frozen dinners, and one of the earliest patents on a type of circuit used in microwave ovens and other small appliances.

So this Westbrook could be a computer mogul, an e-commerce kind of guy. Or . . . hadn't she only a few minutes ago been imagining herself sharing around the money and claiming she'd won the lottery?

If that were the case, then it was even less likely she might have met him. In her parents' hierarchy of worthiness, the old-money families whose current descendants never had to do a real day's work but could coast on the inheritance and investments were the top dogs. Big-money celebrities, sports figures and high-tech dot-commers were next, because while they might not have the bloodline, they had at least earned their fortunes and their way to the top.

But the lowest, the worst, the intolerable were the ones who made their fortunes out of the blue and with little apparent effort. Allison had once overheard her mother and her sister-in-law talking disdainfully about a woman who'd won a million dollars on a game show and was buying a nearby house. This woman even had the temerity to want to join the country club. As Susan Montgomery had put it, "She suddenly has a million dollars and thinks that makes her good enough."

It hadn't been long after that, come to think of it, that Allison had moved out and been glad to go.

No, there was no room in the Montgomery world view for lottery winners – not even those who scored the multi-million-dollar jackpots – or game show contestants, or people who successfully got enormous lawsuit settlements because they'd spilled hot coffee on themselves. A gold-digging bimbo who married an elderly oil tycoon and then had him drop dead a week later of a sexual-overload stroke was more welcome in their society. Heck . . . a woman like that would receive a certain grudging respect, because

she *had* earned it.

If Westbrook was one of 'those' people, it made sense that Allison might have heard his name but wasn't able to connect it to anything. He wouldn't have been a guest at the house, but someone who might have been mentioned in passing, with that lofty arrogance only the truly lofty spoiled rich could achieve.

She had to do something.

Do what?

Allison folded her legs tailor-fashion, braced her elbows on her knees and propped her head up on her hands.

Do something.

Uh-huh, sure.

Call him up, why not? "Hi, Mr. Westbrook . . . you don't know me, but there's someone trying to kill you."

Send him a fortune cookie. *Beware of petite blondes with guns.*

Mail him what she'd found?

That had possibilities. Package it all up, and send it to the Palmyra Hills address with an anonymous letter. When one of his own guns fell out of the envelope, it'd have to make him sit up and take notice.

Except then, the police would get involved. And no matter how careful Allison was, they'd trace it back to her. Somehow. Her fingerprints were all over everything. Even if she wiped off each article, would that work on paper? Didn't the oils from the fingertips soak in and leave an indelible mark?

There would be hairs, fibers from her clothes and carpet. Handwriting analysis of the letter, the address . . . even if she typed them, or used a computer, there were ways to ferret out the truth by the kind of ink, the brand of paper. She watched television. She knew what they could do.

The greater pains she took to cover her tracks, the more it would make the detectives think she had something to hide.

Which, okay, she did. But that was beside the point. She was trying to do the right thing here, damn it! Trying to save a man from being murdered!

It just so happened that she was also a petty criminal.

"Sheesh, Allie-girl," she muttered, using Uncle Bob's pet name. "What's more important here? Your freedom or a guy's life?"

Then there was the scandal to think about, what her family would –

Allison veered her thoughts sharply away from *that*, thank you very much.

What, then? What to do?

She was never going to come up with an answer just sitting here. She needed to get out, away from this mess. She needed to get some air, some movement.

She needed to be Scoot for a while.

Chapter 16

He opened the door to go inside and she was right there behind him. A hard shove sent him stumbling into the darkened room, arms flailing. The bag of Chinese food he'd been carrying flew from his hand and hit the floor. White cardboard containers burst open and spilled fried rice and pork chow mein over the ratty carpet.

"Whoa! Fuck! Hey!" he blurted as his feet knocked into each other and he went solidly to his knees. He landed on a packet of soy sauce and popped it. "What's the fuckin' deal, dude?"

"I'm not a dude," Jade said in her coldest voice. She kicked the door shut, cutting off the daylight and plunging them into even murkier lighting.

The kid with the masses of rusty-wire hair on his head and all over his body, the hulking loser she'd nicknamed Bigfoot, started to rise.

Jade ratcheted the shotgun, and he froze. There was no mistaking that sound. Anybody who'd ever been to an action movie knew that sound.

She didn't care for the shotgun. It was messy and imprecise, hard to conceal, hard to handle. But the important thing was that it made big nasty holes in people, and Bigfoot knew it.

"Don't get up," she said. "Stay right like that."

Still on his knees, he was dumb enough — or stoned into sufficient bravado — to twist his head around and look at her. His eyes were glazed and bloodshot. They squinted at her, then lit up with a low animal cunning. He recognized her. It wasn't hard; she wore a green track suit and a hooded

jacket, but had made no effort to hide the color and style of her hair.

"Look, bitch —"

"Call me a bitch again, and I'll shoot your foot off."

Holding the shotgun on him, she scanned the rest of the room to make sure they were alone.

Bigfoot lived in a scuzzy motel at the bad end of Prewett. It rented units by the week or month, for cash with no I.D. necessary and no questions asked. He had blankets tacked up over the windows, casting the room into a gloomy dimness that hid the worst of the squalor. There was no kitchen, not even a kitchenette. Instead, there was a microwave so old it probably sent out sterilizing beams of radiation whenever it was used. Given Bigfoot's suitability to breed, Jade figured that in his case, a little sterility was a good thing.

The bed folded down from the wall and was a rumpled expanse of sleeping bag, dirty clothes, and dirtier magazines. Pizza boxes, beer cans, empty two-liter soda bottles, and take-out wrappers littered the floor. The closet was a bare bar above a mound of clothes and towels that looked like they might come alive if someone shot a bolt of lightning through them. Posters of bands — grunge and heavy metal — vied for wall space with centerfolds and pictures of pro wrestlers.

The bathroom door stood ajar and the fly-specked low-wattage bulb over the sink shed their only source of light. She didn't really want a close look at his bathroom, but could see enough of it to determine that no one was hiding in the shower, the floor was so grimy that she couldn't guess what color it had started as, and the toilet seat was up. She'd have bet her car that it wasn't flushed, either. And the shower drain would be clogged with a wad of rust-colored hair the size of a dead hamster.

He had himself a fairly nice entertainment setup, a stack of porn videos, a black Rubbermaid container full of video game cases, and not one but two game-system consoles.

Opposite the bed, the disassembled pieces of a bike hung on metal hooks that had been mounted on the wall. He had left his other bike outside, locking it to a metal rack, the modern equivalent of the ol' hitching post. A skateboard, airbrushed with an image of a flaming skull with snakes coming out of the eye sockets, rested against a speaker. At the foot of the bed was a pair of in-line skates with black wheels. He even had one of those shiny silver scooters. Bigfoot covered all the bases.

The smell in here was enough to make her eyes water. Jade tried not to breathe too deeply, wanting get as little of it into her lungs as possible. She didn't let herself think about what might be causing such a stench, just as she

didn't let herself think about the stains on the carpet.

When she had seen him the previous afternoon, Bigfoot had been wearing a rock group tee shirt and black leather pants looped with chrome chains. Today he was in urban commando mode, with an olive-green tee shirt, army-style boot and camouflage pants.

One of his hands twitched toward his belt, where a box cutter hung in a leather loop, and Jade prodded the side of his head with the shotgun barrel.

"Unless you want to make this room even more of a revolting pigsty by decorating the walls with your brains," she said, "you'll forget about trying."

"Jeez, lady! I didn't do nothing!" He had not called her a bitch, so perhaps he could be taught after all, wonder of wonders and hallelujah.

"What's your name?"

"Jon." He said it sullenly, the way he would have – and *had*, she was sure – said it to a teacher or playground monitor.

"All right, Jon. Listen to me. I want to know who that other kid is, and where I can find him."

He didn't bother with pretending not to know what she was talking about. Having a shotgun pressed to his skull, just above his right ear, must have removed any desire to be a wiseass or play games. "The guy who lifted your purse, I don't know who the fuck he is. Seen him around, and I heard some kids call him Scoot. But I don't know him, lady, I don't fuckin' know him."

"Not good enough."

"Fuck! For Chrissake, lady!"

"Seen him around, you said. Seen him around where?"

"Places," Jon said. "The Plaz, the skate park, the library quad at Atherton."

"You go to Atherton?" she asked, not trying to keep the skepticism from her tone.

"To skate," he said defensively. "To ride my bike. I'm not some pussy college student, but they've got good pavement there."

"What skate park?"

"On Pine," he said. "Pine and 3rd, 4th maybe. I don't go there anymore. Used to, when I was a kid. It's for pussies. They won't let you ride your board there unless you wear a fuckin' helmet."

"But you've seen this Scoot there?"

"Sometimes, yeah." He turned his head a little, the shotgun barrel digging into his matted hair, and looked at her out of the corner of his eye. "You're not the first one whose fuckin' purse he's stolen. I seen him do it a few times, and so's everybody else."

"Lucky me," Jade said. "Have you seen him since yesterday?"

"No, dude."

"You're not lying to me, Jon?"

"I swear! I fuckin' swear!"

"You certainly do."

"Huh?"

"Tell me about Scoot."

"I told you, I don't fuckin' know him, already. I heard some of the chicks think he's a fag. A pretty boy; all the chicks are crazy for him, but he looks like a fag to me."

"What does he look like?"

"Told you. A pretty boy. I never seen him up close."

"Do you know where he lives?"

Jon shook his head.

Sighing frustration through her teeth, Jade said, "Do you know who *would?*"

"He doesn't fuckin' hang with us, okay? He's just . . . around. Doesn't say much."

"Does he smoke? Drink? Do dope?"

"Dope," chuckled Jon. "Dude, that's a good one."

She nudged harder with the shotgun, which the shaggy lunkhead seemed to have temporarily forgotten. "You know what I mean."

"I never seen him do anything but soda."

"Who else can I talk to? I need to find Scoot."

"Hey, I'd fuckin' help you if I could, lady. It's people like him who give the rest of us a bad name, all right? Going around fuckin' robbing people, and so the cops start thinking we're all fuckin' criminals."

Jade had, without consciously electing to do so, begun keeping score of his ludicrous profanity. She couldn't help it.

"They're always fuckin' looking for an excuse to bust one of us, dude," he went on. "Like it's against the law to smoke a little pot."

"It is."

"Fuckin' stupid law. It doesn't hurt nobody."

She wasn't about to get into a debate on law and order with him. This was absurd enough already.

"Tell me who might know where to find Scoot," she said, jabbing harder with the shotgun this time.

"Ow! That fuckin' hurts, okay?"

"It'll *fuckin'* hurt worse if I pull the trigger. Dude."

God, how she hated whiners! Here he was, six-foot-something and twice her weight, more covered with hair than a werewolf, and he was whining. If

95

ever she'd needed another reason why she preferred to shoot people without having to talk to them, this was it. They would all whine, or blubber, once they had the gun to their head. And then she wouldn't be killing them for the right reasons.

"Sorry," he said, chastened.

Now, why had that gotten through to him all of a sudden? Was it because she was finally speaking his language? Or had the pressure of the shotgun barrel finally made a coherent impression on that thick head of his?

"I'd rather not blow your brains . . . pardon me, your *fuckin'* brains out, dude," she said. "It'd be noisy and gross. So, if you want to be alive to eat those egg rolls for lunch, I suggest you listen closely to what I have to say."

"Sure, anything, lady."

One hand on the shotgun, she fished into her pocket and drew out a pre-paid disposable cellular phone. She bought them by the half-dozen and never kept them more than a couple of weeks. "My number's already programmed on here. I let you go, and next time you see Scoot, you call and tell me where he is."

His muddy, bloodshot eyes brightened with hope.

"But there's a catch," she said. "If I don't hear from you by Wednesday – that's in four days – I come back and we have another talk. Got it, dude?"

"Yeah."

"I found you this time, so I can find you again if I need to. Don't make me hunt you down. If you do, you'll regret it."

He bobbed his head again. Droplets of sweat stood out in his scruffy red stubble like beads of dew. Maybe the fact that she had bald-faced walked into his room with a shotgun at high noon convinced him she was in earnest.

"Good." She tossed the phone down beside him and backed toward the door. "And it goes without saying that if I find out you've warned Scoot off . . ."

"I'm not a fuckin' moron!" he said.

"Prove it."

With that, she was out the door like an eddy of wind.

Chapter 17

The fall could have been a lot worse. It came at the apogee of a half-pipe jump, which Scoot must have mis-timed.

The skateboard squirted out from under her feet. Scoot's shins cracked with white agony into the concrete lip. The board went skittering wheels-up down the curve Then, like in the old nursery rhyme about Jack and Jill, Scoot went tumbling after.

She fetched up groaning in a heap at the bottom of the half-pipe, the board on its back next to her with its wheels slowly spinning to a stop.

A round of sarcastic applause greeted her performance. Scoot flipped them the finger without looking. She got up and limped to a bench in front of a row of portable toilets, where she sat rubbing her lower legs.

It was all too easy to imagine her shinbones as long splintery sticks. They didn't feel broken, and the pain was already fading, but she knew from past experience that by morning she would have two colossal plum-colored bruises.

The skate park was always busiest on sunny Saturdays. Most of the crowd was made up of kids and families, the younger ones who would put up with the helmet-and-pads rule. But there were enough older participants that Scoot wasn't an anomaly.

Top-forty music thumped from pole-mounted speakers and the cement maze of ramps, bowls, half-pipes and jumps simmered in the sunshine. A few attendants perched on high chairs like lifeguards, ready with whistles and bullhorns whenever they saw someone ignoring the rules posted in red lettering

on a large white billboard.

The park was adjacent to Funway, an arcade that offered miniature golf, bumper boats, batting cages, Laser Tag, singing robot animals and games that paid out in tickets to be redeemed at obscene exchange rates for cheap trinkets. The snack bar served pizza, hot dogs, popcorn, ice cream, soda pop, cotton candy and giant stale pretzels. Funway was *the* spot for birthday parties on this side of town.

Crowded, yes, and if Scoot had been interested in purses today there would have been plenty of mom-purses to choose from. Skateboard groupie purses, too. Not that she was interested. God, no. Right now, she thought she might be cured of her purse-snatching habit forever.

She had been here for most of the day, eating an unhealthy lunch and telling herself that at least her jaw muscles were getting a workout trying to chew a pretzel with the consistency of half-dried adobe. She was sweaty, achy and exhausted.

But she felt good. She'd needed this. Had been getting herself all worked up, tied in knots, about that purse. When really, it wasn't anything she had to worry about.

The thing to do was simply claim, as Allison, that she had found it. And that she'd been so shocked by what was inside that the only thing to do was contact the police.

After all, it certainly was not as if the blonde woman would have filed a report about the purse-snatching. Not with what she'd been carrying, what she'd been doing.

The police would take it from there. The police would warn Benedict Westbrook, and it'd all work out fine.

This was not something that she, either as Scoot or as Allison, needed to involve herself in. True, the wild and reckless part of her had contemplated heading over to Palmyra Hills today instead of to the skate park. Just to see the house, maybe see Westbrook, maybe get an idea of why someone would want him dead. That was the part most intriguing to her. What could he have done? Who would pay that kind of money to kill him? Why?

A case like this, though, was probably the sort of thing that would make the papers. She could read about it later. Read about it without seeing her own name in print.

Scoot had been sitting with sore legs outstretched, but had to draw them back fast as a herd of yelling children raced by. They had sticky faces and frenetic eyes, no doubt on a total sugar high.

As she got up, thinking to move to safer ground, she noticed someone

looking at her. He was a guy she'd seen around the usual skater hangouts. Hard to miss. Big. Hairy. Resembled one of Dr. Moreau's test subjects that had started out as an orangutan. Room-temperature IQ. Camo pants and combat boots. Drawing looks of his own from the attendants because he might be the type to pull out an Uzi and turn birthday parties into bloodbaths.

His beady gaze was fixed on Scoot. The quality of it made her skin creep. Greedy. Predatory.

She did a hasty but surreptitious check to make sure that her clothes were still arranged, that she hadn't torn her shirt wide open in the fall and exposed her bra or something.

Did he know the truth about her? Did he know that Scoot was really a girl?

Her clothes were fine. Baggy stonewashed jeans, sneakers, an oversized tee shirt bearing the logo of the local major-league baseball team. Her helmet hadn't come off, either.

So why the look? Why the predator's greedy stare?

Scoot didn't like it.

Pretending not to be aware of him, she picked up her board and rose from the bench. She threaded her way through throngs of kids and teenagers. Her stuff was in one of the outdoor lockers.

He followed. At a distance, but he was following her all right.

Oh, great.

When she reached her locker, she unpinned the key stuck with a safety pin to the bottom inside hem of her shirt. She opened the locker and grabbed her duffel. By then, the hairy guy was lingering at the end of the row. He had a cell phone pressed to his ear. Seeing her glance his way, he acted – badly – like he was just innocently placing a call.

She hurried for the exit, not like she was being chased but like she happened to need to catch a bus in a few minutes. The parking lot was full of minivans. She wended her way between them, reached the sidewalk of Pine Street, and set her board on the ground.

Lost him. Good.

But moments later, he appeared behind her on a bike.

No coincidence. He *was* following her.

Maybe she was being paranoid. Hell, didn't she have a right to be, after yesterday? She didn't know *why* he would follow her even if he did suspect that there was more to skateboarder Scoot than met the eye.

But he was. She was sure of it.

All right, then. Let him try. Even with wheels, he wouldn't be able to keep up with her.

99

Scoot was off in a flash, building up speed with a series of strong kicks. The skateboard jolted over seams in the sidewalk with a rapid *thud-thud, thud-thud*.

Ahead, a city bus was in the process of disgorging its passengers. Several were kids bound for Funway, happy and excited, carrying birthday presents and gift bags with tissue paper foaming out of the top. Scoot veered around them.

Mailman, dead ahead! Not paying attention. Head down, sorting through a pile of catalogs. Navy blue canvas bag taking up half the sidewalk.

Scoot went off the curb, directly in front of the city bus as its doors hiss-thumped shut and it began to pull back into traffic. The horn, right over her head, sounded like the end of the world. If she fell, the huge tires would crush her into roadkill.

Rather than try and get out of the way, she braced both feet on the skateboard and leaned her back and butt against the front of the rolling steel behemoth. It pushed her along. Her wheels shuddered on the asphalt and the word "whoa!" came out of her in a jittery stutter.

She craned her neck. Through the wide windshield, she could see the bus driver gesturing at her. The horn blew again. The bus slowed as he braked.

"Spoilsport!" she shouted over her shoulder, and kicked off from the bus. She hopped back onto the curb, dodged a man walking a cocker spaniel and a woman with a stroller, and sped around a blind corner.

A shop owner and a delivery man had been nose-to-nose arguing, but both leaped backward as Scoot shot between them. "Sorry!" she called back. But she'd done them a favor, because instead of resuming yelling at each other, they both forgot whatever they'd been fighting about and were joined in brotherhood as they yelled after her.

Another dog, this one no clownishly cute cocker spaniel but a bulldog with a scrunched-up face and a pissed-at-the-universe bark, was tied to a parking meter and tried to take a bite out of Scoot's leg. Avoiding that with some fancy footwork, she damn near ran over a portly man too busy reading the *Wall St. Journal* to look where he was going.

She reached the next cross street and had to stop for the light. There were too many cars moving too fast here for her to risk it. She was a daredevil, maybe, but not suicidal.

Looking back, she saw the bus go through the intersection.

And the hairy red guy come around the corner on his bike.

Shit!

The light went from green to yellow, and Scoot lunged into the street heedless of the last few drivers who tried to make it before the red. A beat-up old Mustang the color of cat puke screeched to a smoking-rubber halt

inches from her, and a man's hand popped out the driver's side window to give her a stiff-fingered salute.

Then she was across, pushing hard, whirring along, trying not to bean anybody with her wildly-swinging duffel. Midway down the block she hung a hard right into an alley. It was a narrow corridor between low-rent apartment buildings, all rusty fire escapes and barred windows and overflowing Dumpsters –

– and three little girls playing jump-rope in the middle of the alley.

"Cinderella-dressed-in-yella-went-upstairs-to-kiss-a-fella," they chanted, two of them turning the long rope while the third, scabby knees showing beneath pink shorts, jumped.

Scoot dismounted at a run, slammed her heel on the back of the board, and flipped it up so that she could catch it by the front end. She trotted to a stop a few yards from the girls, who had left off their chanting to look at her with wide, solemn eyes. The rope lay slack between them, and the jumper stood with one white-sneakered foot on either side of it. She had pink barrettes in her frizzy-dark hair and the Powerpuff Girls on her shirt.

"Made-a-mistake-and-kissed-a-snake," Scoot said. "How-many-doctors-did-it-take?"

The three little girls gave her three gap-toothed smiles. She hopped over the rope and broke into a run, though the jogging motion renewed the pain in her shins in a way that riding the board hadn't done.

At the end of the alley, she looked back. The girls had resumed their jumping and chanting, and she didn't see the guy on the bike.

He hadn't been following her after all.

Relieved, Scoot headed for home.

She changed in the junkyard again, the shadows by now long and cool. Booger the dog was eating kibble in great snuffling gulps out of a stainless-steel bowl big enough to bathe a baby in. The tag on his collar made atonal metallic clinks and clanks.

As she stepped through the fence into the alley, and then onto Dunley Street, she was bathed in whirling pulses of red light from the roof-rack of a police car.

101

Chapter 18

"Follow him," the ice-cold bitch on the cell phone had said. "Lose him, and I'll shoot you in the kneecaps."

Jon had no doubt that the bitch meant every word.

So he followed.

At one point, he was sure he'd lost the little prick. Fury and panic bubbled up in his gut. But then, he'd come around the corner just in time to see the black lightning-bolt skateboard with the electric-blue wheels roll out of an alley and continue on its merry fuckin' way.

He'd been more careful, then. He could be careful when he had to, smart when he had to. People might not think so, but people were fuckin' idiots. They were all down on him because he hadn't finished school. Fuckin' boring school. No use to anybody.

Even his own damn mother thought he was a drug dealer. He told her he didn't, he told her that the reason he got so many calls and had to go out so often in the middle of the night was to buy, sell, and trade bike parts. She could have taken his word for it. But the old shit-queen hadn't fuckin' trusted him, how do you like that? Hadn't fuckin' trusted her own son. She'd even gone searching and found his stash, eighty bucks' worth. Flushed it down the crapper and kicked him out of the house. Said he'd *lied* to her.

Well, fuckin' *duh* he'd lied to her . . . what was he going to do? Tell her the fuckin' truth? For all he knew, she only *said* she'd flushed his stash. For all he knew, the shit-queen might have sold it or used it herself.

That didn't matter now. What mattered was the ice-cold bitch with the shotgun, and that pretty-boy purse-snatcher Scoot.

Jon had seen Scoot go into a junkyard on 7th and Dunley, casual like he owned the fuckin' place. Maybe that was where Scoot lived. A junkyard rat. Living with some drunk fuck of a father in a shack little better than a lean-to, eating canned pork-and-beans.

Yeah, that seemed about right. If he lived in a shithole like this, he'd nab purses too. Who wouldn't?

Jon had been by the junkyard a few times – looking for bike parts, which he sometimes really *did* sell – and knew there was a dog. He pedaled around to the used car lot. Pennants were snapping in the breeze and harsh lights glared across windshields with price stickers like *7,599 Runs Like New* and *13,450 2003* and *5,695 Takes Me Home.* The only salesman Jon saw was busy with a family that had about nine hundred kids, all examining at a mustard-yellow dinosaur of a station wagon with a luggage rack and fake-wood panels down the sides. Fuckin' fake-wood panels, what a joke.

He sidled through the ranks of washed and waxed lemons, walking his bike. At the back were the motor homes. Some were just pickup trucks with camper caps, others were weird silver tubes that looked more like something a robot might land on the White House lawn, and others were more recent models, the fuckin' road hogs that retired old farts drove around in.

Two back-to-back fences divided the car lot and junkyard, chain link on the car lot side and rickety board planks on the junkyard side. Jon propped his bike against the side of an RV and looked over the fence at the jumble of rusted-out hulks, hoping to see the shack where Scoot and Scoot's old drunk fuck of a father lived.

Instead, he saw Scoot.

In a sheltered little nook made by walls of wrecked cars.

Taking off his –

Holy shit!

The fuckin' pretty-boy was a chick!

Jon could not believe his eyes. Or his luck.

Scoot-the-chick had a tall, tight, lean body. Not much titworks, true, and not much ass – J. Lo had the world's most perfect ass, and starred in all of Jon's whack-off fantasies.

But look at those long legs, fuckin' damn! The skimpy exercise clothes she'd had on under her baggy jeans and loose shirt clung like paint and showed off everything. And when Scoot pulled off that dorky helmet and shook out a lot of darkish brown hair . . .

No fuckin' wonder none of the girls had been able to get into Scoot's pants. They would have been in for one big fuckin' disappointment.

He watched as Scoot loaded her skateboard and clothes into her duffel bag and sneaked out through a hole in the board fence.

Fuck! Didn't live in the junkyard after all.

Jon scrambled down, got his bike, and had to go way the hell around to get out of the car lot. The salesman caught sight of him and started to call out, but just then Mr. Fuckin' Brady with all the kids asked a question about the yellow dinosaur station wagon, and the salesman turned back with a big shit-eating grin.

At the mouth of the alley, he saw red flashes and cursed under his breath. But the cop car, parked squarely in the middle of the intersection, turned out to be a fuckin' blessing in disguise. Everyone in the neighborhood was gathered on the corners for the free show. Scoot was walking slowly toward them.

An ambulance was at the curb in front of a diarrhea-brown apartment building. Its rear doors stood open, and so did the building's front door. Two dudes in white smocks came out with a gurney that had a shriveled old man on it. An oxygen mask covered the old man's mouth and nose. A sheet had been drawn up to his chest. An equally shriveled little old lady walked beside him, holding his dry claw of a hand.

The fuckin' 9-1-1 thing, can you dig it? Some geezer had worked himself into a heart attack, and was off to the hospital.

Jon lurked in the doorway of a pet grooming salon that had closed at six-thirty but still stank of wet dog and strong shampoo. He saw Scoot mingle with the neighbors like she belonged there, saw people say hi to her and her give it right back.

Mr. and Mrs. Geezer got loaded into the ambulance. One of the white-smocked dudes said something to a policewoman who, in Jon's opinion, filled out the seat of her uniform pants in an amazing way. Primo ass. Almost J-Lo quality. She nodded, and went back to her patrol car where some beefy cop was leaning on the fender talking to more of the neighbors.

Once the ambulance doors closed, cutting off the view of Mr. and Mrs. Geezer, the crowd started to thin. Jon waited and watched to see what Scoot would do. If she came back this way, she'd see him. She'd seen him at the skate park and had known he was trailing her, and if she spotted him now, she'd guess that her secret was out. Then he'd have to think fast.

But she didn't turn around. She crossed the street and went into the diarrhea-brown apartment building. Nobody gave her a second fuckin' look. Must live there, then.

A thought slithered into his mind.

The ice-cold bitch who had busted into his place and threatened to blow his head off wanted to get to Scoot. It seemed like a lot of fuckin' trouble to go to over a purse . . . unless there was some serious good shit in the purse. Maybe the ice-cold bitch was a dealer. Maybe her purse had been loaded with product.

Whatever the reason, she had to want it back pretty damn bad.

If he could get his hands on it . . . he'd be in charge then, wouldn't he? He'd be calling the shots. Once he had the purse, he could state his terms and see how bad the bitch wanted it back.

And he could get his hands on Scoot at the same time . . .

That'd almost be, what did they call it? Poetic fuckin' justice. He hadn't crossed paths with Scoot all that often, but he resented being tricked. Resented being made a fool of. By a chick, even. So what if she could ride? Who the fuck did she think she was, anyway?

He watched the dregs of the crowd melt away and knew he couldn't linger any longer without looking suspicious.

A mini-movie played inside his head. He saw himself on the cell phone again, cool as Vin-fuckin'-Diesel, telling the ice-cold bitch that he had her purse. That if she wanted it back, she'd have to play the game *his* way. If she tried coming after him with her fuckin' shotgun, she could shoot him, sure, but he'd hide the purse so she'd never fuckin' find it.

Yeah.

And when she showed up where he told her to be, he'd be ready. No bitch got away with talking to him like that. She was some big fuckin' mouth when she had the gun and he didn't, but he knew people. Connected people. Weasel could get him a gun. Weasel could get him a fuckin' *grenade* if he wanted, or a fuckin' rocket launcher.

So the ice-cold bitch would show up and he'd be ready for her. Rough her around some, maybe. Pay her back for what she did to him. He didn't mind so much what had happened at his place, but he minded like *hell* the way she had come right up to him in Century Plaza like she wasn't even fuckin' afraid of him. Made him look bad in front of his friends. They'd laughed about it later, laughed at *him*, Jimmy and Kidmaster-D and Silverdark and the others. Laughed at him.

She had to pay for that. Yeah. Bitch. Pay for it in the only way a bitch like that would be good for. He'd get her down on those knees and make her open up that bitchy mouth, and . . .

Yeah. Fuck with him? He'd show her who was fuckin' with who.

Scoot, too. She deserved it. They all deserved it. And they wouldn't tell a fuckin' soul. They wouldn't dare.

What could they do, call the cops on him? That, he'd like to see.

Chapter 19

The building was abuzz with the story of Mr. Abelard's heart attack.

Allison got one version from Mr. Strevyk on the corner, another from Mrs. Petronile as she crossed the street, a third from Teddi Lace in the lobby – Teddi had been the one to find him, clutching his chest and gasping for air in the laundry room, where he'd gone to look for a lost sock – and Eva Cesare in their shared kitchen.

"The poor man," Eva said, shredding lettuce with the same sure and perfect strokes she might have used while performing surgery. "Smoking like he does, three packs a day at least. I've never seen him without a cigarette in his mouth, have you?"

"Sure, I have," Allison said. She was rooting around in her half of the cupboards, starved from her day's exertions and hoping to find something, *anything* other than that sole can of ravioli. "Mrs. Abelard won't let him smoke inside. He has to either go out front or on the balcony."

The door to Eva's side was open. She kept her apartment as clean as an operating room. It was tidily decorated, too. A cross and a picture of Jesus leading fluffy white lambs over a hill hung on the slice of wall that Allison could see through the doorway. Below it, at a card table, Hector Cesare frowned over a textbook and chewing the end of a pencil so hard that it was a wonder he hadn't bitten it in half.

Her search turning up nothing more interesting than a box of instant pudding, a can of creamed corn, a half-full jar of peanut butter and a packet

of ramen noodles, Allison tried the fridge. Carton of milk two days past the expiration date, tub of margarine, lots of Mountain Dew and a lone orange soda, assorted heels of bread she hadn't gotten around to throwing away, strawberry jam, mayo-ketchup-relish all in a row, and last but not least a plastic container that had originally held cake frosting but now imprisoned some alien leftover life form. Might've been chili. She wasn't about to open it and look.

"I should marry Jamie Tremayne," she said, selecting the least crustlike of the pieces of bread and making a PB&J. "He's always got food."

"You can eat with us," Eva said. "I'm making tacos."

"I've mooched one meal already this weekend."

"Really, there's plenty."

The sizzling aroma of ground beef browning, and the heap of freshly-grated cheese made up her mind for her. "Okay, twist my arm. Thanks. Tell you what, tomorrow night I'll cook."

In the other room, Hector raised his head. "Uh-oh."

"Don't uh-oh me, smart guy," she said. "I *can* cook."

Which was not strictly a lie. She could read directions and follow a recipe with reasonable success more often than not. Now that she could finally remember the difference between the abbreviations for teaspoon and tablespoon, she did okay. Eight or even nine times out of ten, the end result was usually edible.

"Yeah," Hector said. "Frozen hamburger patties."

"Ha, ha. All right, what do you think I should make? Go ahead. Challenge me. I'm not afraid."

"Chicken cordon bleu," he said.

Eva snorted. "Hector, do you even know what chicken cordon bleu is?"

"Sure I do," he said. "But I don't know what Beef Wellington is."

"God, Beef Wellington," Allison groaned. "My father loves that. It's a pain and a half to cook, puff pastry, *soooo* good, and really bad for you, so we'd only have it on his birthday."

"Cool, you can make that," Hector said.

Allison held up her hands. "Not so fast. I've never made it. I've only seen it done."

"Chicken cordon bleu," Eva said, "is breast of chicken wrapped around ham and white cheese, breaded, fried, and baked."

"Or," Allison said, "you can buy pre-made ones and just throw them in the oven."

"Cheater," Hector said.

"When are you going to make us dinner, then?" she asked, lobbing a bit of lettuce at him. "Or are you all talk? Huh? Can you cook?"

"I can make enchiladas."

"He *can* make enchiladas," Eva agreed. "They look funny, but they taste good."

She served up the tacos buffet-style, with dishes of refried beans, lettuce, cheese, salsa, chopped onions, and spicy meat. The shells were crispy, warmed in the oven, and Allison ate two more than she intended.

"Hector is staying here tonight," Eva said when they were done eating. "Our mother and stepfather have been fighting."

"It'll be better once Juan comes home," Hector said. "But today it was pretty bad. I had to get out of there."

Because Eva had cooked, Allison volunteered to do the dishes. Eva protested but gave in, as she had to work that night.

"I swear I don't know how you do it," Allison said. "School, shifts at the hospital, and keeping a job. It's a miracle you don't explode. Me, I have to be at the store at nine tomorrow to help Uncle Bob tag all the new donations, and I'm whining."

"That's nothing," Hector said. "We go to seven o'clock Sunday services at church, too."

"Great, now I feel extra guilty."

Hector chuckled. "Church will do that."

When the kitchen was clean, Eva put on her sky-blue uniform and headed out. Allison said good night to Hector and shut the connecting door. By comparison to Eva's, her apartment was in need of federal disaster relief.

She put off housework to made her weekly duty-call home, which she always tried to do on Saturday nights because her parents would be out at the theater, the opera, the ballet, or some political function. She talked briefly to the housekeeper, then to her brother Andrew and finally, to Missy for almost an hour.

With that out of the way, she straightened up, lugged a load of laundry down to the first floor laundry room, forgot her soap and had to run back up, got the load started, and sat down to decide what to do about the buttercream-leather purse.

Tomorrow, she would take it to the police. She'd been dithering around for too long already. Let the police handle it, let the police worry about it. Allison "Scoot" Montgomery was done. Having that hairy guy on the bike following her had spooked her. It was all preying on her nerves, and taking the fun out of her main joy in life.

Come to think of it, she realized with dismay, she'd seen him in Century Plaza too. He had been in heavy-metal attire instead of wanna-be Rambo, but it was the same slab-muscled orangutan all right.

He had seen her take the blonde's purse, and now he was following her? That was too disturbing even to consider.

She sat cross-legged on the floor with the purse in her lap, debating what to do with the contents. Try to clean her prints off? The problem with that was that she'd also be cleaning the blonde's prints off, and the blonde might be of great interest to the police.

True . . . but the greater interest the blonde was to the police, the greater their interest in the circumstances of her purse being stolen would become. And the greater their scrutiny of Allison.

If she dumped it anonymously at the 10th Street Station, they wouldn't necessarily know to connect it to her. Her prints weren't on file anywhere that she knew of, and as long as she was cautious from here on out . . .

No. Too dangerous. Better to wipe everything and hope for the best.

But that wouldn't give the police a lead on the blonde.

"Damn it, damn it, damn it," muttered Allison. "Doing the right thing gets a lot harder when you're a criminal."

Then, like a bursting ray of light, she thought of the miniature tape recorder. The blonde must have been the one to put the tape in the machine, and Allison had not taken it out. Her prints would be nowhere on the cassette. But the blonde's would have to be.

Satisfied, she got a box of tissues and a spray bottle of watered-down blue window cleaner and proceeded to swab everything she had touched. Since she didn't have latex gloves, she made do with her ordinary winter knit gloves.

At last, she was left with the envelope of money, and that same dilemma.

She really, *really* wanted to keep the cash.

It was really, *really* wrong to keep the cash.

Once, she had amused Missy by fashioning devil and angel puppets out of red and white socks and putting on little skits with them. Sometimes she had rested the puppets on her shoulders and made them talk in funny voices. Those puppets were still at the house, in Missy's room to remember her weird big sister by. Allison raised her gloved hands to her shoulders nevertheless, and worked her fingers like mouths.

"That money doesn't belong to you," the sweetie-syrupy angel-voice said. "It's wrong to keep it."

"It's wrong to steal purses," the gruff-raspy devil-voice said. "But you do that all the time, and you keep the money."

"This is different."

"No, it isn't."

"This is blood-money! Tainted! Dirty money!"

"All the better reason to keep it and put it to good use," the devil said. "Help people with it."

Allison stopped, shook her hands, looked at them. Whenever the devil started saying things about helping people, she knew something was way off-kilter.

She inhaled, held it, let it out. "All right. I'm going to keep it. I'm going to find ways to spread some around so no one can figure out what I did, but I found it, I'm going to keep it. F.K. Finders-Keepers."

All of the other items went back into the purse, which she put in the seat of the recliner and left her gloves lying over the arms so she wouldn't forget and leave new prints. She'd have to think of some clever explanation as to why she'd be wearing winter gloves on a warm day, though.

The envelope of cash, she returned to its hiding place under the recliner's cushion. Then, biting her lip thoughtfully, she masking-taped it to the back of the recliner's elevating foot pad, and closed it all up.

She changed into socks, cotton drawstring pajama pants and a camisole top, then climbed into bed with a J.A. Jance novel and a bag of peanut M&Ms. After a few chapters, she put both on the shelf by the lamp, switched it off, and snuggled under the blanket.

The building was never silent, but the noises were familiar enough that she was able to tune them out.

In her dream, she and Jamie were on the top of a bluff, the landscape falling away below them in a steep rocky precipice toward the dark-green tops of pine trees. A zip line stretched from the bluff down at a sharp angle toward a river below. Jamie stood next to her, legs all hard muscle in snug biking shorts, excellent legs. He urged her to go ahead and go first, and he'd be right behind her. She hung onto the triangular trapeze-thingie with white-knuckled, sweaty-palmed hands, the wind blowing her hair back from her face and making her eyes water, terrified but unable to say no or step back. Boulders, dislodged from the side of the cliff, bounced downhill with a rolling, grinding sound.

All at once she was wide awake, her hands clamped into tight fists around nothing, the wind still blowing her hair.

She opened her eyes. More light than usual streamed in from the building next-door, because her curtains belled out in the draft from the open sliding glass door that led to the little balcony.

That door had been shut and locked when she went to bed. She was sure

111

of it. She'd triple-checked. But the lock was a flimsy thing, and the door didn't fit well in its frame. It could be wobbled until the lock came loose, and then trundled back on its tracks. When it was, it made a sound very much like that of the boulders in her dream.

In the deepest corner of darkness, over by the bathroom, a large and hulking shadow moved.

Allison kicked off the covers and shot out of bed like she'd been fired from a cannon. She hit the floor running. It was a small room and she'd be at the hall door in a couple of strides –

Something flung into her legs from behind. It made a terrific metallic clatter. She tripped, fell, and hit hard on her belly. Winded, she thrashed free of the metallic thing – it was the folding tray table she kept beside the recliner to hold drinks, snacks, and the remote control.

Sucking in a new breath, she was about to shriek for help when someone knee-dropped onto her back. A hoarse, coughing groan burst from her. In the next apartment, Mr. Kaminski's television blared on and on about the latest kitchen gadget that could be yours for only nineteen-ninety-nine, but wait, there's more!

A hand seized her hair. Another clapped over her mouth. The weight on her back moved, straddling her, knees digging into the sides of her waist. Her first crazy thought was that it was the blonde woman called Jade. But Jade had been tiny, and whoever was on her was big, heavy.

She bit hard on the hand over her mouth. She tasted dirt, sweat, oil, pizza. The grip on her hair became a fist and yanked. Some strands ripped loose from her scalp but the rest held. Her head was forced back. The other hand squeezed her jaw with nearly bone-cracking force.

This wasn't happening. This was a nightmare. Her strange, scary-pleasant dream about Jamie had taken this dark, awful turn . . .

No, she wasn't dreaming! She was awake, and approaching panic.

The man – it was a man, had to be, too strong, the hands too big to be a woman – let go of her jaw and Allison gasped for air. He looped something around her throat and pulled it tight, cutting off her breath just as she started to inflate her lungs.

Her fingernails scrabbled at it. A wide strap. Leathery. A belt? She was strangling, choking. Her windpipe was closed to a pinhole. She bucked and thrashed, struggling, clawing at the belt and the floor, trying to drag herself out from under him.

Then he wrenched her over onto her back and gave the belt another yank, and she couldn't breathe at all. "Fuckin' hold still," he snarled.

Looking up at him, she saw wild matted hair and camo fatigues. It was *him*, the guy on the bike, the one who'd followed Scoot. He had found her again, found where she lived, knew her secret.

She got a finger under the belt and tried to loosen it. He smacked her hands away, then punched her in the face. It was like a bomb going off inside her skull. The back of her head hit the floor. Bright lights exploded in front of her eyes. The world flickered. She went limp, dazed and incoherent. Hadn't she done this already today? Hadn't she knocked her head at the skate park?

He groped at her chest, then tore her camisole top apart like tissue paper and his filthy, callused hands were on her bare breasts. He grunted. Still straddling her, he sat back with his weight resting on her pelvis and unfastened his pants.

Allison was distantly aware of this, distantly aware that the son of a bitch meant to rape her, but her main concern at the moment was the fact that she couldn't breathe. Her vision was a foggy field, her ears both ringing and feeling stuffed with wads of cotton. Her chest burned and throbbed.

His weight shifted again, sitting on her thighs. The drawstring of her pajama pants popped as he tugged.

Once again, she worked a finger under the belt. It loosened. Even as she took in a welcome breath, the air flooding her tortured lungs, she got the belt over her head and off so that he couldn't yank it tight again.

"Hey!" He snatched for it, missed.

Her throat felt lined with sandpaper. She wheezed and hacked.

He struck her again, a glancing blow off the cheekbone as she jerked her head aside. She swung the belt at him. It whistled through the air and slapped across his face. He howled and rocked back in shock.

As he did, Allison lunged out from under him with all her might. Rug burn scoured a layer of skin from her back. He overbalanced and toppled sideways, crashing into a small freestanding bookshelf. It toppled, spilling books, knick-knacks and her collection of trinket boxes everywhere.

But he was off her, and she scrambled to her feet.

"Help!" It came out a raspy croak. Pain tore through her abused throat like a cluster of fishhooks.

"Fuckin' bitch!" He threw himself after her.

Allison backpedaled and swung the belt again. It smacked his arm. He caught at it and almost got it away from her.

"Someone help me!" This time it was a thin teakettle squeak.

"I'm gonna fuckin' kill you!"

She backed into the low coffee table that held her television, and without

a moment's debate flipped the whole thing over. The television hit the floor and the screen smashed.

He rushed her, roaring like a wounded bear. Allison cracked him another one with the belt, with the buckle end. It gouged a furrow in his cheek but it didn't slow him. She leaped sideways and he tumbled over the upended coffee table, splitting it with a noise like a splintery gunshot.

Mr. Kaminski banged on the wall. "Do you know what time it is?"

"Help!" Allison coughed, and now her throat felt lined with a cheese grater.

As she ran for the hall door, the hairy guy heaved up out of the coffee table wreckage like a breaching whale. His hand closed on her pajama pants. With the drawstring broken, they slid down her legs and entangled her, and she went sprawling again.

All of the knives were in the kitchen, she didn't have anything like pepper spray . . .

She rolled over, sat up, and that was when he tackled her. His weight drove her down onto her back, with him on top. She felt something stiff prodding at her thigh.

Revulsion sparked new strength and she hammered blows at his head. She hit him in the ear, over the eyebrow, on the chin. Her attack rattled him enough to let her twist away again, and she fetched up against the recliner with a jarring jolt. The purse fell on her, heavy as a sack of bricks, dumping its contents all across the carpet.

His hand got her hair again.

Allison screamed. This time it was a shrill, splintery cry, louder than any of her previous efforts.

"Did you hear me?" Mr. Kaminski called, pounding on the wall again. "I'll complain to the manager. I'll call the cops!"

The guy whirled her around and slammed a fist into her stomach. She curled up into a helpless ball and heard animal noises barely recognizable as coming from herself: moans, sobs, ragged panting.

"Okay," he said, his own breathing labored. "Okay, you fuckin' bitch. You ready for it? You fuckin' better be, because you're gonna get it."

Chapter 20

He shoved her legs apart. Allison tried feebly to bring them together but her limbs wouldn't obey her mind. She was consumed by the paralyzing fireball of pain in her stomach, where he'd punched her.

All she could hope for was to pass out before he did what he was about to do.

The kitchen door shuddered under a solid impact. The bolt and cheap fixture, screwed to the wall, snapped off. The door flew open, blinding light poured in. Hector Cesare charged into Allison's apartment with Eva close on his heels.

They stopped short, aghast, at the sight that met their eyes – the room trashed, broken furniture everywhere, and Allison mostly naked on the floor underneath a huge hairy brute.

Hector spat something vehement in Spanish. Eva screamed Allison's name at the top of her lungs.

"That's it!" Mr. Kaminski yelled through the wall. "I'm calling the cops!"

"Get off her you *bastardo*!" Hector shouted.

"Stay the fuck away from me, bro!" He jumped up, hauling at his pants. His face was scarlet and as he towered over Hector, he seemed to swell up with rage like the Incredible Hulk.

Quick as a cat, Hector bent and scooped something off the floor. He pointed it at the guy. It was the gun, the ivory-handled one from the buttercream-leather purse. "Don't make me shoot you, man!"

"Hector, no!" croaked Allison.

"Put the fuckin' gun down!"

"The police are coming," Eva said. "We'll wait for them."

"Fuckin' hell I will. You gonna shoot me, huh, bro? Come on. Come on and shoot me. You pussy. You're not gonna fuckin' shoot anyone. You don't have the balls."

He took a step toward Hector, reached out for the gun, and Hector shot him.

The gun was a thunderclap, kicking back hard in Hector's grasp. The red-haired guy staggered back, making a surprised glottal bleat. His calves collided with the recliner and he spilled into it. He touched his chest, and stared with dumb incredulity at the blood on his hand.

Hector threw down the gun as if it had bitten him. His face twisted in horror.

"Fuckin' *shot* me, dude," the guy said in a faint, faltering voice.

"Oh, shit!" Allison heard herself say.

Eva pushed past Hector and ran to the recliner. "Give me that towel! Have to apply direct pressure . . . somebody call the paramedics."

"I didn't mean to do it," Hector said. He was very pale.

"Give me the towel!" Eva ordered.

Allison, on unsteady legs that felt composed of loose springs and Silly Putty, got the towel she'd left draped on the back of her desk chair. She handed it to Eva, who folded it into a pad and held it against the red-haired guy's chest.

Someone was trying to batter down the hall door, and the frantic gabble told her that half of the building's tenants were out there. Mr. Kaminski must have made good on his threat because sirens warbled nearer.

She looked down at herself. Her camisole top hung in flaps from the satiny spaghetti-straps, hiding nothing. Her panties were mercifully still on, but her torn pajama pants were bunched on the floor like a shed snakeskin. She got her robe from the hook on the bathroom door, struggled into it and tied it shut. Then everything caught up with her, and she sank onto the edge of the bed, shaking.

"Hector, get the door," Eva said. "We need help here."

He opened it and neighbor-faces gawked avidly in at the damage. Teddi Lace elbowed her way through, telling everyone to stand back, stand back and let her by. She stopped in the doorway, mouth falling agape.

Allison buried her head in her hands. Her stomach churned sickly and throbbed around the place where he'd punched her. It felt like she had swallowed lava, which had seared its way down her throat and then cooled

into a stony mass in her midsection. She hurt all over from other injuries, too many to count.

She couldn't *think*. Everything had gone abysmally wrong. A guy was shot and bleeding in her recliner. Shot with the gun from the purse, from the purse that had dumped out all over the floor. He had broken into her *home*, attacked her, tried to rape her, damn near beaten and strangled her to death, and Hector had shot him. He was bleeding in the recliner, Eva working feverishly to save his life. In the recliner, which had the envelope of cash taped to the underside of its foot cushion.

There were excited, upset people all over the place. She picked up parts of what was being said. Eva and Hector telling how they'd been awakened by the commotion and burst in to find Allison being attacked. Mr. Kaminski, puffed up with importance, claiming to have known something bad was going on so he'd called the police.

In the middle of it all, a woman sat down beside Allison. "Miss Montgomery?"

Dully, Allison lifted her head. It felt like it was made of lead and weighed ninety pounds.

The woman beside her was the same police officer she had seen earlier in the evening, when she'd arrived home as Mr. Abelard was being carted off to the hospital. Tony Rugerro's partner.

"Yes?" she tried. No sound came out. Allison cleared her throat, but that sent such a wave of molten agony rolling through her that tears ran from her eyes.

"That's okay," the woman said. "Just nod or shake your head. My name is Sandy. Sandy Flyte. I'm a police officer. We're going to get you to the emergency room —"

Allison shook her head. It hurt, but not as much as trying to speak had.

"You've been assaulted."

She nodded.

"Do you know that man?"

She started to shake her head, changed her mind, shrugged. "I've seen him around but I don't know his name," she whispered harshly.

Officer Flyte lowered her voice. "We'll need to have someone examine you."

"He didn't rape me," Allison said. "Hector and Eva got here in time."

"You've been pretty badly hurt, and we need to get you taken care of. And then we're going to have to ask you some questions."

"I'm all right."

A sympathetic look crossed Officer Flyte's face, and Allison supposed that she must look pretty terrible. He had hit her so many times she had lost

117

count, and her neck felt swollen up like that of a bullfrog.

The room had cleared out. The red-haired guy had been bustled away by efficient medical personnel, leaving the recliner with a dark crimson puddle soaking into the upholstery. Teddi Lace had shooed the rest of the neighbors away and paced, chain-smoking, in the hall. She stole anxious looks in at Allison every time she passed the half-open door.

"Where's Hector?" Allison rasped.

"Next door," Officer Flyte said. "My partner's questioning him."

"He saved my life and was defending himself," she said as forcefully as she could, ripping each word out through her tortured throat. "You can't arrest him."

"No one's under arrest."

The policewoman's tone was soothing, but Allison wasn't soothed. This was a living hell . . . a cop in her apartment, and that damned stolen purse still right there on the floor! And Hector Cesare being interrogated for doing a good deed!

"That guy would have killed me," she said. "He choked me."

"I know. Maybe you shouldn't try to talk right now."

"I have to!" Allison's voice did not just crack on the high note, it shattered. She cupped her palm over her throat and moaned.

"It seems pretty clear to us that Hector acted in self-defense," Officer Flyte said. "We're just wondering where the gun came from. His sister swears it was on the floor when they came in. Did the man who attacked you bring it?"

Oh, how tempted she was to say yes, to blame it on him! But they'd find out, and the only thing worse than telling the truth to the cops was getting caught lying to the cops.

"It's mine." She closed her eyes as she whispered it, waiting to be struck by lightning. When no lightning was forthcoming, she opened one eye.

Officer Flyte looked serious. "Yours."

"I got it yesterday." Not *technically* a lie.

"Do you have a permit?"

She shook her head and tried to swallow a mouthful of nervous saliva. It stung like acid going down, and she blinked away more tears.

"I'm going to have to take the gun," Officer Flyte said, but sounded sympathetic again. "We can sort the rest out tomorrow, but in the meantime is there anyone we can call for you? Anyplace you can stay? I imagine you won't want to stay here."

"She'll come home with me," Uncle Bob said from the doorway.

Allison's breath hitched as she saw him. She wanted to run to him and

hug him and have him tell her that everything was going to be okay, but at the same time she was consumed with embarrassment. Someone had phoned him, woken him up with this news, and he'd driven right over. Probably speeding and blowing through stop signs.

He wore pants, moccasins with no socks, and a white undershirt beneath a fleece jacket. His hair was uncombed, his face was stubbly and he still had pillowcase-lines imprinted in his skin.

This time she couldn't hold back the tears. Uncle Bob picked his way through the ruin of the room and sat on her other side, putting his arm around her.

"There, Allie-girl," he said. "It's okay."

He urged Allison to lean against his shoulder, and she did so, still crying and hating herself for it. She'd always wanted to impress Uncle Bob, to make him think she was smart and sassy and spunky. Now she was a blubbering wreck.

"You're her father?" Officer Flyte asked.

"Uncle. Bob Sherwood."

"From the second-hand store," she said, nodding in recognition.

"I came right over. Can you tell me what happened here?"

Allison was sniffling and fighting to get herself under control. Officer Flyte gave her another sympathetic look.

"Maybe we can do that in the hall while your niece gets dressed and packs a bag. Are you all right for that, Miss Montgomery?"

"Yes," whispered Allison, wiping her eyes and blotting her nose on the sleeve of her robe. "I'm sorry . . . I . . ."

"Allie-girl, don't be," Uncle Bob said. "You didn't do anything wrong."

"Have you called them?" she asked in a watery croak. "Mom and Dad?"

"I didn't want to scare them until I knew the details. You go on and get some clothes, get some stuff together, and we'll worry about that later."

He patted her, then went with Officer Flyte into the hall and closed the door most of the way. She heard Flyte's low voice sketching it out for him, and imagined Bob nodding, listening grimly.

Alone for the first time since waking to find the guy in her room, Allison saw with fresh alarm the contents of the stolen purse scattered over the carpet. She quickly collected the photos and papers that had fallen out of the manila folder and slid it into a wicker basket amid copies of *People* and *Entertainment Weekly*. She popped the tape out of the tape recorder.

Everything else that had been in the purse, except for the money taped under the recliner, she crammed back into it. She didn't want it anymore, wanted it out of her house. It was bad luck. She stepped out onto the balcony.

119

A ladder was propped against the rail. Here was how he'd gotten inside. Anger churned in her, and she was for one moment viciously glad that Hector had shot him. She hoped he *died*, the rotten bastard!

She leaned over, aimed, and depth-charged the purse into one of the large trash cans Teddi kept in a chain-link enclosure on the side of the building.

That left the money.

She thought about leaving it, not wanting to go anywhere near the blood-soaked recliner. But as soon as she left, the cops would probably be crawling all over the room. They might take the chair with them, or have some crime scene cleanup crew haul it away.

Out in the hall, Officer Flyte was telling Uncle Bob about the gun. Then she heard his reply, which was rueful.

"She was just Friday evening asking me if I knew anything about guns. I asked why and she wouldn't say, but I got the idea some creep had been bothering her. Following her around, like those stalkers you hear about."

Flyte sighed. "That was the impression I got, too. Do you know where she might've gotten a gun?"

"No. I thought there were waiting periods and all."

"There are, but between you and me, someone who knows where to look can buy damn near anything in this town."

"My niece is a good girl, Officer. I hope she's not going to get in trouble over this."

Hoping so, too, Allison gathered some clothes and went into the bathroom to dress. When she looked in the mirror, she wished she hadn't. It was a stranger's face, looking shell-shocked and battered. She had a puffy black eye, a bruised cut on her cheekbone, and drying blood crusted around a split lip. The mark of the belt was a livid red weal across her neck. Her hair was a nightmare, but her hair was the least of her concerns.

She had scratches, too, scratches she hadn't even noticed until she slipped out of the robe and the torn camisole. His chewed, dirty nails had left them on her shoulders, breasts, belly and thighs.

All at once she felt filthy, disgusting and filthy. She fell to her knees by the toilet and vomited until she was dizzy and dry-heaving. The acidic taste of puke clogged her sinuses. Her hair was hanging in it.

Sobbing some more, she rested her brow on the cool porcelain rim. Finally, the worst of it passed and she was able to get up again.

Maybe she was supposed to make this quick, but Allison could not bear to have the remembered feel of his hands on her body a moment longer. She shed everything she'd been wearing, even her socks, and climbed into the

clawfoot tub for a shower. Hot as she could stand it. Hotter, even, until steam turned the small bathroom into a Turkish sauna and her skin was a boiled-lobster red.

Chapter 21

Eva was waiting tentatively in the kitchen when Allison emerged from the bathroom. "Allison?"

"How's Hector?" The steam had helped ease her throat, and though it hurt to talk, she almost sounded like herself again. Almost.

"Fine," Eva said. "They are not arresting him."

"He saved my life, Eva. That crazy bastard would have killed me."

"Who was he? Do you know?"

Allison shook her head and repeated what she'd told Officer Flyte. "I've seen him around here and there." She paused. "And . . . yesterday . . . I thought he was following me for a while. Then I didn't see him, and figured I was being paranoid. I guess I wasn't, huh?"

"But you are all right? Your eye looks bad. And your poor neck."

"I'm fine. Or I will be." She looked past Eva, but the apartment on the other side appeared empty. "Where is Hector? You said they didn't arrest him."

"No," Eva said, and frowned. "But Teddi hit the roof when she found out I had been letting him stay here without paying any rent. She threw him out."

"What?" In her outrage, she spoke too loudly, and pain like a sliver of glass lodged in the soft meat of her throat.

"It is all right," Eva said. "He's with Jamie Tremayne."

"Jamie? Jamie was here?"

"I wouldn't let him come up. I thought you would not want him to see all this."

"Oh, God."

"He knows you are not hurt, though," she explained.

"Does the whole neighborhood know?"

"This is the most exciting weekend for Dunley since the election-day riots," Eva said seriously. "First Mr. Abelard and now you."

She groaned. But she didn't have time for this. She had to . . . "Listen, Eva, will you do me a favor?"

"Of course, Allison."

"This is going to seem weird."

Eva's lips quirked. "Really?"

Kneeling by the recliner and trying to ignore the ripe, coppery slaughterhouse smell of the blood, she said, "Just don't ask me any questions or tell anyone about it, okay?"

"I promise."

"I want you to hang onto this for me," she said, unsticking the envelope from the underside of the foot cushion. She was glad to see that no blood had seeped down that far.

"Is it drugs?" Eva asked, her voice even as she eyeballed the envelope.

"No."

"You swear to God and the Holy Mother?"

"I swear to God and the Holy Mother, it isn't drugs."

"Because I won't keep drugs for you, or for anybody."

"I wouldn't ask you to," Allison said.

Not without some visible reluctance, Eva took the envelope. "All right."

"Thank you, Eva. And thank Hector for me. He really did save my life."

As she got up, her foot kicked something small out from under the recliner. It whirled into view. It was a cell phone, the pre-paid disposable kind. Allison didn't own one. Nor had she found a phone of any kind, though she'd expected to, in the purse.

But the guy . . . one of the times she'd looked back to see if he was still following her, *he* had been talking on a cell phone. This had to be his, dropped in the scuffle.

Feigning nonchalance, as if it was hers, she picked it up. She got her trusty familiar duffel, which still had her skateboard, helmet and pads in it. Not sure how long it would be until she was allowed back in her apartment, she left those items in there and added a few changes of clothes and other odds and ends. And the tiny cassette from the miniature tape recorder.

Uncle Bob, Teddi Lace and Officers Flyte and Rugerro were waiting down the hall by the stairwell. Though the other doors were all shut, Allison

got the crawling sensation of many curious eyes socked up against peepholes and watching her as she walked by.

"We figure he came in by the balcony," Officer Rugerro said as she neared them.

"I heard the door open," Allison said. "Felt the breeze. That's what woke me up."

"Your uncle is going to take you to his house now," Flyte said. "Someone from the department will contact you tomorrow. Later today, really. And we'll have you come down to the station and make a statement. Just going over what you told us here tonight."

"Oh!" Allison blurted, then grimaced and spoke in a harsh whisper. "The . . . the guy . . . is he going to be okay? He's not . . . he's not dead or anything, is he?"

"He was alive when they loaded him into the ambulance," Rugerro said with a glower that made her think he wasn't exactly glad of this fact.

According to neighborhood lore, when he'd heard about what Needles had done to the flasher, Rugerro had taken the tattoo artist out for a beer. He had also reportedly busted the nose of Tina Wendmeyer's ex-boyfriend when that ex had shown up at the 7-Eleven threatening to rearrange Tina's face. Rugerro was no one to fuck with when the neighborhood was concerned.

"I think the bullet went into his lung," Eva said. "It was a sucking chest wound. And he lost a lot of blood."

"Lucky for him you were here," Flyte said.

"Yeah, good job," Rugerro said, like he was trying to sound as if he meant it but really would have been just as happy – maybe happier – if Eva had not been so quick to provide emergency medical care.

Fifteen minutes later, Allison was in Uncle Bob's living room, surrounded by rock and roll memorabilia. The crowning glory of his collection was an antique but still functional jukebox, loaded with records. He had stacked them randomly. Jazz and sixties' protest songs and big-band classics and fifties' beach music and disco. It was always a musical adventure at Uncle Bob's.

She called Jamie, who was wide awake and waiting to hear from her. Talking fast despite the clawing pain in her throat, so as not to let him get a word in, she assured him that she wasn't hurt. This was fudging the truth a little because by now she felt like she'd put in a year in a torture chamber. She thanked him for volunteering to give Hector a place to stay. Told him she would see him tomorrow.

"If you can stand the sight of me, that is," she said. "I'm not exactly ready for a photo shoot."

124

"Allison —"

"Tomorrow, Jamie. Please?"

"But I —"

"Tomorrow," she said. Right then, she couldn't stand to hear the distraught concern in his voice. It would make her cry all over again. "I'll see you tomorrow."

Uncle Bob came back into the living room as she hung up. He held a tray with two steaming mugs and a plate of brownies.

"Warm milk," he said. "With a splash of vanilla extract, a dash of cinnamon, and a squirt of that phony whipped cream out of the can. I didn't have any cocoa. So, for our chocolate, we'll have to eat these double-fudge walnut brownies."

"Wow," Allison said. "You didn't have to —"

"Stop telling me what I do or don't have to do," he scolded gently. "I had enough of that on the way over here in the car. Allie-girl, did you honestly think I was going to let you spend the rest of the night in that building?"

"I could have stayed with Eva."

"Not hardly. Not happenin', as the kids say."

She curled her hands around the mug, which had a white dollop of whipped cream melting over the side. "What about Mom?"

"What about her?" He blew into his own mug, sipped, wiped away a foamy mustache.

"Does she have to know about this?"

"She is your mother."

"She'd freak out," Allison said. "So would Dad. They'd say that I never should have moved out on my own, and they'd want me to come home."

"They can't make you do anything. Wasn't that what your big rebellion was all about? Showing them that you could take care of yourself?"

"And then this happens," she croaked. "Some nutjob breaks into my apartment and almost kills me . . . that's taking care of myself?"

"Allie, you're an adult," he said. "A young one, maybe, but you're over twenty-one. If you don't want to tell them, you don't have to."

"But you think I should."

"Family is family." He shrugged, took a brownie. "Wouldn't they want to know that you're okay?"

"I *am* okay. Besides, the only one who'd care is Missy, and I don't want to scare her. It's better this way."

"If that's how you want it." Bob chewed for a while; the brownies were moist and dark and dense.

Allison took one, found that opening her mouth that far hurt her split lip,

and broke a piece off to nibble on.

"Are you ready yet to tell me about it?" Uncle Bob asked.

"There isn't much more to tell," she said. "I don't know him."

"Tony Rugerro said they found a bike in the alley behind your building, next to the ladder he must've used to get up there. By the looks of that ladder, he probably got it from Sam's junkyard, and it was a wonder it didn't break apart under him."

"Too bad it didn't," Allison said.

They chewed brownie and sipped warm milk for a while. Allison found the trickle of the milk down her throat simultaneously soothing and excruciating.

"I've seen you sometimes, out riding that skateboard of yours," Uncle Bob said.

"You have? But . . ."

"Oh, you're dressed like a boy, sure enough, but I know it's you. What your mother would say about *that*, I'd like to hear."

"I wouldn't," Allison said.

The fact that Bob had recognized her didn't upset her much. He was more observant than most people gave him credit for, especially his own sister. Everyone thought he was a harmless eccentric with a thing for moldy oldies, but he saw a lot from his store.

"Anyway, I've seen you with whole crowds of kids, some of them on skates or those scooter-things or bikes. This guy, maybe he was from that crowd?"

"Yeah. I think he was." She told Bob how she had seen the red-haired guy around occasionally, how she'd seen him at the skate park. "And then it seemed like he was following me. I thought I lost him after a couple of blocks."

"The gun, though, Allie. Where'd the gun come from?"

She studied the carpet, which was burnt-orange shag mashed flat by years of wear and tear. "That's . . . that's kind of . . . tricky."

"If I'm going to help you, I need you to be honest with me. Where did you get it? Did you buy it?"

"I . . . sort of . . . found it."

"Found it?" His eyebrows climbed toward his comb-over. "Found a loaded gun?"

"Sort of."

"Did you steal it?"

"Well . . ."

"Allie, I'm not going to be mad at you," he said, setting aside his mug and half-eaten brownie. He put his hands on her shoulders. "But the police are going to ask these same questions, and you'll have to have a better story than

126

'I sort of found it' to tell them."

Allison's head felt plated with iron, it was so heavy. She couldn't lift it to meet his gaze. "If I told them the truth, though, they'd arrest me."

"Tell *me*, then."

"It was . . ." She swallowed thickly, like she was trying to choke down a sticky wad of guilt. It hurt her throat. "It was in a purse. I stole a woman's purse on Friday, and the gun was in it. That's why I asked you about guns. I didn't know what to do. I should have gotten rid of it. I meant to get rid of it, and then all this had to happen. When the guy and I were fighting, we knocked everything over. The gun fell out of the purse. And then when Hector and Eva came in, Hector saw it and picked it up. I tried to tell him not to, but I wasn't in time."

He let go of her shoulders and sat back, and Allison wanted to peek and see if he was about to get mad at her after all. But still, her head was too heavy to lift, and she could only sit with her neck bent, staring miserably at the ugly orange carpet.

"I'm guessing this isn't the first time?" he asked, still speaking gently.

"The first time there's been a *gun*," she said.

"But not the first purse."

"No." She braced herself for him to demand a full accounting, an entire explanation of her life as Scoot and Scoot's illicit activities. In a way she'd made him a part of it too by disposing of the purses through Sherwood Second-Hand.

"Does all that have anything to do with this guy? Was he . . . in on it with you?"

"No!" Now she looked up. "Nobody was. Just me. No one else. I mean, sure, there were some people who saw me do it now and then, and he might have been one of them, but no one was in on it."

"All right," Uncle Bob said. "I believe you."

Allison drank more milk and let the warmth trickle down her throat, trying not to wince. "I'm sorry, Uncle Bob. I know you promised not to be mad, but if you are, I understand. I let you down. You trusted me, and gave me a job and told Mom and Dad you'd keep an eye on me, and I've let you down."

"You haven't let me down, Allie-girl. I'm glad you told me, and I'm not mad."

"Really? But—"

He made an exasperated snort. "Do you *want* me to be mad?"

"Well, no," she said.

127

Though, weirdly, she felt the same flicker of disappointment she'd always felt in her shoplifting days whenever she once again strolled past an oblivious security guard. What was *wrong* with her? Did she, secretly and deep-down, have some crazy masochistic streak that *did* want to be caught? Mrs. Oberdorfer, who watched Dr. Phil religiously, would probably say that it was her child inside, Little Allison, crying out for attention, for discipline from stern fatherly types. She shuddered.

"We still need to think of what we'll tell the police," Uncle Bob said. "Without mentioning purse-snatching. Let me think for a minute."

He got up and turned on the jukebox. It came alive with a whir. Neon sputtered, then steadied into a multicolored luminescent glow. Through the convex glass bubble on the front, Allison could see levers moving as a new record was brought to the top of the stack and the needle-arm descended into the groove. A fifties-sounding car song came on, something about a girl dying on the railroad tracks with her boyfriend's class ring held tight in her hand.

Cheerful, Allison thought. A hell of a cheerful way to end the night.

128

Chapter 22

Jeanette hadn't been expecting him to call her at all, let alone later that very same day. She'd figured he would try to run, try to hide from her, and had admitted to herself that if he did, her chances of actually finding him again were slim.

So she had been downright shocked when the cell phone chirped while she picked unenthusiastically at an early dinner. She hadn't eaten lunch, and only coffee and half a toasted bagel with cream cheese for breakfast, yet she wasn't the least bit hungry.

She didn't like this. Didn't like not being in control. Hated elements of random chance. Hated flukes and freaks of fate. This was why she never went to Las Vegas.

Even as a child, she had developed an abiding distrust of games that relied on the luck of the dice or the draw. She couldn't stand having her next move determined by a random number, to be told by the fall of the dice where to put her piece on the board.

And now, this. This random chance, this freak of fate. One instant of bad luck – to be spotted and targeted by Scoot the purse-snatcher – and everything was hanging by a thread.

Bigfoot, for all of his apparent Neanderthal wit, had proved to be either clever or lucky. Or both. Whichever, he had found the kid called Scoot and agreed to follow him home.

Feeling like an oncoming disaster had been narrowly averted, Jade tore

129

into the rest of her meal with a voracious appetite. She was at a seafood place by the lake, which she had chosen more for the view than for the cuisine. But now that her taste for food had returned, she devoured the grilled shrimp and the blackened salmon and the Cajun-flavored rice.

Out on the water, clean white sailboats moved serenely across the deep mirror-green water. Closer to shore, some fools on powered watercraft zoomed and sped . . . the rich, nautical version of skateboard kids, and if she'd been out on her boat enjoying a peaceful Saturday afternoon when one of them whizzed by, she'd be tempted to pick them off with a harpoon gun. Or a torpedo.

She could see the baronial estates of Palmyra Hills, picture windows turned to shimmering gilt by the sun, the grounds so painstakingly manicured that they made her own once-a-week landscaped yard look like the wilderness. Even the mansions right on the lakeshore, mansions with cordoned-off swimming areas, boasted pools as well.

Her place was nice. More than she needed. She certainly didn't need a fourteen-bedroom palatial monstrosity with custom everything and half a dozen live-in staff. She would have rattled around like a button in a clothes dryer. She didn't *want* servants who might notice and remark upon the odd hours she kept.

Still, the palatial homes were nice to look at. Nice to dream about. Nice, even, to aspire to, if she ever decided that she needed to raise her fees or take on ten jobs a year.

Provided, that was, she could salvage *this* job and not have to go groveling and apologizing to Rayburn and his employers.

Bigfoot had not called back by the time she finished her dinner, so she ordered coffee and a slice of key lime pie for dessert. Impatient now, she kept checking the phone to make sure it was on, that it was getting a signal. Every time she checked it she worried she might have turned it off by accident, and had to check it again, until she had to push the phone to the other side of the table, close her eyes, and take some nice deep steadying breaths.

When she opened her eyes, she was looking at her target.

Jeanette blinked.

He was still there.

The man from the photographs.

She had only given them a cursory look, but she had a good memory for faces. It served her well in her chosen career.

Of course, in this part of town there might be hundreds of good-looking blond men with bronze tans, athletic bodies and megawatt smiles.

Almost as many men like that as there would be women. But it was him. She was sure of it.

He and a gorgeous brunette in a red cocktail dress were being shown to a corner table. Her target was dressed with casual "I'm rich so I can do what I like" insolence, foregoing a suit in favor of comfortable linen pants and a plum-colored polo shirt. His hair was tousled and his tan was more golden than ever, as if he had just stepped off his sailboat . . . or out of an aftershave commercial.

His date did not look as though she had stepped off a sailboat. His date looked as if she had been in a salon since eight a.m., getting worked on by a team of experts borrowed from Nicole Kidman. She had a flawless café-au-lait complexion, ebony hair, and the large, striking, deep sapphire-blue eyes of a Disney cartoon princess. The diamonds in her ears and around her neck were simple and tasteful but still might have financed a trip to Europe. The young woman looked passingly familiar to Jeanette, as if she'd seen that face before, perhaps on the cover of a magazine or in a movie.

Sipping her coffee, Jeanette watched the couple take their seats. Her nerves were yammering, but outwardly she was cool as ever.

Here was that very element of luck she had just been thinking about. Random chance, pure coincidence. He had come right into the very restaurant where she was having dinner. And here she was without the gun.

Not that she would have shot him even if she'd had it. She couldn't haul a gun out of her purse, blow him away and run for it. For one thing, her car was in valet parking. For another, *she* chose the time and place. That had always been the way, that was the way, that would always be the way she did this.

Control. It was all about control. Having it, being in it.

The maitre-de addressed the target as "Mr. Westbrook." His date called him "Ben." He didn't look like a Ben. He looked like a Chet, or a Chip. Something preppy. But now she at least had a name for him. That was a step in the right direction.

Watching them, she caught herself wondering if the brunette — he called her "Sophia" — was the one who'd hired the job. She cut off that line of speculation fast. It wasn't her business. God, she hated these personal ones.

Maybe this was a sign. She had allowed herself to be lured into taking a personal one against her better judgment. Lured by the money, lured by the challenge she'd seen smoldering in Rayburn's cobalt eyes. And almost from the moment she'd agreed, it had all gone hideously wrong.

No personal ones.

In the old days, they'd been plenty personal. Deirdre Vaughn had been

131

the first one to hire her to get rid of a bad husband, but she hadn't been the last. Deirdre'd had friends, and discreet word had gotten around to many an eager ear.

There had been a rash of deaths that year in that particular social circle. Husbands who slipped in the tub. Husbands who were stabbed during muggings gone too far. Husbands who were shot, presumably by muggers, when leaving the little love nests where they kept their mistresses. Husbands who didn't see to it that their cars got regular maintenance. In one memorable case, a husband whose death was ruled accidental, an experiment with autoerotic asphyxia gone tragically, humiliatingly, fatally wrong.

One of those bereaved widows had waxed remorseful, and told her friends that she wanted to confess. Jeanette had killed her. She'd hated doing it, but the act had convinced the rest of the women of the benefits of continued silence. They had quietly gone on to enjoy their insurance settlements.

That had been the end of Jeanette's connection with any of them. She was no longer a friend of a friend, doing a favor for a modest amount of cash. Even Deirdre withdrew from her. And Jeanette had vowed that from then on, she would not get involved in anyone's personal life.

The trouble was, she'd found that she had a knack for murder. And a fondness for it. There was a strange paradox in how alive she felt when killing someone else. As if it was her way of showing the world, one person at a time, that she, Jeanette Kurrell, was more important than the rest of them.

With no other burning interests, she had started taking more jobs. Building up her connections. Letting word get around. She'd started small, but she was good.

And only the impersonal ones. The ones where she only had to worry about greed, and gain, and envy. No jilted lovers. No battered wives. No broken hearts. Only lowdown dirty avarice and callous necessity. She heard a lot of speeches that went, "It's regrettable, it truly is, but . . ."

Businessmen and politicians were her clients these days. Corporations, too. The occasional university professor or scientist in the cutthroat world of academia. Prior to yesterday's meeting with Rayburn, her last job had involved a scientist. The poor, foolish, stubborn idealistic son of a bitch had actually invented a weight-loss drug that worked, that was cheap and safe and effective. As far as the enormously lucrative weight-loss industry was concerned, he had to go.

Having never struggled with her weight, Jeanette hadn't felt any qualms about killing him. Now, as she ordered a second piece of pie so she could watch her target a little longer, she hoped she wouldn't be sorry for that later.

By the look of it, Mr. Westbrook and Sophia were not married. Dating, Jeanette thought, and not for very long. They were still in the parry-and-riposte stage of courtship that made her think they hadn't yet slept together.

Which meant that Sophia most likely wasn't in on the murder plot. She appeared genuinely interested in and attracted to Ben, and wasn't seething with the buried fury required to crave someone's death badly enough to hire it done. She was too young, as well. A woman that young didn't think in terms of hiring a killer. If she wanted her lover dead, she'd be the one to do it herself, in a fit of passion.

If there was a Mrs. Westbrook, though . . . or if lovely Sophia had been seeing someone else, someone who was the jealous type . . .

She had to stop this. It was useless wheel-spinning, getting her nowhere and only complicating things. Her job was simple. Westbrook dead by his own gun. Rayburn hadn't specified that it should look like a suicide – in the personal ones, people didn't *like* it to look like a suicide because that often meant no fat payoff from the insurance company. So, that meant Jeanette was free to do it her own way.

He looked like something of a ladies' man. Flirt with him, get him alone, and pow? She'd done that before. But he did seem quite captivated by his date – who could blame him? – and might prove to be one of those rarest of men . . . the faithful kind.

They had drinks and appetizers, and by then the restaurant was filling up with the later crowd. Jeanette had drunk three cups of coffee, feeling the buzz, and eaten more pie than was good for her. Jon still had not called. The waiter was giving her the evil eye, clearly wanting her to shove off so he could fill her table with a couple or group whose bill, and consequently tip, would be higher.

Just as well that she didn't have the gun. She'd been too visible here, though from the moment Sophia had walked in, it wasn't like many people were paying attention to *her*. She paid, left an adequate tip, and retrieved her car from the valet. Down the block, she pulled to the curb and dialed the phone she had given to Bigfoot.

Nothing. Had the idiot turned it off?

She drove around for a while, fingers drumming the steering wheel, humming under her breath, fidgeting with the radio. Nerves and too much coffee . . . this wasn't like her, and she didn't care for the feeling. She felt too edgy, too high-strung, too out of control. In a mood like this, she might do something stupid.

The sun went down, the city lights came on and turned the lake into an onyx teardrop in a dazzling diamond choker. She found herself by Century Plaza again. The downtown streets were full of people from opposite ends of the spectrum. Men and women in evening clothes going to the theater or opera, grubby bums panhandling on streetcorners.

When he'd called, he'd said he'd found Scoot at the skate park on Pine Street . . . but that Scoot was leaving. She'd told him to follow, and to call her back when he knew where Scoot lived.

But he hadn't called. Why hadn't he called? Where the hell did Scoot live? It had to be in town. Punks on skateboards didn't commute back and forth from the suburbs.

He might have lost Scoot.

Jeanette gripped the steering wheel.

If he had, if he'd lost Scoot, it would be just like him to be too cowardly to call her up and say so. He would be afraid of making her mad. And with good reason.

So . . . where was he, then? Was he still out there in a desperate scramble, hoping to pick up Scoot's trail again? Or had he decided that his only chance would be to cut and run?

She turned onto Prewett, which was even more garish by night with flashing neon signs everywhere. Two muscle cars were revving at a light, preparing to race. Hookers paraded up and down the sidewalks in heels and tight miniskirts, most of them too fat or too thin, smoking, chewing gum. A blood-red strobe light pulsed outside Club Dracula, where an overflow of black-clad Goths grinned inhuman vampire-grins at passers-by. A fight had broken out in front of a strip club and a trio of teenagers in gang colors had broken into a parked car.

Smiley's Motel had a large sign with a bright yellow winking smiley face, and offered "Free Adult Movies, Hourly-Nightly-Weeky Rate's, Kitchen Unit's with Frig," complete with misspellings and misplaced apostrophes. It had been dismal when she'd seen it by daylight. Now the peeling paint, weedy sidewalks and cracked windows were concealed by shadow, but not enough to make anyone mistake this place for the Ritz.

It was a two-story U-shape around a sunken patch of dirt that might have once featured a pool but now featured beer cans and crack vials. The arms of the U faced the street. Bigfoot's room was around the back.

As Jeanette's car rolled slowly past the filled slots, a door flew open and a drunken woman reeled out, shouting obscenities at a naked man in the doorway. Naked . . . except for the cowl, cape, and utility belt of a Batman costume.

"I fuckin' told you, you sick fuck, no sick fuckin' stuff!" the woman shrieked. "Motherfuck!"

The Eskimos, Jeanette had always heard, had something like ninety different words for snow in their language. Here on Prewett, the entire language seemed to consist of maybe two dozen variants of "fuck."

She grimaced. She used to like Batman. Had, as a little girl, sometimes thought how cool it would be to be Catwoman when she grew up. So much for fantasies. A mostly-naked Batman with a potbelly and a half-mast erection was almost enough to turn her celibate.

Bigfoot's unit was dark, but that didn't mean anything. Half the units at Smiley's were dark, and she was willing to bet that plenty of them were inhabited. By pallid subterranean creatures, maybe, or giant rats.

Two guys were sitting outside of his door. She could tell even in the poor lighting that neither of them was him. Neither was a hairy red Bigfoot. One was young, stocky, six-foot and black. The other was a scrawny, scabby little monkey.

Though she didn't have *the* gun, she had *a* gun. It was not in the glove compartment, but in a plastic box under the passenger seat. The box was a variation on the old hollowed-out-book gag, except that it had once held audio tapes, an unabridged reading of Dean Koontz's *Mr. Murder*. Like making the lunch reservations under Dufarge, this was another of Rayburn's ideas of a joke.

Jeanette opened the plastic box. Inside, the ridges that had once held tape cassettes in neat little slots had been cut away to provide room for a compact 9-millimeter. It was one of her favorite guns, fitting well in her hand.

She had gone home to change after her last visit here – had been tempted to burn her track suit for fear of what lice, germs and vermin it might have picked up in Jon's pigsty of a room – and was now in a smart beige linen suit and jade-green blouse. She looked like an Avon lady, a church volunteer, or a social worker.

The jacket's pockets were roomy, so she slipped the gun into one and kept her hand on it as she got out of the car. If need be, she'd shoot through the pocket. It would wreck the jacket, but she could live with that.

The black kid said something to the scabby monkey, and they both laughed. They had crude, sneering, sexist laughs.

"Is Jon around?" she asked.

Her tone, indifferent and unafraid, took them aback.

"Haven't seen him," the black kid said. He stood up. "Haven't smelled him neither. But hey, baby, what you need him for?"

The other guy, the scabby monkey who looked fifty but was probably only a hard-used thirty, only stared at her. He had hard, starving junkie's eyes and several days' worth of stubble.

Inspiration struck. "I'm his new parole officer," she said dryly. "Mind stepping aside so I can see if he's home?"

The black kid threw a guilty look down. There on the cracked and weed-grown sidewalk in front of the door, strewn between where he and the scabby monkey had been sitting, was an assortment of drug paraphernalia. He looked back at Jeanette and drew himself up in a macho posturing stance. Daring her to bust them.

His bravado was so transparent it was funny, but she didn't want to push him. Pushed by a small white woman, a kid like this could turn mean. She acted as if she didn't notice the stuff on the sidewalk.

"What happened to Ramirez?" the scabby monkey asked.

"Ramirez?"

"Jon's *old* parole officer."

She sensed a trap, and said, "I don't know anything about that. I'm just here to do my job. I'd appreciate it if you'd move, so that I can."

"Tellin' you, he ain't here," the black kid said, but he shuffled out of her way. "Hey, Weasel, man, I'm thinkin' like Abraham Lincoln it's time we beat feet 'cause I could use me somethin' to eat. Whatchoo say?"

The scabby monkey – Weasel – didn't move. He ogled Jeanette, but his eyes were so empty and dead that it was like being leered at by a corpse.

She stepped up to the door, thinking that if Weasel laid a finger on her, she would stomp her heel into his crotch. She'd have to disinfect her foot and burn her shoe if she did, which would be a shame because she liked these shoes. But, like the linen jacket with the gun in the pocket, she could buy a new one if she had to.

At the last minute, Weasel did hitch himself sideways. She rapped on the door and raised her voice. "Jon?"

There was no answer, not even the tense hush of someone holding his breath and hoping she'd go away. Of course, it was hard to tell with what sounded like orgies and barroom brawls going on in the rest of the units. She knocked again.

"Told you," the black kid said.

Jeanette didn't get the impression that they were hiding anything either, at least, not anything about Bigfoot. He wasn't here. She could try getting a spare key from the manager – the parole officer story would probably hold up in a place like this – but it would be no use.

136

"If you see him," she said, "tell him I was here. I'll try him again tomorrow."

"You can try me anytime, baby," the black kid said, regaining some of his swagger now that she was leaving without busting them for possession, or possession with intent to sell.

She wanted to smile and tell him that if he called her 'baby' again, she'd shoot him in the eye. But she ignored him, and walked back to her car. The vehicle's engine caught with an almost relieved sound, as if it knew that it would have been stolen, stripped, or at the very least spray-painted with gang tags had Jeanette left it unattended much longer.

With no other ideas at the moment, she headed for home.

Where the message light was blinking on her answering machine.

"Hello, Jade." A voice like rough velvet.

Her heart momentarily stopped.

He knew. Somehow, incredibly, unbelievably, Rayburn *knew*.

Then a few things occurred to her in quick succession – Rayburn was just doing his *Charlie's Angels* shtick, which he reserved for times when he was in a good humor. Rayburn surely *wouldn't* have been in a good humor if he knew about her troubles. Further, this was the plan. This was the routine. She had set it up herself.

According to the routine, Rayburn or one of his associates would contact her, via this private, unlisted number she kept only for her jobs. No specifics, just a query-call to see if she was available and interested. A meeting would be set up. At the meeting, the vital information would change hands. And then, sometime in the next day or two, she'd get another call.

This call. This preliminary follow-up.

Normally, she would use that intervening time to go over the information and make her preliminary plan. When the follow-up call came, she could ask further questions to refine her plan.

"Are you there?" Rayburn's voice asked on the recording. He waited a few beats, then went on. "I was just calling to check in, but I'll have to try and reach you again later. I do hope everything's going well. And that you're still thinking about it."

Despite everything else, Jeanette flushed. His dinner offer. She had almost forgotten. Understandably, perhaps . . . it would have to take the biggest disaster of her professional career to drive thoughts of a date with Rayburn out of her head.

"Talk to you soon," he said, and there was a click as he hung up.

Chapter 23

She dialed Bigfoot's cell phone again to no avail. Where was he? What was he up to? It seemed like forever since he had called to report having found Scoot at the skate park, so where had he gone after that? Had he been spotted? Had Scoot seen him, and gotten away from him?

If that was the case, Bigfoot was exactly the type to not want to own up. He wouldn't call back and say, "Oh, by the way, I lost him."

"I *fuckin'* lost him," Jeanette murmured to the empty house. "Dude."

Which meant he was either still out there looking, or, more likely, he had cut and run. The phone was probably in a trash can somewhere.

He couldn't and wouldn't go far without his stuff. All his worldly possessions were in that fleabag motel room. But would he go back there? He'd be paranoid, he'd be sure that she'd be watching his place. And he'd be right, which was the most aggravating part of it. She hated being predictable. Especially hated being predictable to a semi-literate scumball drug user.

Well, then, fine. She wasn't going to do it. Was not about to spend the night staking out Smiley's Motel. That part of town, she'd be lucky to be alive by daybreak. She'd find Scoot some other way.

"But that doesn't mean you're off the fuckin' hook, Bigfoot," she said. "Oh, no. There might not be any money in taking care of you, but I promise you I'll get plenty of job satisfaction all the same."

She was too wired to even think about sleep and there was no way she'd return Rayburn's call.

138

In the upstairs bedroom that she'd converted to a gym, she did half an hour on the treadmill, half an hour of free weights and ab crunches, fifteen minutes on the stationary bike, and fifteen minutes of stretching.

After her shower, she slipped into an emerald-green silk robe and blended a fruit-and-yogurt smoothie, then sat down to watch the eleven o'clock news. National political bullshit, a local Amber Alert for a missing six-year-old believed snatched by his father, international political bullshit, a multiple-with-fatalities collision that had closed down part of the interstate for three hours earlier in the evening, military bullshit, a pop diva's marriage-of-the-week, weather forecast for continued sunny and warm, colorful local man riding a unicycle cross-country to raise money for male breast cancer awareness, sports bullshit.

Still no call from Bigfoot, and no answer.

She flipped channels for a while, watched most of a true-crime docudrama about a woman who'd murdered her way through five husbands, then watched all of another about a man who'd tried to hire someone to kill his father so he could inherit the family business. Sloppy jobs, all of them. They should have hired a professional.

At one in the morning she turned off the television.

Tried Bigfoot again. Nothing.

Jeanette went up to her office and got online. Finding Scoot would be a longshot, but she tried anyway. No luck. Next, she did a search for Ben Westbrook, and spent a couple of hours wading through various websites and articles.

Ben, as it turned out, was short for Benedict. He lived in Palmyra Hills and was a big-shot collector of antique weapons. But she didn't learn much that would help her kill him. No convenient museum openings or historical society functions coming up. No wife, never been married. No information about the ravishing Sophia.

She still did have to kill Westbrook one way or another. She'd accepted the job. If it meant losing a quarter of her promised fee . . . even if it meant not getting the extra money she'd been promised . . . that was too bad. She'd have to do it anyway.

It was the gun, more than the money, that worried her most. Someone had a reason for wanting Westbrook shot with his own gun. Was the job connected to his collection somehow? A rival antique-weapons buff? What was it about *that* gun in particular? Was it a gun with history?

An old commercial popped into her head. She couldn't even remember what product it had been for, but it had involved a history geek obsessed

with an old duel.

Was this that kind of thing? Had the gun been used in a famous duel? The gun used to shoot Lincoln, or something crazy like that?

She went back to one of the historical websites and looked for pictures matching the ivory-handled pistol, but came up dry.

Her initial impulse of a plan had been to break in somehow and make it look like Westbrook had walked in on a prowler and in the course of a struggle been shot with one of the pieces from his own collection. She imagined a manly room with dark paneling and crossed cavalry sabers over the mantle, glass cases full of neatly-labeled hardware and accessories. Deep wingback chairs, leather studded with dozens of little brass tacks. Maybe a few animal heads on the walls.

She'd discarded the notion. Collectors wouldn't keep their prizes loaded.

At some point she became aware she was dozing over the keyboard. It was after six in the morning and her eyes felt like they'd been rolled in fine sand. Her nervous adrenaline had leached away, and a heavy lethargy had settled into her muscles and limbs.

Logging off, switching off, turning off.

Halfway to her bedroom, the cell phone rang.

Chapter 24

The warm milk didn't help.

Allison's sleep was thin and restless. She kept waking with a start and a painful gasp, sure that someone was in the room with her. The first time, she saw Uncle Bob's life-sized cardboard stand-up figure of Elvis in the corner and almost wet the bed.

She wrestled Elvis into the hall, but still spent the next few hours tossing and turning and getting up to check that the window was locked.

At six, when the eastern sky was beginning to turn pale, she gave up and got dressed. She moved quietly around the amiable music-memorabilia clutter of the guest room, trying not to knock anything over.

The guest room technically wasn't a guest room. It was a shrine, a museum. The bed was a rollaway that normally stayed in the closet, and had been set up in the middle of a cleared space barely large enough for it to fit. Allison was sure that not having any part of the bed up against the wall had contributed to her uneasy rest. She'd felt like she was on an island, or floating unanchored on a raft, out in a dark, dark sea.

Her body ached all over. Slowly, carefully, moving like a little old lady, she dressed in sweatpants and a white sweatshirt advertising a Rose Bowl now seven years gone.

She could still taste the toothpaste from when she'd brushed before bed, but it was a faint residue under a nasty coating. She shuffled into the tiny bathroom, avoiding her reflection.

Her throat burned and throbbed. There were pain-relievers in the medicine cabinet and she took three ibuprofen, thinking that she'd heard somewhere that ibuprofen reduced swelling. Each pill felt like a boulder going down. A boulder covered with jagged outcrops of stone. Obsidian-stone. Volcanic glass.

Then, because it was better to know the worst and view the damage, she closed the medicine cabinet and looked squarely at herself in the mirror.

"Damn," she whispered.

It was pretty bad, even allowing for the unflattering light. Her face was lumpy, bruised, and unfamiliar. The marks on her neck had darkened. Sunglasses and a turtleneck would only make her look like a battered woman trying to hide what had been done to her.

And she was supposed to go to the police station like this?

Well, maybe they'd take one look at her and feel so sorry for her that they'd go easy in their questioning.

She went back to the guest room to put her little overnight bag back in her duffel, and as she was doing that she saw the phone at the bottom. The pre-paid cell phone. She took it downstairs with her.

The house was old and creaky, and every stair tread that squalled under her made her pause, listening for an interruption to Uncle Bob's snoring. She felt bad enough for screwing up his night's rest already. But he snored on, undisturbed. He might not have heard if a jet buzzed the roof.

Downstairs, she sat by the front window and watched the sky brighten. Then she turned her attention to the phone and switched it on.

The display screen came alive and informed her that there were missed calls. She brought them up. All were from the same number, at various times through the night and even into the wee hours of the morning. Someone had really wanted to get in touch with the guy.

Allison fiddled with the keypad until she got the "return call" option. She held it to her ear. It rang once, then again, and then was answered.

"It's about time!" A woman's voice, sounding wide-awake despite the early hour.

"Um," Allison said, faltering. "Hello?"

"Who is this?" Instantly alert, and sharp as a blade.

"Who's *this?*" Allison countered.

"Let me speak to Jon."

"He's . . . um . . . not here."

"Well, where the hell is he?" She sounded like an older woman, angry, mature . . . and weirdly familiar. "Who are you, and how did you get his phone and this number?"

"I'm . . ." Allison trailed off as recognition dawned.

"Hello? Are you there?"

She felt like she'd been dipped in liquid nitrogen. The woman's voice . . . it was impossible. It couldn't be. How . . . ? What . . . ? Her mind did not so much spin or reel as it skidded, like tires on a sheet of black ice.

It was the blonde. The voice from the tape. The woman named Jade. The killer.

Somehow, it was *her* on the other end of the line.

Allison didn't know how that could be, and grasped mentally at straws. She hadn't listened *that* closely to the voices on the tape . . .

A lie. She had concentrated intensely on those voices, trying to absorb every nuance, once she understood what she was hearing.

"Damn it," the woman said. "I'm not in the mood for stupid games. Let me talk to Jon."

"How do you know Jon?" Allison asked. Her own voice was thick and odd, and not just because of her throat.

"Put him on the phone."

"I can't. He's not here."

"Then who is this?"

What could she say? "I'm . . . um . . ."

She heard the blonde grumble something about idiotic drugged-out kids.

"His girlfriend," Allison blurted.

"That figures. Where is he?"

"Out."

The blonde hissed in annoyance. Allison had thought herself awake before, but now she was sitting tense as a wire on the edge of the chair, fingers locked around the phone, heart skittering, mouth so dry she could barely work up the spit to say even those few words. She knew she should hang up, that this was too dangerous even for her tastes. The woman on the other end was a *killer*. Had somehow sent Jon after her. How much did she know?

"He told me about you," her mouth said, seemingly independently of her sliding-on-black-ice brain.

"What?" The word snapped through the phone like a whipcrack.

She *had* to find out how much Jade knew. "You're looking for Scoot."

"Yes," Jade said, with a tight, clipped tone that made her sound like she was striving to hold onto her temper. "He's got something that belongs to me."

Tentative relief thrilled through her at the knowledge that part of her secret was still safe. "You mean, he took your purse."

"That's right."

Allison closed her eyes. The spinning tires in her mind caught traction and raced. She'd seen Jon place a call from the skate park. Saying what? Saying he'd found Scoot and was going to follow Scoot home. Then he'd lost the trail and hadn't wanted to admit to it . . . and somehow caught up with Scoot again.

He must have seen Scoot go into the junkyard, and either spied as she changed – she squirmed with revulsion – or guessed when he saw Allison come out. And then what? Why hadn't he called back and told Jade that Scoot was really a girl?

She could envision the cold-voiced woman on the other end of the line getting Jon or someone like him to follow Scoot. She couldn't wrap her head around the idea that Jade would tell Jon to *retrieve* the purse. Not with what was in it. Jade must've only wanted him to *find* Scoot, and then planned to take over from there herself. But Jon had gotten ambitious.

"So, like, what's in there anyway?" Allison giggled the vapid, empty giggle of a skater groupie.

"Look, maybe you can help me." The voice warmed, became just-us-girls conspiratorial, and if Allison had really been the dippy skater-girl persona she was pretending to be, she would have been taken in by it. "I really need to find Scoot, or Jon. Can you tell me where either of them are? Jon was supposed to call me when he found him."

"Gee, I think Scoot lives over on the south side somewhere," Allison said. "I see him on the bus, you know, the 62?"

"Does Scoot have a real name?"

"Well, duh, like, probably!" Again with the giggle. "I don't know it, though. Maybe Kip. I think I heard someone call him Kip once."

"Who are *you*?"

"Steffi." The names popped out. Kip and Steffi were another couple of skater-kids she had known, back when she'd still been learning her way around. Kip was tall, lean, and hot, and had gone off to college in another state. Steffi had been his girlfriend, though rumor had it that he'd turkey-dumped her when he came home for Thanksgiving.

"And what about Jon? Are you at his place?"

"Yeah."

"Where's he?"

"I told you, out. He said he had to see a guy about some stuff. He's been gone all night."

"He left the phone?"

"I just found it under the bed."

"You've been there all night?" The sharp edge was back.

Allison got a precarious feeling. "Not *all* night, I guess. It was pretty late when I got here. What time is it?"

"Never mind that. Did anyone come by?"

The urge to hang up was stronger than ever. She suddenly felt that Jade was seeing right through her stupid act and stupider lies, was playing with her, stringing her along. "Um . . . not that I know of."

"You're sure."

"Yeah, why?"

"When Jon gets home, tell him he needs to call me. It's important. He knows why."

"Okay. Hey, I better go."

Before Jade could reply, Allison jabbed the buttons to end the call and turn off the phone. She dropped it onto the rug between her feet and put her hands over her face.

She had the shakes again, and was beginning to seriously reconsider her self-conception of a daredevil and risk-taker.

The skateboard stunts, the shoplifting, even the purse-snatching now seemed childish and moronic. Only risky on the surface, but safe underneath, the way a roller-coaster might scare the hell out of you but you knew, deep-down, that it was a controlled situation and nobody was really going to get hurt.

She'd had a few close calls and a few minor injuries pursing her various interests these past few years, but always, down-deep, she'd known she wasn't *really* going to get hurt. If she took a bad fall on her board, the worst that was likely to happen was a broken wrist. If she got arrested for shoplifting or purse-snatching, nothing *too* terrible would come of it. Especially not once they found out who her parents were. Oh, she'd be in plenty of trouble with her family, yeah, but no one was going to throw her in *jail* for it.

Now, though . . .

Now she was playing with fire. Now, the risk was real. Now, she could get her impulsive butt killed.

Her apartment had been broken into. She'd been beaten up and nearly raped. She had just gotten off the phone with a cold-blooded murderer. The police would expect her to come and talk to them on matters a lot more serious than a few stolen purses.

And a guy had been shot. Might even be dead.

Allison went even paler as she thought about that. Hector had shot Jon. Eva and the paramedics had saved him, but for all she knew he could have died on the operating table. If he was dead, she was responsible.

If he wasn't, though . . . if he wasn't, what would he tell people?

Chapter 25

The drowsiness was gone like a fog whipped apart by a sudden high wind.

Jeanette dashed to her room, threw off the robe, and put on the same track suit she'd been wearing when she'd paid her earlier visit to Bigfoot's place.

She was out the door into the early light of what would shape up to be another summery day according to the weatherman, into her car and on the road less than fifteen minutes after the brain-dead slut hung up.

Ten minutes after that, she was cruising Prewett again.

Gone was the hectic, dirty, festering activity of the previous night. The street was all but empty, the buildings along it looking like piles of roadkill so unappetizing that even the flies turned up their noses. Smiley's in particular was a gangrenous open sore.

Thankfully, there was no sign of Batman. Or of Weasel or the black kid who'd been camped in front of Bigfoot's door last night.

She drove past, then parked a block over, in front of a food bank on the corner of Dunley and 2nd. The posted hours showed that the food bank didn't open until ten on Sundays, but a few other cars occupied the slots that angled up to the curb. She got a small café mocha at a coffee kiosk to blend in with the few others out and about, and walked into the manager's office of Smiley's like she owned the place.

A tinny bell, mounted above the door, jingled. But the sound was lost in the way-too-enthusiastic patter of some morning-show hostess desperate to prove she was pretty enough and vivacious enough to be put on weekdays

instead of weekend mornings.

The office had cheap tubular-chrome furniture and a scarred wooden counter that served as the front desk and divided the small room into two smaller halves. The desk was unmanned at the moment, and she could hear water running somewhere nearby.

Jeanette flipped up the hinged section of the counter, stepped into the rear half, and surveyed the keys hanging on grimy metal rings from a pegboard. She chose the one that read 'Main' and was at the door before the water gurgled to a stop.

The bell jingled again. From the back, a man called, "Be right with you!"

Without answering, Jeanette let the door swing shut and strolled around to the rear of the building.

Bigfoot's room was 119, and the key didn't give her any trouble at all.

That, though, was the last part of her plan to go right.

The room was empty. Not empty of *crap*, no . . . in that regard it was exactly as she'd seen it before. Piled high and strewn from hell to breakfast with trash, porn and junk. But empty of people.

No brain-dead slut. No *sign* of a brain-dead slut. No sign that a girl of any sort had spent much time in here at all. There were no panties on the floor, no used condoms stuck to the wall. Besides Jeanette, the only women present were bare-assed and beaver-shot on the walls and the covers of magazines and DVD cases.

She had come in pumped up and gun in hand, not entirely sure whether she intended to take the slut hostage or leave a vivid reminder waiting for Bigfoot. To abruptly have *neither* option threw her badly off her stride. She looked around the room in disbelief.

"Hey!" she barked. "Where are you?"

Rustle-rustle! Then a stack of moldy pizza boxes fell over as a body darted out from under a pile of garbage.

A rat. She saw at once that it was a rat, nasty and brown and beady-eyed, and almost blew it to bits anyway. It scurried for the open door, slid around the jamb like a brown wad of snot, and was gone in a flick of diseased-looking pink tail.

"Son of a bitch," Jeanette said.

Rather than put the gun away – that being the sort of thing people did in movies after being startled by a cat, bird, or whatever, only to relax and *then* be jumped – she made a circuit of the room, kicking stuff out of her way.

It *was* empty. She even held her breath and checked the bathroom. Which was every inch as purely vile as she had previously suspected, and harbored

millions of living things far down the evolutionary scale, but no people.

She didn't see the pre-paid cell phone anywhere.

"The bitch wasn't here," she said to the pouty-lipped silicone bimbos on the wall. "She was never here. Where *was* she?"

A shadow partially blocked the open doorway.

Jeanette still had her gun in hand, and it was pointed at Weasel's face before she knew she meant to do it.

He goggled at her, absolutely stunned. "The fuck?" he slurred.

Weasel, still in the same torn, rumpled, dandruff-speckled and food-stained clothes as she'd seen him in last night, stood there with a key in one hand and an empty cardboard box that had once held Soft Roll toilet paper in the other. He was, like Smiley's and most of Prewett Avenue, even uglier by day's harsh and unforgiving light.

"Where is he? Where is the stinking shithead?" she demanded.

His bloodshot eyes nearly crossed as he tried to focus on the gun. "The fuck?!" he repeated, astounded.

She was to him in four strides. At the last minute, Weasel's street-savvy survival instincts took over and he tried to run for it, but he was too late. She caught him by the collar. And although Jeanette was only five-two and a hundred and ten pounds, she matched Weasel for size and more than matched his slack, wasted frame when it came to strength and fitness. The box went flying. She hauled him backward and flung him on the floor, then slammed the door and stood over him with the gun aimed at the center of his scabby, receding hairline.

"The fuck?" Weasel groaned, there on the floor.

"Tell me where Jon is."

"The fuck I will."

Aha, she'd gotten two whole more words out of him.

"The fuck you *won't*," she said.

"Won't fuckin' shoot me. You're a fuckin' parole officer!"

"No, I'm not."

"The fuck?"

God! She thought she might have to shoot him after all if he said that one more time. "Last chance, Weasel."

"The fuck you know my name?"

Her finger tightened on the trigger.

"Okay, okay, hold your fuckin' water!" Weasel cried, raising his hands. He had dropped the key. "Jon called me this mornin', okay? 'Bout an hour ago."

"And?"

148

"Wanted me to come here and get some stuff."

"What stuff?"

Weasel got a sulky look. "Nothin'."

"Nothing?"

"His mom might come over. He din' wan' her see him livin' like this." Weasel nodded around at the centerfolds and stacks of magazines.

"Oh, really?"

The gun hadn't wavered but Weasel's eyes did. "And, okay, he's got some fuckin' recreational, okay? He don' sell it, but he don' wan' his mom findin' it. Said I'd get rid of it for him."

"Wait," Jeanette said. "His *mom?*"

"What? So he's got a mom, so fuckin' what? *I* got a mom."

She found that she did not even want to imagine what kind of women could have birthed and raised sons like this. "And she's coming here why? Where's Jon? Why doesn't he come and clean out his own porn?"

"He's in the fuckin' hospital, okay?"

This threw her for a loop. "The *hospital?* What happened? Did he crash that damned bike of his? Was he hit by a car?"

"Shot," Weasel said, and looked from the gun to Jeanette accusingly.

"The fuck?!" she said. "Where?"

"In the fuckin' chest."

"No, not where on his body did he get shot, you moron, where —"

"Century Medical," Weasel said.

"No, again. Where *was* he when he got shot?"

"Fuck'f I know. Dunley Street someplace, I think. He din' tell me the whole fuckin' story, okay? Said he'd been shot, some guy shot him, he hadda have surgery. An' his mom was comin' to get his shit, okay?"

"Shot," marveled Jeanette.

Then the bottom dropped out of her stomach. Shot. By some guy. Shot. And she had a very bad feeling she knew which gun had done the shooting.

She looked down at Weasel, who hadn't budged from where he'd landed when she had thrown him to the floor. He lay there in a litter of trash and pornography, watching her. Not afraid. He had never been properly *afraid*, not even with the gun leveled at him, and now a cocksure insolence was growing in his eyes.

He didn't think she would shoot him, especially now that she'd gotten what she wanted to know. He didn't think she had the guts.

She shot him.

Chapter 26

"Connect me with Rayburn, please."

She hated to do it, but she had no more choice. Not after what happened with Weasel. Not after what she'd seen in the morning paper, and heard on the radio news.

"Jade, is that you?" His voice was warm and he sounded genuinely pleased to be speaking to her, and Jeanette regretted that she would probably never hear him sound quite that way again.

"It's off," she said.

"Pardon me?"

"The job. It's off. I can't do it."

He paused for several beats. "Jade, if this is because of —"

"It's not because of that," she said. She sighed. "There's been a problem."

"What kind of a problem?"

"I don't have the gun. The police have the gun."

He paused again, then said, "Jade, this isn't anything to joke about."

"Damn it, Rayburn, do you think I would joke about it?"

"Maybe you'd better tell me what's going on."

She was in her car, and leaned her brow against the curve of the steering wheel while holding the phone to her ear. "It's embarrassing. My purse was stolen. My purse with everything in it. The gun, the money, *everything*."

"Are you serious?"

"Yes, I'm fuckin' serious!" She clapped a hand over her mouth. "Sorry.

It's the company I've been keeping lately. A kid swiped my purse right after we had lunch on Friday. I've been trying to find him ever since. I got another kid to look for him, and *that* kid is in the hospital now. Shot. By, I'm willing to bet, the gun that you gave me."

The news reports had been sketchy, with no names given as of yet. Some of the details didn't add up. A man broke into a Dunley Street apartment in the middle of the night Saturday, sexually assaulted a young woman, then was shot by the woman's neighbor. In the ironic sort of twist that the news loved, the med student sister of the shooter had performed emergency first aid and been able to keep the intruder alive until paramedics arrived. He had been taken to Century Medical and was out of surgery, though still in critical condition.

She relayed all this to Rayburn. "I only wanted him to find Scoot, and I intended to take care of it from there myself. I never told him what was in the purse but even a piece of slime like him would have guessed it had to be important. Maybe he thought that if he could get his hands on it, he could . . . I don't know, blackmail me or something."

"But instead, he ended up shot."

"I'm not saying it was undeserved. I would have done it myself once I knew where to find Scoot." She raked her fingers through her hair, letting the platinum-blonde strands sift against her cheeks. "The part I don't understand is the sexual assault. The best I can figure —"

"Excuse me for interrupting, Jade," Rayburn said, and her heart sank. Now he sounded cool and clipped. Businesslike. Not at all the same man who'd invited her to consider dinner with him. "Are you *certain* that it was the same gun?"

"Not one hundred percent, but if it is, we're screwed. The police will figure out who it belongs to, and then our man will know something's up."

"What about the money?"

"I don't know," she said. "Scoot must have it. Along with . . . along with the folder you gave me, *and* my tape."

Rayburn swore softly.

"But we don't need to get worked up over nothing," Jeanette said. "These are burnt out pot-head slackers we're dealing with. Even if Scoot listens to the tape and looks at the information, he's not going to put it together. He'll probably see the money and forget everything else."

"We cannot be sure of that. And there is the matter of the money, Jade. You agreed to perform a service for a price. You were paid a quarter of the offered fee up front. Now you're telling me that you aren't going to be able

to deliver –"

"Oh, for Christ's sake, Rayburn!" she cried, exasperated. "You'll get the money back, if that's all you can think about. I'll cover the loss of the twenty-five grand."

"The Company was getting a tidy commission for arranging this, Jade, and now it's fallen through."

"Fine, I'll cover your lost commission, too! How much? Ten percent? Twenty? State the time and place and I'll deliver it, in cash."

"It isn't only the money," he said. "What about our man? Even if this Scoot person is, as you say, a burnt out pot-head who won't suspect what he has, our man is going to know something's up."

"There isn't anything I can do about that," Jeanette said heavily.

"And if the folder and the tape *do* wind up in the hands of the police –"

"They won't be able to connect them to us. I didn't have any identification in the purse."

"Thank God for that, at least." His voice went even cooler. "Because if they do find you, Jade, and you give them *us* . . ."

"I know how this works, Rayburn," she said, feeling nettled that he even thought that he had to threaten her. "The police won't find me. They might get prints off of my things, but my prints aren't on file."

"What about the tape?"

"It's not like we used our real names. The best they could hope for would be to figure out where we were, track us to the restaurant. But you paid cash, the reservation was under Dufarge thanks to your sense of humor, and they won't have anywhere to go from there."

"Descriptions," he said darkly.

She started to object, then bit her lip. The hostess. Fascinated with Rayburn, undressing him with her eyes. If the police got to her, she would be able to describe him in loving detail. As for a description of Jeanette, it would go one of two ways. Either she had been a complete nonentity to the hostess, who would have seen Rayburn and only Rayburn and dismissed everything else . . . or the hostess had taken point-by-point careful inventory of Jeanette, jealously comparing, searching for faults, trying to see what a man like Rayburn might want.

"There's no way they'd get that far," she said. "It'd only be background noise of a crowded restaurant. If they want to canvass every single eatery in the city, let them try. They won't know what we look like from our voices alone."

"All right, so maybe they won't find me," he said. "What about you?"

"The same logic applies."

"But these kids saw you. They'll be able to describe you to the police."

Shit! Jeanette clenched the fist that wasn't holding the phone. "What's Scoot going to say? Tell the police that he got the gun from a purse he stole?"

"What about the other one?" pressed Rayburn. "If he spills his whole story to the police, there won't be much you can do."

"If they even believed him."

"Can anyone back him up?"

She thought of Weasel, and the way he had flopped over with a look of surprise only beginning to register on his face. Weasel wouldn't be talking to anyone ever again, unless it was by Ouija board. The only other one who had seen her looking for Bigfoot was the rhyme-talking black kid. Not the most credible witness in the world, and also someone who would want to have as little to do with the cops as was humanly possible.

Or Bigfoot's brain-dead slut of a girlfriend . . . where was *she*? She'd said she was at his place, but his room had been empty. And if he'd had a girlfriend there, why call Weasel to come and hide his drugs and porn?

"Not really," she said to Rayburn. "It sounds too crazy. The police will think he's psychotic or stoned. And *he* won't know that the gun was from my bag."

"I don't like it," Rayburn said. "This is a real mess, Jade."

"Yes," she said, careful to keep her tone even and not give in to sarcasm. "Yes, I know it is."

"What are you going to do?"

There it was. Not "what are *we* going to do?" but "what are *you* going to do?" She was on her own. As always. And while she hadn't really expected any offer of help from Rayburn or the people he represented, she was more than a little disappointed all the same. Part of her had hoped that *he* would stick up for her, maybe join in the search for Scoot and help her get this all back on track.

"At this point," she said, "I can't exactly walk away."

Because even if good old Bigfoot hadn't told the police what he knew, he would as soon as Weasel's body was found. And Weasel's body *would* be found, soon. Bigfoot's mom — Jeanette's mental image was of a rawboned hillbilly woman with long snarls of rust-red hair, bad teeth, and rolls of fat over a core of tough hardship-born muscle — would find him when she showed up to gather her son's belongings.

On the plus side, Jeanette thought sourly, maybe she'd done them a favor. Odds were, his mom would be so distracted by finding a corpse in the room that she might overlook the naked women on the walls.

Once Weasel was discovered, the police would be even more involved.

153

They'd want to know who shot Weasel while his buddy was in the critical care unit. They'd interrogate him. If the story about the little blonde lady with the shotgun hadn't already been told, it'd be told then.

All that, though, really was secondary. Bigfoot could tell the police anything he liked and it still wouldn't lead them to Jeanette. She could change her hairstyle, change her look, change her habits. Move away and start over, if she had to. It wouldn't be the first time.

But damned if she was going to let these skateboard kids get the better of her. Damned if she was! They had made her look incompetent. Had made her look bad in front of Rayburn, and just at a moment when it seemed like things might be shaping up interesting between them.

Could she still salvage anything from this debacle? Maybe, if she acted fast.

"And if it's too late for salvage," she murmured, "there's always revenge."

"Jade?" asked Rayburn. "I didn't quite catch that."

"I'll take care of it," she said. "I'll get you the money, and if you still want me to deal with our man, I can find some other way to do that, too."

"I'll have to check with a few people first," he said. "This changes everything."

"Tell me about it."

"And . . . Jade?"

"What?"

"I'm really very sorry this had to happen," he said. His voice was warmer now, and touched with heartfelt regret.

"So am I. This'll be the end, won't it?"

"The end?"

"Of our association."

He hesitated. "My employers aren't usually very big on second chances."

"I thought so," she said. "Have someone call me when you know where I should drop off the money. Goodbye, Rayburn."

She disconnected, and dropped her phone into the passenger seat, and sat there with her head against the steering wheel with her eyes closed.

A light tap at the window made her jump. She whipped her head up and around and stared at her own reflection in duplicate, mirrored in the shiny silver shades of a motorcycle cop.

154

Chapter 27

They hadn't hauled her off to an interrogation room like in the movies, some place of all industrial sheet-metal and furniture bolted to the floor, with one window a long pane of one-way glass. She wasn't cuffed, wasn't sweating under a spotlight, wasn't even getting the good-cop / bad-cop routine.

Instead, Allison was in a comfortable conference room, with nice paneling on the walls and a long oval table surrounded by swivel chairs. A cup of silty police-station coffee sat in front of her, catching the overhead light in rainbows on the oil slick floating on its surface.

None of this made the experience any easier. She only refrained from gnawing her nails by a supreme effort of will. The sudden slam of a door nearly made her leap out of her seat.

There *were* two cops. The plump and smartly-dressed woman had introduced herself as Detective Victoria "please call me Tori" Bryland. She seemed friendly enough, but if they all of a sudden did decide to do a routine, Allison was sure that Detective please-call-me-Tori would excel at being the bad cop despite her generous mouth and ready smile. Her partner was short, thin and balding, with a wrinkled navy-blue suit and sad puppy-dog eyes. His name was Detective Philip Mindersohn. He had not, for the record, offered to be called "Phil" or even "Philip." He had not, in fact, said much of anything at all.

The two detectives were on the other side of the table. Next to Allison was Uncle Bob's lawyer and bowling buddy, Joe Peters. Like Uncle Bob, he

was portly and red-faced, but had a steel-grey gaze as sharp and intent as that of a jeweler looking for flaws in a diamond.

Uncle Bob was waiting elsewhere in the station. He'd gotten up at seven, made Allison a breakfast of mushy oatmeal and soft-boiled egg – all she could eat with her throat so swollen and sore – and promptly got on the phone. He had talked to the station to set up a time for Allison to meet with the detectives who'd been put in charge of the case, and had arranged for Joe Peters to meet them there.

"It seems pretty self-explanatory," Detective "please call me Tori" Bryland said. "With the statements from your neighbors, the ladder outside, the damage to your apartment, and the injuries you yourself sustained, I don't think anyone would argue that Mr. Cesare's actions were justified. Our only loose end is the gun."

"I bought it," Allison said. "It was stupid. I know it was stupid. But . . . I . . . I guess I wasn't thinking straight."

"Where did you buy it? Do you have a receipt?"

"There was a guy," Allison said, feeling her way carefully through the story she and Uncle Bob had worked out. "Over on Prewett Avenue. I've seen him around. Selling things. You know, watches, radios."

This much was true; there were plenty of people on Prewett who, when the sun went down, sold dubious stuff of all varieties out of the trunks of their cars or set up card tables on the sidewalk.

"Do you know his name?"

Allison shook her head.

"What did he look like?"

"Tall, pale, dark-haired," she said, now departing from the truth completely. "His hair was slicked back and he had on a black trenchcoat and sunglasses. He looked kind of like *The Matrix*."

"And he was selling guns?"

"I asked him if he knew where I could get one. He didn't want to tell me at first, like he thought I might be a cop, but finally he said he sometimes had guns and wanted me to come back in an hour. So I did. I gave him a hundred bucks and he gave me the gun."

Was she over-explaining? She'd heard that people with something to hide would get too nervous and let their mouths run. Prickles of sweat broke out along her hairline. She hoped that any tension in her voice would be masked by the hoarse, raspy sound of it. And that any nervousness would be taken to mean she was still rattled by the previous night's ordeal.

"The gun . . . was it loaded?"

"He said it wasn't." Allison shrugged. "I didn't check. I don't know anything about guns. I figured I'd get some bullets somewhere else."

"So you bought the gun on Friday evening," please-call-me-Tori said, consulting a page of notes. "Not knowing it was loaded, you took it home to your apartment. What did you do with it?"

"This is going to sound so dumb," Allison said, "but once I got it home, I was scared of it. I mean, I didn't even know for sure if it was loaded, but I was afraid it would just . . . go off. So I put it in a box on my bookshelf."

"Then, Saturday night, you woke up hearing an intruder."

She nodded.

"He attacked you," please-call-me-Tori continued, "and you fought with him."

Allison shuddered and instinctively touched her neck. It felt like she was wearing a collar made from a wraparound hot water bottle. "He choked me with his belt."

"Your neighbors heard all the noise and came in through the connecting kitchen."

"Hector kicked in the door, I think. The bolt's pretty flimsy."

"Which was when Mr. Cesare saw the gun on the floor, where it had fallen?"

"Right. We crashed all around my apartment. Everything was knocked over."

"Is Miss Montgomery going to be charged with possession of an unlicensed firearm?" Joe Peters asked.

"The gun was a stolen piece," please-call-me-Tori said. "It belongs to a collector of antique weaponry. How much did you say you bought it for?"

"A hundred dollars."

Detective don't-call-me-Phil spoke up. "You got quite a bargain. Something like that would normally go for upwards of seventeen hundred."

"Detective Bryland, you didn't answer my question," Joe said. "Will Miss Montgomery be charged?"

Please-call-me-Tori exchanged a glance with don't-call-me-Phil. "Under the circumstances, I think we'd all like to avoid that. However, I still have some questions of my own."

"Hector's not going to be in trouble, is he?" Allison asked. "He was trying to help me. I don't want him to be in trouble."

"I'd like to ask you about Jon Wharton."

"Who? Oh . . . the guy?" She felt her neck again. "Is he going to be all right?"

"He'll live," please-call-me-Tori said. "He suffered a collapsed lung and considerable blood loss. The bullet also broke a rib. But he came through surgery well, and regained consciousness early this morning. He's being held

in critical care, but he is also under arrest. Mr. Wharton isn't being as cooperative as he could be. He won't admit to breaking into your apartment though we have his bike, and his prints on the ladder. He denies having been following you at all."

"What does he say happened?" Joe Peters asked.

"That he doesn't remember." The detective's generous mouth tucked down in a scowl. "He seems of the opinion that if he can't tell us anything, he won't be held accountable for anything. Apparently, he's already making plans to move back home with his mother as soon as he gets out of the hospital."

"Is that likely?" Joe asked with a disapproving frown.

"No." Here, the detectives exchanged a weighted glance.

The back of Allison's neck prickled. She didn't like that way they were looking at each other, as if trying to decide what they should say and what they should keep secret. It meant they suspected something. Even if they themselves didn't know what it was they suspected . . . they suspected *something*.

She wished she had never gotten into this. It was all Scoot's fault, damned daredevil Scoot who couldn't resist snatching a purse every couple of weeks or so.

No, that wasn't fair. Scoot's recklessness might have set the dominoes falling, but Allison had done all the thinking from that point on. If you could call it thinking. Allison had decided not to turn the contents over to the police. Allison had decided to keep the money. Allison had decided to stay silent about her phone conversation with the murderous blonde. Each of those decisions only dug her in deeper.

Right now, there was a chance she could wiggle out of this. But as that thoughtful, weighted glance between detectives went on and on, becoming a proper *look*, a silent-communication-bordering-on-telepathy kind of look, the worse she thought that chance might be becoming. Slimmer and slimmer. Forget suspecting. They *knew* something.

"You've said that you don't know Mr. Wharton," don't-call-me-Phil said.

A leaden feeling sank through her guts. Maybe she had been wrong about the good-cop / bad-cop thing after all. Maybe those sad puppy-dog eyes weren't as doleful as they seemed.

"Not by name, but I've seen him around," Allison said.

"Do you have any idea why he would break into your apartment?"

"Here, now," said Joe Peters. She was glad that he, too, had noticed the change. "This had better not be leading up to one of those 'you brought it on yourself' moments. If you're inferring that Miss Montgomery somehow encouraged this lunatic, then —"

"Mr. Peters," please-call-me-Tori said, holding up a placatory hand. "No one is saying that."

"Maybe not," he said, "but I've heard it before."

"Not from me," she said.

"How could I know why he came after me when I don't even know him?" Allison asked. "I woke up and he was just *there*. I'm sorry he got hurt, but it wasn't my fault. And it wasn't Hector's fault, either."

Joe Peters patted her arm, but his gaze was still on the detectives. "What's this really about?"

Don't-call-me-Phil dipped his head toward please-call-me-Tori, as if indicating that she should go ahead. She took a deep breath, looking like someone bracing herself to do an unpleasant chore, and spoke.

"This morning, Peggy Wharton, Jon's mother, went to the motel where Jon had been living. She intended to pick up some of his personal effects. When she got there, she had the manager let her in. They found a dead man in the room."

Allison's eyes bugged. Her scalp felt like it was suddenly contracted by a quick tug on a drawstring. "What?" she croaked.

"Shot," don't-call-me-Phil said. "Once. In the head."

Immediately, Allison had a flashback to her conversation with the blonde, Jade.

And what about Jon? Are you at his place?

Yeah.

That had been at around five o'clock. Had the blonde rushed right out to the motel? And, not finding 'Steffi,' killed someone else?

Joe Peters was aghast. "So this Wharton character didn't just attack my client, but *killed* someone?"

"We don't think he did," please-call-me-Tori said. "The other man, who right now we only know by his street name of Weasel, was discovered at eight a.m. He had only been dead for a couple of hours. Jon Wharton was in the hospital from two a.m. onward."

Allison wrapped her arms around herself and leaned forward over her knees. She had gone cold all over. For a moment, she had been sure that they were going to say that this Weasel had been shot earlier, with the same gun. That wasn't possible; she *knew* it wasn't, but she had expected it anyway.

"Allison? Are you all right?" Joe Peters touched her arm.

"I'm sorry," she said. "I . . . it's . . ."

Please-call-me-Tori nodded. "We're sorry to put you through this when you've already been through so much. But we need to figure out exactly

what happened, and some of this is still confusing us. It seems like there's a piece missing."

They asked her a few more questions, but she kept stressing that she didn't know Jon Wharton, had never met him, had only seen him here and there around the neighborhood. She repeated her story about having thought someone was following her, and how it had prompted her to get a gun.

As she spoke, she kept thinking about the folder stuffed in among her magazines. If they found that, with photos of Mr. Westbrook the antique weapon collector, what would they think? That she, Allison, had amassed information on him and then had stolen the gun from his collection for some reason or another?

Had they found it? She didn't know what might have gone on in her apartment after she'd left with Uncle Bob. She'd given the envelope of money to Eva and taken the cassette tape with her – it was in her jacket pocket right now. Had they returned and done a thorough search? If so, they wouldn't have been able to miss the folder.

And what about Jon Wharton? Had he *really* denied everything, said that he didn't remember, gave no reason for his presence in her apartment? Or had he looked up at them from his hospital bed and told them about Scoot? Were they playing with her? Giving her some rope and seeing if she had enough to hang herself?

She finished, and held her breath. This would be the moment when they would blow apart her feeble, fragile story like a house of cards.

"Thank you for coming down to the station, Allison," please-call-me-Tori said. "I don't think we have any other questions right now. Are you sure that you don't want to see a doctor?"

The words filled her with hopeful relief. She didn't dare let herself trust that hope too much, for fear they would abruptly yank it out from under her.

"It looks worse than it is," she said, skimming her fingertips over her face and trying to sound brave.

She had, before being ushered into this room, submitted to being photographed by Officer Flyte. The pictures would go in a file as evidence. Just what Allison had always wanted. No debutante ball for this Montgomery daughter. No off-the-shoulder ball gown, corsage, tuxedoed date. Instead, there'd be her name on a file containing photos of her, all bruised and battered.

Lovely. Her parents would be ever so proud. Assuming they found out, which was something that Allison was seriously hoping to avoid.

"Are we done here, then?" asked Joe Peters.

"Miss Montgomery will have to testify at the trial," don't-call-me-Phil

said. "If we need anything more from her before then, we'll be in touch." He got up, and the others took their cues from him.

Hardly able to believe it, still waiting for that other shoe to drop, Allison slowly rose from her seat. "I . . . I can . . . uh . . . I can go?"

"Unless there's anything else you want to tell us," please-call-me-Tori said. Her steady gaze said that she knew Allison was holding something back, and that now was the time to spit it out.

This was it. This was her last chance to come clean. If she walked out of the room without confessing about the blonde, the purse, the phone and the rest of it, she would never be able to own up later. She would have lied to the police and gotten away with it, and if they ever found out they would never trust her again.

And what did she think that she, Allison, could do, anyway? This was no game. This was real. People had been hurt. Someone had died. The blonde called Jade was a murderer. The police needed to know about her. Needed to stop her before anyone else ended up dead.

But even if she told them now, she'd get in trouble anyway. They wouldn't be content with just a little bit of the truth. They'd want it all. Everything would have to come out. Scoot, the purses, the shoplifting, *everything*. There'd be no way to keep that quiet. Her parents would be told. It'd probably be on the news and in the papers.

"No, nothing," she said, and swallowed with a painful twinge. "Thank you. I wish I could have been more help."

She felt them watching her go, their suspicion boring into the back of her skull like drill bits. It was all she could do to keep a normal pace and not scurry or bolt from the room.

Joe Peters walked with her out into the reception area, where Uncle Bob sat waiting. He stood as Allison came in. His genial face was knotted in concern. She rushed to him for a hug.

"There, Allie-girl," he said, holding her and giving her a comforting pat, like he had done when she was a little kid with a skinned knee. "Let's get you out of here."

"Can I go home?" she asked.

"We'll go home, absolutely. I promise, I'll get some of that stuff cleared out of the guest room and —"

"Uncle Bob . . . I mean . . . home to my own place. My apartment."

He stopped as he was steering her toward the door, and looked at her. "You're sure you want to go back there? After everything?"

"Yes." She wasn't sure, not at all. But she *had* to.

"If that's what you want, Allie." He looked over at Joe Peters. "And . . . ah . . . if it's fit for human habitation."

Allison remembered the blood-soaked chair, and fought down a gag. The world went briefly grey and fuzzy. She had to stop for a second and regain her bearings. "Oh. Right."

"I called a cleaning service this morning," Joe said. "They promised to have it done by four o'clock." He checked his watch. "It's only two-thirty, so you might want to go have a late lunch or something first."

"Lunch," Allison said weakly. Lunch was the last thing she wanted right now.

"That sounds good," Uncle Bob said. "Then we'll swing by my house to pick up your bag, and I'll drive you home. Okay by you, Allie-girl?"

"Great." She managed a thin smile.

"Join us, Joe?"

Joe agreed, and after some debate between him and Bob – Allison, with no appetite, didn't get involved – settled on the Red Robin out by the mall. While they waited for their burgers and fries, Allison sipped at a strawberry lemonade that stung her throat like acid. She rejected it in favor of a milkshake, letting the creamy frozen treat slide in slow soothing decadent spoonfuls.

Joe made a quick call to the cleaning service. He ascertained that the chair had been removed, and her apartment cleaned.

"That quick and all," Uncle Bob said, impressed. "I thought with it being a crime scene –"

"Could we talk about something else, please?" asked Allison. "Anything else. Even bowling, okay?"

Chapter 28

Jeanette stared into the cop's mirror shades and felt her life flash before her eyes. Seeing once again how miserable, sucky and empty it had been only made her more determined to cling to it.

Her gut reaction was to floor the gas pedal and burn rubber out of the lot where she'd pulled over to call Rayburn. Or of drawing the gun she'd used to shoot Weasel and letting the cop have it right between the eyes . . . *then* flooring it.

He was a recruiting-poster perfect young officer, with a dusky complexion and a jaw Tom Cruise might've envied. His long, lean body could have been designed to show off his uniform. He was hatless, black hair cropped short. The brass tag affixed to his pocket read "Avery."

Behind him, idling, was a patrol car. A chunky older cop filled the passenger seat, observing through the windshield as he ate not a doughnut but one of those nutritious energy-bar things. By the look on his face, he found it to be about as appetizing as a piece of cardboard. He would be slow, too slow to get his lard ass behind the wheel in time to give chase if she roared away. They might already have noted down her plates. She could change her plates. Could ditch the entire car.

Officer Avery rapped on the window again. She could see his eyebrows over the sunglasses, raised inquisitively. He smiled. It wasn't Rayburn's smile. Avery's teeth were the tiniest bit crooked, which was probably why he had been forced to resort to a career in law enforcement instead of modeling. Maybe, once he had earned the money for some cosmetic dentistry, he would

trade the beat for the catwalk.

The smile, even with its minute imperfection, was open and friendly. Her apprehension ebbed, but only a little.

She rolled down the window. "Yes?"

"You okay, ma'am? I saw you sitting here with your head down and got worried."

"Fine," she said, hesitated, then added with a heaving sigh, "Well, not so fine, really." She held up the phone. "I just had an argument with my boyfriend."

His handsome face creased into lines of sympathy. He doffed the shades, revealing eyes as warm and dark as cocoa. "Oh, hey. Sorry to hear that."

"Am I blocking the way?"

"No. I wanted to check and make sure you were all right, that's all."

"That's very kind, Officer." She mustered what she hoped looked like a brave it-hurts-but-I'll-get-through-it smile.

"I'd arrest him for you if I could," he said. "It *ought* to be a crime to upset a pretty lady on a nice day like this."

Holy God, was the cop flirting with her? Seeing her as a freshly dumped blonde and thinking to score on the rebound?

It was all Jeanette could do to keep from screaming with laughter, and she wondered what the hell had happened to her lately. Always, she'd prided herself on being cool, being in control. And now, all because of Scoot, her composure was shattered and her nerves were twanging like banjo strings. Her emotions kept bounding from one wild extreme to another.

"Thank you, Officer," she said. "I shouldn't keep you from your duties. You've probably got dangerous bad guys to catch."

"Guess so," he said, and slid the sunglasses back on. To hide a touch of disappointment in those cocoa eyes? "Hope you and the boyfriend work things out." He almost sounded like he meant it.

"I'm sure we will."

Jeanette could hardly believe it when he sketched her a dashing little salute, then turned and ambled back to the car, whistling. He got in, said something to the other cop. The other cop snorted and looked over at Jeanette. She waved. Both of them waved back, and then drove off.

"Jesus," she murmured, resting her forehead against the upper curve of the steering wheel. "That, I did not need."

She waited until the patrol car was good and gone before starting up her engine. The close call and surge of adrenaline had left her starving, so she made a sandwich shop her next stop. A large diet cola, a chicken club wrap, and a bag of chips later, she was on her way once more.

It was after three when she reached her destination. After taking a slow cruise through the neighborhood, Jeanette parked half a block from Dunley Street, in a lot between a bowling alley and a thrift store. She locked her car – she always drove the anonymous late-model Honda Civic on these trips; it was a medium-beige that could pass for white, tan, gold or light green depending on the lighting.

With her keys and phone tucked in the pocket of her track suit, and her gun staying in the audio book case under the seat, she set off down the sidewalk.

The thrift store should have been open, but was dark and the sign was turned to 'Closed.' Glancing in, she saw the usual racks of used clothes, the usual ugly furniture, the usual broken, crappy toys. It reminded her of her childhood, of having to wear those clothes and sit on that furniture and play with those toys, and she angled across the street to get away from the unwelcome nostalgia.

On this, the south side of 6th Street, was a place called Needles & Nails, offering "tattoos and body piercing while you wait." Jeanette frowned. Of *course* it was "while you wait;" what the hell else would someone do? Drop off their skin to be tattooed and come back to pick it up later?

Next door to the tattoo parlor was the Luv Shak, with crotchless panties and see-through nighties and miniature bull whips on display in the window. Then a cigarette store . . . class all the way here on 6th Street.

Everybody she saw looked equally poor and disreputable. This was the world she had wanted so badly as a child to get away from. To rise above. Kids in hand-me-downs, alcoholic men with tempers, women overweight from only being able to afford cheap, greasy food.

It wasn't like Prewett. Prewett was sleazy but defiantly proud of it. As if there was a certain sneering joy in seeing how low you could sink. This neighborhood had the feel of desperation, of mostly decent people fallen on hard times and trying with varying degrees of success to brake their slide. A lot of the people looked old, fixed-income and dispirited.

The cross street was Dunley. Weasel had said Jon was shot over on Dunley, and the news had mentioned him breaking into an apartment. She could see three apartment buildings. One was directly across the street, old and dismal. The other two, closer to Pine than to Dunley, were newer and nicer.

She looked both ways, up and down Dunley. A 99-cent emporium, a diner, a dog groomer, a locksmith, a used bookstore, a hot dog stand and a junkyard. Straight ahead on 6th, she saw a bar, a teriyaki place, and a psychic.

Maybe she should ask the psychic how to find Scoot.

Scoffing under her breath, she wandered around looking for evidence of a break-in and a shooting. There was no helpful yellow police tape in evidence on any of the apartments in the vicinity, and she finished up at the used bookstore. It was open, with a few people browsing the stacks.

Jeanette pretended to do the same while she listened in on their conversations. She reasoned that the event would be a hot topic among the locals, excellent gossip fodder, and she was right. Within ten minutes, she'd learned that the crappy corner apartment building was where it had happened, and that the intruder had been shot by someone named Hector.

Hector.

No wonder Scoot went by a nickname. What sort of parents in this day and age tagged their kid with Hector?

"How is he?" a white-haired lady with a sweet, dimpled face asked the wheelchair-bound guy behind the counter. "The police aren't giving him trouble, I hope."

"He had to go to the station and talk to them again today," the young man in the wheelchair replied. He was handsome in an appropriately bookish, unconventional way, with dark-blond hair pulled back in a ponytail, but his mouth was set in a grim line and his eyes smoldered with anger. "I don't think they're going to charge him. They'd better not. All he was doing was defending Allison."

"Eva says that the man who attacked her is lucky to be alive." The old lady shook her head and clucked her tongue. "Poor Allison. Have you heard from her? Is she all right?"

"She called me from Bob's last night. God, it makes me *sick!*" He slammed a fist on the counter, causing books to fall over and a small cloud of dust to arise. "If *I'd* been there, that jerk wouldn't *be* so lucky."

"Now, Jamie –"

"Please don't 'now, Jamie' me, Mrs. O. You didn't hear her. She could barely talk from him throttling her, and Eva said she was beaten to a pulp."

Peeking at them from the mystery section, idly running her finger along a row of book spines, Jeanette frowned.

What the hell was this? Allison? Who was Allison?

All right, yes, Bigfoot Jon was a hairy ape and a pig and ten other kinds of animal, and she could easily see him knocking a woman around, even raping one if he thought he could get away with it. Aside from providing drugs to the brain-dead Steffi or renting the strutting disease-factories on Prewett, that might be the only way someone like him could ever get any sex.

But why last night, of all nights? Why, when he'd been so close to finding Scoot, had he taken time out to go after this Allison? Crime of opportunity? Had the dumbshit broken into the wrong apartment? Caught some pretty

girl in her underwear and just gone berserk with lust? He was a brute, but was he *that* stupid?

"How could something like this happen?" Mrs. O. fretted. "We try to keep things nice, just a few nice and peaceful blocks in the middle of all this city with its noise and crime. Our little haven. Our little corner of the world. Everybody knows everybody else. We all do our part to look out for one another. And then some horrible stranger comes along."

"If I'd *been* there . . ."

Mrs. O. gave him a kindly look that Jeanette could read all too well, even from here. It said, without coming right out and putting it into words, that it was nice of him to feel that way but what, really, could he have done? Him being in that chair and all.

What she actually said out loud was, "What matters is that Allison will be fine, and Hector too. I am no fan of violence, of course, but it would be a real shame if Hector got in trouble for doing what was only right. It's like with that dirty man who frightened my granddaughter so. He got his arms broken, and maybe that was wrong, but I'd stand before the throne of the Father Almighty and say he deserved it."

Jeanette wished they would quit with the speeches and tell her how to find Hector.

The damage was most likely already done. The gun and everything else would be in the hands of the police. They would have contacted Westbrook. They'd be trying with every means at their disposal to figure out who the owner of the purse was. Who the people on the tape were.

Still, there was a slim chance that Hector hadn't been entirely honest. He wouldn't want to confess to a career in purse-snatching. He might have spun some yarn about where he got the gun.

No matter what, she had to know. Had to find him. It was this not-knowing that was driving her crazy. This sense of not being in control. She couldn't walk away and leave it like this. Even if nothing ever came of it, she'd spend the rest of her life with her mind worrying at it like a dog with a bone.

"Is Hector still staying with you?" Mrs. O. asked Jamie.

Jamie shook his head, dashing Jeanette's spark of hope even as it ignited. "I offered, but he said he was going to go home."

"He's tried so hard, that boy. The family he comes from, it's a wonder he isn't mixed up with crime or drugs."

Jeanette stifled a bitter laugh. Not mixed up with crime? Since when?

"He said he had never picked up a gun before in his life," Jamie said. "But if he hadn't, who knows what might have happened? That son of a

bitch would have killed him, and Allison too."

"It's like we aren't safe in our own homes anymore," Mrs. O. said, and sighed with the weight of all the world on her stooped, frail, elderly shoulders. She shuffled off into the dusty stacks, leaving Jamie rearranging the books on the counter with perhaps more force than was strictly necessary.

Jeanette left the bookstore a few minutes later and headed back toward the corner. As she neared the Dunley Apartments, she saw a car pull up and let out a tall, slim girl with a chestnut-colored ponytail. The girl was moving slowly, with an invalid's stiffness, and as she turned to say something in through the open door to the driver, Jeanette saw that her face and neck were blotched with fresh bruises.

This, she surmised, had to be Allison. Even in a neighborhood like this, she doubted there would be more than one beaten, half-throttled girl out and about on the streets. Jon had really done a number on her.

Allison reached into the back seat of the car and got out a heavy duffel bag. The man behind the wheel tooted the horn and drove off. Allison waved. Then, with a quick glance around – Jeanette watched sidelong, pretending to fix her attention on the view visible through the dog groomer's window, a chubby young man wrestling a soapy mutt – the girl ducked her head and hurried toward the apartment building. She moved like she wanted to get inside before any of her neighbors saw her. No wonder. It couldn't be fun, being the talk of the town.

Despite the recent trouble, no efforts had been made to beef up the building's security. Jeanette passed by and took a cursory look. The front entrance had a lock that could be jimmied with a paper clip, if it even bothered to latch shut at all thanks to a warped frame. The fire doors at the end of the downstairs hall and the bottom of the stairwell were both propped open by doorstops, no doubt in direct violation of code.

Inside, the small lobby was threadbare brown carpet and peeling paint. It was stylishly furnished with a couple of large fake plants in terra cotta pots, a vinyl couch mended with strapping tape, a coffee table listing toward one uneven leg, an untidy pile of the Sunday paper, two mismatched chairs, a row of mailboxes and a large corkboard for posting messages.

Jeanette saw the girl, Allison, disappearing up the stairs. A quick scan of the intercom buzzer buttons mounted by a speaker on the wall beside the front door revealed no Hectors. There was a "Vance, H." on the fourth floor, though. Hector "Scoot" Vance.

An alley ran around the back of the building. Balconies jutted out over it like fungal growths, those shelf mushrooms that sprouted on rotting logs. A

chain-link surround enclosed a bunch of large metal trash cans with the lids off, and burst-open bags suggested that some of the tenants tried their luck hoping to score a basket rather than bother with walking all the way down the stairs, disposing of their trash, and walking all the way back up.

So this was where Scoot lived.

She started on her way, meaning to come back later when she would be at less risk of attracting attention, then stopped short. Her gaze was drawn back to the garbage cans.

Something looped down over one of the rims. A strap. A familiar buttercream-colored leather strap.

Forgetting caution, Jeanette unhooked the latch on the chain-link gate and pushed it open. It squalled on rust. A thin, scruffy cat streaked out of the space behind the cans, hissing balefully. She ignored it.

The strap belonged to her purse. She pulled it out from under a few plastic bags of kitchen trash, none of which had yet broken open or split and spilled their festering contents. The purse was clean aside from a few specklings of coffee grounds and one Popsicle wrapper pasted to the side.

The zippered opening gaped wide. It was not, as Jeanette had expected it to be, empty. She dug through the contents feverishly. Compact, lipstick, tape recorder, other personal effects. But the manila folder was gone. The envelope of cash was gone. The envelope with the gun was gone.

She experienced a moment's jubilation at the discovery of the miniature tape recorder, a moment that lasted until she realized that the tape inside was gone.

Scoot must have listened to it. And what? Decided to hide it? Decided to destroy it?

Hoping for the latter, hoping to find a crushed case and loops of filament-thin tape tangled through the garbage, Jeanette bent over the cans again.

Movement above her made her glance up. Someone had just come out onto a second-floor balcony.

It was the girl, Allison. That bruised face was impossible to mistake. She was holding something small in her hand, poking at it with an outstretched finger. It looked like a cell phone.

Jeanette didn't move. She couldn't yet figure out how this girl was connected to Bigfoot, or to Scoot. All she knew was that she'd be hard-pressed to explain why she was digging through the trash.

Allison held the phone to her ear, her bruised face wearing the expectant, apprehensive look of someone waiting for a call to go through.

With a bright electronic chirping, the cell phone in Jeanette's pocket began to ring.

169

Chapter 29

The cleaners had been and gone, as promised. The recliner was missing, leaving a conspicuously empty place where it had been. The television was gone, too, and the shards of broken screen vacuumed up. The carpet was still damp and smelled faintly of rug shampoo. The scattered books, trinket boxes, and knickknacks had been picked up and put back on the shelf, though of course not arranged the way they had been.

It gave Allison a strange feeling to know that other people, people she'd never met, had been in her apartment going through her stuff. It was for the best of reasons, of course . . . not with any bad intentions. Still, it creeped her out.

She supposed that it was only poetic justice. Didn't she get her main thrills in life by going through other people's stuff? And with intentions far less benign?

Her throat hurt worse than ever despite another dose of ibuprofen. At lunch, while Uncle Bob and Joe Peters gorged on mushroom-bacon cheeseburgers and endless baskets of seasoned steak fries, she'd supplemented the milkshake with clam chowder to avoid causing herself any more pain. The soup, combined with her lack of sleep and the stress of the trip to the police station, had left her sleepy. All she wanted to do was crawl into bed and nap for about five or six hours.

First, though . . . first she had some calls to make.

She'd promised Jamie Tremayne that she would get in touch when she got home. Normally, especially since their dinner and that kiss, she would

have been eager to talk to him. Now, though, she was dreading it. She wanted to see Jamie, wanted to hold him and have him put his arms around her.

But she didn't want him to see her like this. She looked like shit. She should've taken Uncle Bob up on his invitation and stayed hiding out at his house until the bruises faded and she was halfway presentable again.

It wasn't just concern over her looks, either. She hated this sensation of being in way over her head. And of feeling things, sharklike things with lots of teeth, swimming around in the depths.

Bad enough that she'd gotten herself into this situation. Worse to think that she could be endangering the people she knew and cared about. She had already dragged Eva and Hector Cesare into her drama, not to mention Uncle Bob. The last thing she wanted was to get Jamie mixed up in it as well. She was glad she'd chucked the purse. It had been an impulsive move, but at least now it was out of her apartment. Out and gone. When the trash men came on Tuesday, it'd be gone forever. Good riddance.

The rest of it had to go, too. She'd found, to her relief, that the folder with the information on Westbrook was still tucked in among her magazines, looking undisturbed and undiscovered by both the police and the clean-up crew.

"I'm done," Allison said to the quiet apartment. "Quits. Finito. I don't want anything to do with this. He can look out for himself, whoever the heck he is. Screw civic duty. I just want my life back."

So resolved, she would tear up that folder and dispose of it first thing tomorrow. Same with the tape, which she still had in her pocket. She didn't care what might or might not happen to Benedict Westbrook. By now, he would have heard from the police and it was *not* the problem of Allison Danielle Montgomery. Allison Danielle Montgomery was not going to get involved. She was through. Let the rest of the chips fall where they may, she just didn't give a damn.

All she had to do was convince someone else of that.

Going out on the balcony to get away from the smell of the rug shampoo, she placed her call before her resolve could falter or her bravado could fail.

The phone rang in her ear.

At the same instant, from the alley directly below her, she heard a sudden jingling chime.

She leaned over the rail and looked down.

A pair of disbelieving jade-green eyes looked back up at her.

The phone rang again.

There by the trash cans stood a petite blonde in a black track suit, black running shoes, and warm-up jacket with the hood pushed back. Her platinum

hair shone in the sun, the brightest thing in the alley. She was in the chain-link enclosure, the buttercream leather purse dangling from her hand.

Neither of them moved. They stared at each other. Allison felt like she'd been turned to stone, paralyzed by Jade's gaze as surely as if Jade had been a Gorgon straight out of Greek myth.

The phone rang for a third time.

Slowly, Jade's free hand dipped into her pocket. She raised the phone to her ear, thumbing a button. "Hello."

Allison heard it twice, once from the woman and once through the earpiece, in a curious sort of sound-doubling that only added to her whirling sense of unreality. She couldn't bring herself to speak.

"Your name's not Steffi at all, is it?" Jade asked with bitter chagrin and accusation clawing through her voice.

"I . . . um . . ." Her mouth worked, but she could not seem to form words.

"Is it, Allison?"

"Oh, shit," Allison whispered.

"Oh, shit indeed. I think you'd better start talking."

"Um . . ."

"What *really* happened here last night?" Each of Jade's words cut like a razor honed from glacial ice. "You were in on it, weren't you? All three of you."

"What?"

"But it went wrong, didn't it?"

"I . . . I don't know what you're . . ."

"Spare me the bullshit. You just give a message to Scoot for me."

Allison staggered. For an instant she thought she might drop the phone straight off the balcony and onto Jade's head. She clung to the rail, her knees weak. "A . . . a message? You . . ."

Had she heard that correctly? Was she understanding what she thought she was understanding? It couldn't be.

"Tell him," Jade continued relentlessly, enunciating each word with crystal-clear precision, "that I know who he is, and I want what's mine."

"You . . . you *what?*"

"I know who he is," she repeated, as if she thought Allison might be thick in the head.

Not that Allison, stammering like a dolt, was giving her any evidence to the contrary. "You . . . you know who . . . who Scoot is?"

"That's right. And I don't care what sort of deal you and Jon had with him, or how it went sour. We can put all this behind us, forget the whole thing, as long as he gives me back the rest of my things."

"Which things?"

Jade flapped her hand in irritation. "Don't play games with me. Not the gun; I know the police have that. I want the rest. The money, the tape, the folder."

"Wait a minute," Allison said, still trying without success to make sense of what she was hearing. It was as if Jade were speaking some language tantalizingly familiar to, but not quite exactly, American English. "How do you –?"

"Just tell him, and give him that phone. I'm done dealing with you. I'll talk to Scoot directly."

"But –"

"I'll call him tonight, at seven o'clock."

"I can't do that!" Allison cried.

"You'd better. You must know by now what kind of person I am."

"Yes, but . . ."

Jade snapped the phone shut, and although they were only a few yards apart, looking right at each other, easily within earshot of ordinary conversation, that decisive snap ended Allison's fumbling attempts to speak.

Those green eyes were still fixed on hers. They were narrowed into deadly, hateful slits. Then Jade turned in a swirl of disheveled platinum-blonde hair. She strode out of the alley.

Allison stared after her. She was on that mental patch of black ice again, wheels spinning without getting any traction.

This was absurd. This was insane!

She went back inside and flopped on the bed.

What had just happened?

Somehow, Jade had come *here* . . . how? Why? She knew that Allison had been 'Steffi,' but not that Allison was Scoot. She thought that Scoot was someone else. Some guy. But who? How could Jade be so close to the truth and still so wrong?

It was an impossible mess, a quagmire, and Allison didn't know how to get out of it. Give the phone to Scoot by seven o'clock? Scoot *had* the phone, had it right this minute! But what else was she going to do? Admit to Jade that she, in fact, was Scoot? How well would *that* go over? Jade wouldn't believe her . . . and if by some miracle she did, what then?

A woman like that wouldn't appreciate being tricked or fooled any more than she had already been. She'd kill Allison as much out of spite as out of a desire to snip the loose ends.

The only other crazy idea that popped into the whirling confusion in her mind was that she could get someone else to pretend to be Scoot on the phone. But the only one she could trust enough to ask would be Jamie, and

that was not something Allison was about to do. Not Jamie.

She could run. Just cut and run. Leave all her stuff here and *go*. Somewhere. Anywhere. New York. California. Orlando, Florida. Montreal. Mexico. She had a passport and twenty-five thousand dollars of an assassin's money to spend. Paris. Cairo. Tokyo. Maybe the moon or Mars would be far enough to run.

How about home? Home to the big house, to Daniel and Marian, to Missy and the twins and the country club?

A shudder wracked her. Home? That wasn't home. *This* was home. Dunley and 6th. She didn't want to give it up. This was her real life.

You must know by now what kind of person I am, Jade had said.

Yes. She did. Jade was the kind of person who would murder a man for money. Jade was the kind of person who would rush out after a phone call, expecting to find 'Steffi' wherever Jon parked his bike, and when she didn't find Steffi there, would shoot a guy named Weasel in the head. What would she have done if she'd found the elusive Steffi? Shot her, too, probably.

Scoot would be as good as dead no matter who Scoot turned out to be. But what would Jade do if Allison didn't come through?

"I have to get out of here," she mumbled. "Right now."

Where to go? Not back to Uncle Bob . . . he had been understanding, but she wasn't about to drag him deeper.

She thought of Officer Flyte, or Detective please-call-me-Tori Bryland, both of whom had been sympathetic and might listen. But they had only been sympathetic when they thought they were talking to a naïve young woman who had been beaten up, who had been ignorant enough of the law to buy an unlicensed, stolen gun. That was forgivable. The real story would not endear her to them.

Definitely not her parents. Not her brothers. Not her ballerina sister. Absolutely not Missy, who should never hear about any of this.

Eva?

Eva was her friend, and already partly involved. She owed Eva a little more honesty.

She got off the bed, went through the kitchen, and knocked on Eva's side. No answer. So much for that.

Except . . .

On a Sunday afternoon after everyone's sleep had been interrupted, the rest of the building was somnolent. Not even Mr. Kaminski's television was on. Allison tried the door and it slid obligingly open to reveal the tidy, quiet room on the other side. Eva was a kind, trusting person. Eva didn't lock her

side of the kitchen.

And Eva had no idea that Allison had given her an envelope containing the price of a new car.

It was sitting in plain sight on top of the dresser, on a crocheted doily. It made an odd addition to an alabaster candle holder, a statuette of Christ with eyes uplifted in prayer, a silver-framed photo of a teenaged Eva in a white dress, a pad of note paper shaped like a dolphin and a red ceramic pot full of pens and pencils.

Allison felt more like a thief than ever as she tip-toed across the room to retrieve the envelope. The masking tape was still stuck shut and it felt as packed with cash as ever – and she got a twinge of shame that she could possibly have suspected Eva of opening it, let alone taking anything from it.

She tore the top sheet from the notepad and scribbled a quick note to Eva. *Dear Eva, thanks for hanging onto it for me, I had to go out for a while, see you later and thanks again to you and H. Your friend, A.*

Now that confiding in Eva was not feasible, Allison felt better. She hadn't really wanted to tell this sort of thing to Eva anyway.

However, she did have to talk to someone. Not to get help. Just to have a friendly ear, and maybe to get some advice. There was only one other person besides Uncle Bob that she knew she could trust.

Ten minutes later, she was in front of the Readmore Bookstore, with her duffel bag in hand, just like she was on her way to the junkyard to change into Scoot. She entered the musty, papery-smelling dimness and blinked as her eyes adjusted from the glare of the afternoon sun.

"Allison!" Jamie wheeled toward her, then quit pushing and coasted to a stop as he saw her face. His expression flickered through a multitude of emotions.

In the aftermath of her encounter with Jade, she had almost forgotten. She turned her head away and yanked the elastic band out of her hair, letting it fall in concealing waves over her puffed, purple cheekbone.

"No," Jamie said, and reached out a hand that she could barely look at, let alone take. "Don't, Allison. Don't hide from me."

"I warned you I didn't look so hot," she said, her voice made even hoarser by impending tears. It hadn't been the shock and horror he'd shown that had done that . . . it was the concern . . . and something else.

The Readmore closed at five o'clock on Sundays. Now, at quarter 'til, it was already empty but for the two of them. Jamie rolled past her, flipped the sign from 'Open' to 'Closed,' locked the door and lowered the blind, and came back.

He stopped in front of her. "Allison . . ."

175

"Jamie, I'm in trouble," she said. "I'm in so much trouble."

"What can I do?" He reached out again.

When she still didn't take his hand, he rolled closer and took hers. He had considerable strength in his upper body, which shouldn't have surprised her as much as it did. Hadn't he pulled her right into his lap the other day?

Jamie drew her two faltering steps toward him. She dropped her duffel – it clunked when it hit the floor, weighted down by her skateboard and all her gear – and put her other hand over her battered face. Her breath caught. She sniffled.

God, she was on the verge of tears! She hadn't expected that. Didn't want to break down and cry in front of him.

"Allison," he said in a soft tone.

He thumped first one leg and then the other to the floor. With his left arm, he pushed hard on the armrest of his chair. Shakily, he levered himself upright. At last he was leaning heavily on the counter but standing, *standing* in front of her.

She gaped at him through a watery veil of tears. "Jamie . . . but you can't . . ."

"Come here." He drew her against him.

Allison let him do it. She felt his arms encircle her and it was the last straw. The remnants of her will crumbled. She put her forehead on his shoulder and wept while he stroked the loose spill of her hair.

"I'm so sorry for what happened," he said, tilting his head against hers. "I wish I had been there to help you. I never want to see you hurt, Allison, never."

"It isn't that," she said between sobs. "There's something else . . . something worse. I don't know what to do."

"Whatever it is, I'm here for you," he said. "No matter what. I promise."

She looked at him – looked *up* at him, because standing, even leaning in that awkward scarecrow stance, he was taller than she had expected. "I . . . I didn't know you could . . ."

"I can. Sort of. Sometimes. I have metal leg braces and crutches that I can use, but most of the time I don't bother. They make me look like a . . . cyborg or something. Scary. A clanking robot, lurching along. In the chair, I'm just a cripple."

"You're not," she said. "You're a hero."

"Some hero," he said wryly. "Look at me. I'm standing here with my arms around a beautiful girl, and I'm about to collapse."

"My hero, anyway."

"Again, some hero. I wasn't there when you needed me."

"Please, Jamie, sit down. I don't want you to hurt yourself."

"And I don't want you to hide your face from me. Agreed?"

"Agreed."

As he lowered himself into the chair, she bound her hair back in the ponytail again.

"You don't have to do that," he said. "Your hair is pretty. I don't think I've ever seen it loose."

"I've never seen you without your ponytail, either," she said.

"Later, I promise. Here, come in the office. You can tell me what's wrong."

The bookstore's back office was reached via a wide doorway behind the counter. A large desk that looked like a mahogany door with table legs screwed to the corners was stacked high with cardboard boxes, milk crates and shopping bags full of traded-in or donated books. A library-style trolley, half-full of paperbacks, sat at one end. The only available seating was a futon with a denim cover.

A pair of old-fashioned wooden crutches leaned against the wall. Jamie saw her look at them and nodded. "I keep them here in case I need help getting up off the couch," he said. "Have a seat."

She did, and he maneuvered himself from the chair to the futon beside her. His arm went around her again as if it was the easiest and most natural thing in the world.

"You might not want to do that when I tell you what I have to tell you," she said, loathe though she was to give up the welcome, warm comfort.

"I don't think there's anything you could tell me that would make me feel that way."

"We'll see about that," she said, and told him the whole story.

Chapter 30

Jamie listened to every word without interrupting, his only response being an intrigued, interested look that grew more pronounced with each revelation.

When she was done, Allison sat back and regarded him with wary expectation. "Well?"

"Wow," he said.

"Wow? Is that all?"

"You've got to give me a minute to let it all sink in."

"Okay." She needed a minute herself, really. She already felt better for having gotten it all out, but at the same time was wondering what she had been thinking to tell him so much. He wouldn't let her walk away now. He'd insist on being with her, on helping. He couldn't leave her to face this alone.

It would, she thought, serve her right if that was exactly what he did. If he gave her a hearty commiserating clap on the back and said, "Gee, Allison, that's a hell of a tale, thanks for sharing, thanks, see ya, bye." It would be just what she deserved.

"So you think this woman – Jade – killed someone this morning," he said after a long, thoughtful pause.

"Yes," Allison said.

"You should call the police."

"But I'd have to tell them how I got myself into this mess."

"Yeah, they'd probably like to know."

"I'd be arrested! I stole her purse –"

"For God's sake, Allison, do you really expect her to press charges?"

"What about all the other purses?"

"Slap on the wrist," Jamie said, and he sounded mildly annoyed with her, as if she was quibbling over petty meaningless details and ignoring the bigger picture. Which, in fact, she was. "If they even care about that at all. You'd be giving them a murderer. A serial killer."

Allison shivered. "A serial killer?"

"Well, maybe not," he amended. "She doesn't sound like a psycho, like the ones you hear about on the news. But a repeat killer, at the very least. A multiple-murderer. An assassin. You can't possibly believe that this is the first time she's done this. From everything you told me about the tape, and your conversations with her, it sounds like she's done this plenty of times before. If you can hand the police a way to tie up who-knows-how-many unsolved murders, the last thing they'll care about is you swiping a few handbags."

"It isn't that easy," she said, though she knew he was right. "I don't really know anything about her. She didn't leave her driver's license in her purse."

"Fingerprints, her voice on tape, and you've seen her. More than once. Are you telling me you couldn't describe her? That'd give them a good place to start."

"What if they don't catch her, though? She knows who I am. She knows where I live. She'll come after me." Allison touched her bruised cheekbone. She already didn't feel safe in her own home, and to have a professional killer mad at her was enough to ensure she might never feel safe again, anywhere.

"We're not going to let that happen," Jamie said. "The police will catch her. They'll protect you. Besides, you have other places you can go."

"I don't want to bring Uncle Bob any more into this than I already have. And my family . . . I don't want them to know at all."

"There's me."

"You've done too much already."

"Don't push me out of this, Allison. Don't even think that." He squeezed her hand almost hard enough to hurt.

"Jamie . . ."

"And you have a lot of friends in this neighborhood," Jamie said. "You know how they rally 'round."

"Oh, sure," Allison said. "When it's something like Needles breaking the arms of that pervert, or even the way they supported Hector for shooting Jon . . . because those were bad guys. Bad guys getting what was coming to them. And when Mrs. Oberdorfer, or Needles and Tisha, or anybody else finds out what I've been doing, they'll think that *I'm* a bad guy, too. That if

some killer shoots me in the head, I'll be getting what's coming to me, too."

"They won't."

"They will! And then I won't have anywhere to go, anyplace I can call home."

"Allison." He took her by the shoulders and made her look at him. "I'm sorry to say it like this, but . . . this isn't about you."

"What?"

"If you don't go to the police, that woman is going to get away with what she's done. She's going to get away with murder. What if she *does* come after you, and kill you? Then she'll get away with that, too. And she'll go whack this Westbrook guy and *he'll* die, and even if she leaves him alone, what about all the other people after him? You think she'd quit? She'd just move on to the next job. And you'll be responsible."

She blinked at him, feeling thunderstruck, and the only thing that came out of her mouth was incredibly childish and inane. "Well, if I'm dead, I won't care, will I?"

"Won't you?" he countered.

"What, is this an afterlife thing? God's going to punish me?"

He shrugged. "Nobody knows for sure."

"I never would have guessed you as the religious type," she said, thinking that if anything, he should have refused to believe in, or outright turned away from, any good Lord so merciful as to stick him in that awful wheelchair.

The corner of Jamie's mouth lifted in a slantwise grin. "It's a miracle I'm even alive, so who am I to doubt? I should have died in that accident."

Her gaze shifted to his legs, which looked so normal. A little thin, maybe, the muscles not as toned as the rest of him. Then, feeling guilty for staring at him like that, she blushed.

"You've never asked how I ended up on wheels."

"I thought it'd be rude and nosy." And, though she couldn't bring herself to say it, she'd always just figured he had been born that way.

He smiled. "You'll steal and paw through some stranger's purse, but it's rude and nosy to ask a friend about himself?"

"Well . . . I . . ."

"Remember the other day, you came over and caught me watching adventure racing? I used to do it."

"You did? With the . . . rock climbing and the kayaking and the freezing your butt off in the remote wilderness?"

"Yeah." Jamie's smile softened into a faraway expression, part nostalgia, part bitterness for what was lost, part exhilaration. "It seems like such a long time ago. I was outdoorsy as a kid. Hiking with my dad, mountain biking,

white water rafting. Mom hated it, thought he was going to get both of us killed. She was a city girl. The funny thing was, *that* was what killed them. The city."

"The city killed them?"

"They were mugged one night coming home from a restaurant. It was their twenty-fifth anniversary. I was in college. The way I heard it was that Dad thought he could take the robber. But as fast as he was, he couldn't beat a bullet."

"Oh, Jamie, I'm so sorry!"

"School seemed meaningless after that," he said. "I wasn't learning anything that I couldn't learn from books. So, with the insurance money and what I got from selling the house, I dropped out of school and became an adventure racer. Bought all the highest-tech gear. Flew all over the world. South America, New Zealand, Russia, everywhere. I was getting pretty good. Good enough to compete. My dream was to get on a team for the *Eco-Challenge*, the big one by Mark Burnett."

"The *Survivor* guy, sure," Allison said, recognizing the name.

"Then, my luck ran out," Jamie said.

"You don't have to tell me —"

"I know."

"Okay," she said. "If you're sure."

He got that faraway look again. "It was a biking leg. I was with my girlfriend and her —"

Allison jumped a little, and Jamie laughed. She started to blabber some apology, but he gestured her to silence.

"Yes, I even had a girlfriend," he said. "Kirsten. Another racer. She and her brother Kevin were rising stars on the circuit, and we all sort of fell in together. Kevin was the driving force, though. We all saw what we were doing as a personal challenge, but Kevin really had a conquer-the-world thing. Nothing was ever good enough. He was the one who had to go higher, faster, more extreme. But even when he was being Captain Ahab, he had a way of encouraging us to go to lengths we would have thought were impossible."

"Was she pretty? Kirsten?" She was disgusted with herself to find that as Jamie revealed his tragic past, what most hooked into her like cat claws was jealousy at this mention of a girlfriend.

"Honestly? Not really. Tough, healthy, tanned, strong, fit . . . but not really pretty. It didn't matter, though. There are so few female racers that any of them are considered a good catch."

"Like in skateboarding," Allison said. "A lot of groupies, not many girls who actually get on a board."

"It was late," he said, and she could tell that he was seeing another place

far removed from this musty book-smelling back office. "Sunset. Gorgeous country. We were up in the Canadian Rockies, in a part of the world where you could almost believe you were the first explorers on a new planet. The only signs of civilization we could even see were the contrails from jets. Kevin wanted to make the next marker by dark, and we'd had some delays along the way. A rockslide that we had to get off our bikes and climb over, carrying them. Winds, some snow."

Allison felt awestruck by his simple words, and at the knowledge that Jamie Tremayne, pleasant Jamie from the bookstore, had once led a life far more filled with risks and thrills than her own. She also felt juvenile and stupid. What was Scoot and a skateboard compared with this?

"So we pressed on," Jamie said. "At twilight, at that elevation, everything was unearthly. The snow on the mountains seemed to glow like moonlight, though the moon wasn't up. The first few stars were out, and the last of the sunlight was this clear gold that made all the colors and details leap at you. The air was icy-crisp and sharp as a scalpel. I was bringing up the rear, behind Kirsten. My front tire hit a rock, and when I bounced over it, I came down on a patch of ice. That was it for me."

"What happened?"

"I don't remember," he said hollowly. "I remember everything right up until that point. How the stripes on Kirsten's suit were this iridescent green, almost neon. How my leg muscles ached, but it was a good ache, the kind you get from exercise, the kind full of pride and accomplishment. I remember how hungry I was and how much I was looking forward to stopping for the night. Then there was the rock, and the ice, and darkness."

"What about Kevin and Kirsten?"

"They heard me go over. They told me later that my bike flipped, then slid, and went into a ravine. I hit at least three trees, and the last one kept me from going over a forty-foot drop. The bike *did* go over. I saw it later and it looked like a metal rag some giant had wrung out."

"Oh, my God," Allison murmured. To think that he could have died . . . long before she even had the chance to meet him . . .

"I was in a coma for nineteen days," Jamie said. "Kevin and Kirsten got down to me, called for help, and waited with me. They had me airlifted out by helicopter. I'd broken both legs — the left in two places, the right in four. Crushed three vertebrae. Broken one arm and dislocated the shoulder. Nine ribs, one of which punctured a lung. And to top it all off, I fractured my skull. My helmet was cracked clean in two."

She put her arms around him, and though she knew those injuries had

been years ago, and had long since healed as much as they were going to, she did so carefully. As if she would hurt him. Her eyes were wide and her chin was quivering with retroactive fear and shock for what had happened to him.

"The doctors didn't think I would ever come out of the coma, or that if I did, I'd be so brain damaged that I would have been better off dead. They got in touch with my closest relative, an aunt on my father's side, and started sounding her out about organ donation."

"You're kidding!" Allison gasped.

"Hey, they move fast when they've got a live one," Jamie said. "So to speak."

"They would've . . ."

"Harvested me," he said. "Heart, kidneys, corneas —"

"That's revolting!"

"I was a young guy, prime of health except for being a human jigsaw puzzle. No sense letting all that good material go to waste, if it could have helped some other people live a better life."

"It's so . . . vulturish. Were they trying to get your aunt to pull the plug?"

He went grim. "Kirsten told me later that they were leaning on her pretty heavily. Poor Aunt Sarah had only met me three times, one of them at my parents' funeral, and she didn't know what I would have wanted. She took so long to make up her mind that I came out of the coma and ruined the harvesting team's hopes."

"Good!" Allison said vehemently.

"I spent another month in the hospital, had a bunch of surgeries. Then eight months of rehab and physical therapy." He spoke lightly, glossing it over, but Allison was sure that those had been months and months of raw torture and sheerest living hell.

"Jamie, I'm so sorry."

"It could have been worse. I lived. I surprised everyone by not being a vegetable, by not showing any lingering signs of brain damage at all. But they told me I'd never walk on my own again. In a way, it would have been better to be brain damaged, because I wouldn't have known what I was losing."

"Don't say that," she said, holding him tighter, as if she could somehow undo his pain with her embrace.

"The kid I was then thought so, anyway," he said. "For that Jamie, it was the end of everything. No more races. Stuck in a wheelchair for the rest of my life. Not even able to stand upright without help. It was worse than being dead. I came pretty close to suicide a few times."

She squeezed her eyes shut, hardly able to bear thinking about it. "And . . . and Kirsten?"

183

"Kirsten couldn't handle it," he said, and she heard the buried heartache beneath his mild tone. "She stuck with me until I got out of the hospital, but the more people kept telling her how brave and devoted she was, sticking with me despite the fact that I'd be a cripple for the rest of my life, the more it got to her. So she left me. I hated her for it at the time, but I understand now. If it had been me, the Jamie I was then, if our situations had been reversed, I probably would have done the same thing."

"So she just . . . just dumped you? What did you do?"

"There wasn't much I could do. I survived. I went through those months of physical therapy. Everyone kept saying how lucky I was to be alive, and eventually I came around to believing them. I thought I'd take the miracle a step further, and prove the doctors wrong by regaining full use of my legs. That didn't work out. I did get back more use than they thought. I'm not totally dead from the waist down, thank God."

"Thank God," she echoed, and blushed again.

He paused and gave her a raised eyebrow and an evaluating look.

"Um. You were saying?" she asked.

"The hospital bills ate up most of what I had left from my parents," Jamie said. "Aunt Sarah invited me to come and live with her, but I felt like I'd been too much of a burden on her anyway, and I wasn't up to getting to know a bunch of cousins when I was still so mad at the world. I'd done a lot of reading, and discovered I could escape from things through books. So, with the money I had left, I bought the bookstore. Three years later, I'm still here. And there you have it. The story of Jamie Alan Tremayne, in a nutshell."

"Your middle name's Alan?"

"Yes. What's yours?"

"Danielle. For my father."

"Allison Danielle. That's pretty. Are you all right?"

"Why?"

"You're so pale," he said.

She placed her hands along the sides of his face, brought his head down, and kissed him, a light, brushing kiss that hurt with bittersweet tenderness on her bruised lips.

"I'm glad that you survived," she murmured. "I'm glad you're here."

"And I'm glad you're here," he said. "I'm overdue for some good things in my life."

They kissed again, him being careful and her striving against him, throwing pain to the winds. What was her pain compared to what he'd suffered? She clung to him and turned it into a deep and searching kiss that left them both

breathless. When it was done, she leaned her forehead against his and shut her eyes. A familiar sensation of excitement and adrenaline was tingling through her. Here was a risk she hadn't taken in a long time, a thrill that wasn't going to get her killed or land her in jail.

"So," Jamie said, sounding a little unsteady himself. "Now you know all about me."

"Not quite," she said. "You promised . . ." She reached behind his head and undid the black velvet ribbon.

His hair fell loose, framing his face in honey-gold waves, and the tingle shot through her again – excitement colored with smoking lust. She almost threw herself on top of him. Never mind anything else.

He must have seen it in her eyes, because he drew back from her with what looked like true regret. "As great as this is, Allison, there's still Jade to think about. She's expecting to talk to Scoot when?"

"Seven o'clock tonight."

"And it's after six now."

"Is it?" she asked, shocked. Her gaze followed his to a clock on the wall, and sure enough, the hands stood at ten after six.

"We need to decide what we're going to do."

Chapter 31

Jeanette saw her leave the apartment building, striding down the sidewalk at a brisk pace that only the person who had frightened her would recognize as a near-run. To anyone else, the girl named Allison could have just been late for an appointment or worried she'd miss a bus.

A heavy duffel bag swung at her side, and this disturbed Jade. Was Allison, or Steffi, or whatever she wanted to call herself, splitting altogether? Leaving town? *Was* she worried she'd miss a bus? A Greyhound to another state?

But Allison didn't matter. Scoot was what mattered.

By five o'clock, evening was descending over the city like a flight of dusky moths. Most of the shops in the neighborhood were closing. Jade returned to her car, waited until the bulk of the street and sidewalk traffic had eased, and then calmly set about breaking into the thrift store.

She wasn't concerned about setting off an alarm, and didn't need to be. The back door, which was marked 'Emergency Exit Only' and opened onto an alley, had a cheap lock that broke after only two hard strikes with a hammer from the toolkit in the trunk of her car. No braying sirens split the air, no lights flashed. Who would bother installing an expensive system to protect a bunch of donated junk?

The store had been closed all day and there was the slim chance that it was because the proprietor was doing inventory. However, once Jeanette was inside, she found the place utterly deserted.

The scent of it brought back her childhood again, that unwelcome rush

of memories. Musty upholstery. Harsh, cheap detergent. The poor-sweat of customers who'd handled the items on display. Rust. Mildew. She could almost see herself here, that younger Jeanette, pushing the cart for her mother while Mitchell kicked and squalled in the seat and Carrie and Deena pleaded for naked Barbie dolls in plastic bags, or threadbare stuffed animals. Their mother would be loading the cart with school clothes for them . . . mostly with the knees out or the cuffs frayed or splotched with bleach stains or missing buttons.

Shuddering, she forced those thoughts out of her mind and set about a purposeful search. The overhead fixtures were out, but enough light came in through the wide front windows to allow her to make her way through the store easily enough. Her petite stature made it easy to duck down unseen behind the stacks of cookie tins, wicker baskets, board games and holiday decorations on the shelves that topped the racks, if any pedestrians should happen by.

In the ladies' wear section, she selected the best outfit that she could assemble from the choices. The idea of putting on the clothes turned her stomach, but she had been seen by too many people in the black track suit, and it wasn't right for what she needed now.

She started with dark grey slacks, in the middle ground between dressy and casual. They were too long, but she found a pair of nearly-new black suede slouch boots to tuck them into. A plain white blouse with fake pearl buttons went under a vee-necked sweater in a green, white and grey diamond-shaped pattern, one sleeve bearing a cigarette burn on the inside of the elbow.

In all her younger years she had never once gotten lice or ringworm from thrift-store clothes, the thought of such vermin nagged persistently as she dressed in the plywood stall of the changing room. She stuck the track suit and hooded warm-up jacket on a spare hanger and jammed them onto a rack. The sneakers, she shelved with the other shoes. Everything that had been in her pockets went into a black purse with a strap she wore crossing her body from shoulder to hip. She suspected that she would carry her purses like that from now on.

By the time she was done changing, no police cars had been summoned by any silent alarm or keen-eyed passerby, so Jeanette let herself out the same way she had come in. Instead of returning to the car, she walked down the alley toward Dunley, behind the ugly backsides of the 6th Street businesses.

She saw two stray cats and a homeless woman, and then she was back on Dunley across the street from the used bookstore. She had watched Allison long enough to see the girl enter the bookstore, and remembered how the wheelchair-bound clerk had sounded so protective and fond of her.

Strange. He had struck Jeanette as an intelligent, literate guy. Not the sort who would run with a brain-dead slut like Steffi. Nor had Allison seemed much like Steffi in person. So what was *she* doing with Bigfoot? Or had it all been some sort of weird mix-up that Jeanette couldn't yet fit together?

The bookstore was dark, the 'Closed' sign in the door. Jeanette headed for the apartment building, moving like she knew where she was going and belonged here as much as anyone.

Getting in wouldn't be a problem . . . an elderly man with his pants hiked up to his armpits had propped the front door open with a rolled newspaper as he exerted himself into a stroke lugging groceries from a beat-to-shit old station wagon illegally parked at the curb.

Jeanette stood back out of his way as he went past, arms trembling to support a box full of canned goods – creamed corn, stew, soup, tuna. "It's . . . for . . . my . . . sister," he said. "Food . . . bank. She's . . . a shut . . . in. Fourth . . . floor."

"Let me get the elevator for you," she said, darting around him to thumb the button. In the wall, gears groaned and cables creaked, and before the doors even slid open, Jeanette knew that she wouldn't get in that thing if her life depended on it. The prospect of plunging down the shaft wasn't nearly as daunting as that of being trapped in the claustrophobic little cage, unable to get out, having to wait for rescue.

"Thanks!" wheezed the old man. "Going . . . up?"

"I'll take the stairs," she said, smiling and giving him a cheerful little wave.

Allison's apartment was on the second floor. Jeanette got out, nose wrinkling at old, familiar smells not much better than those of the thrift store. A cat box, diapers, the yellowed-newspaper stink of old people, stale cigarette smoke, frying onions.

The only person in the hall was a little boy, sitting on the carpet playing with a toy garage and a bunch of Matchbox cars. The door behind him was open, and the source of the frying-onion smell as well as the sound of a *Seinfeld* rerun on the television.

"Hello," the little boy said.

"Hi."

She didn't linger, kept on going. When she glanced back, the kid had lost interest in her and gone back to his cars.

The row of intercom buttons out front had shown an 'Arnold Kaminski' in 211 and an 'A. Montgomery' in 206, and no other A-names. 206 lined up with Jeanette's orientation of where she remembered the balcony being, and moments later she was at the door.

Now she had to move fast. The kid wasn't much of a witness, only two

188

or three years old and paying more attention to his cars, but even he was bound to remember if the nice blonde lady took too long getting through the door, or had to do something as dramatic as kicking it down.

This lock, though, opened readily enough after a few pokes with a slim strip of metal that Jeanette kept with her for just such an occasion. She let herself in, glanced back again, saw the kid trying to drive his cars up the wall, and shut the door.

Allison's apartment was dark and quiet, and the smell of carpet shampoo hung in the air. Jeanette drew the drapes across the window that gave onto the balcony, then switched on the lamp.

She saw what was missing first. No television. And an odd sense of absence to the furniture, as if some large piece should have been present but wasn't. A sunburst clock hung askew on the wall, the hands pointing almost straight up and down as it ticked its way toward six.

Bigfoot had been here. Had been shot here. That was why the place smelled of wet carpets and shampoo. That was why some of the furniture was missing, either broken in the struggle or hauled away later with bloodstains. Jeanette had seen plenty of gunshot wounds and knew all too well how they bled. There was a lot of what Rayburn liked to call 'the claret' in a person.

But what, *what* had Bigfoot been doing here in the first place? What did Allison have to do with Steffi have to do with Scoot?

She was missing something. Overlooking some vital part of all this. And it was driving her crazy.

The tape cassette was not in the recorder. Scoot had listened to it, she was sure. And the fact that he'd taken it out suggested that he had either given it to the police, or hidden it for his own reasons. Had he hidden it here?

Hastily, she tossed the apartment. She found nothing to suggest that the girl who lived here was involved with any guy, let alone a stoner like Bigfoot. She examined a collection of small trinket boxes, some of which were very nice, expensive and imported. Some of the pieces of jewelry were quite good as well, and that in itself made her wonder all over again what this girl was doing involved with Bigfoot. Why hadn't he yet ripped off her good pieces and hawked them to support his drug habit?

The furnishings, though, could have come right from the thrift store. The clothes likewise, though there were some nicer outfits.

The books were mostly thrillers and mysteries – J.A. Jance, James Patterson, Jonathan and Faye Kellerman, Sharyn McCrumb, Janet Evanovich, Tami Hoag, the ubiquitous King and Koontz – with a few fantasy and romance standards by Anne McCaffrey, Robert Jordan, David Eddings and Katherine

189

Kurtz. By the look of them, they had been purchased at the used bookstore.

She found a letter in with a stack of mail, and read the childlike printing with growing curiosity.

Dear Allie, I miss you, when are you coming home? David is going to tennis camp this summer and Steven to music camp so it will be boring here. Mom says it won't because I will have Danny to play with but Danny is a baby and he bites me. I drew you a picture so you remember who I am. Love, Missy.

In with the letter was a fairly skillful drawing showing a large house and a family, and a red-haired girl with sad eyes.

The envelope was embossed, with an ornate calligraphy M and the return address stamped into the upper corner in gold leaf. That was when Jeanette's brow really furrowed. She knew that neighborhood. It made Palmyra Hills look like tract housing and her own gated community look like the ghetto.

What in the world was a daughter of that kind of wealth and privilege doing living in a place like this? How had she gotten hooked up with a loser like Bigfoot?

Most of all, what was she, Jeanette, missing? The more she learned, the less it all added up.

She flipped through a bunch of celebrity gossip magazines in a wicker rack, more in the interest now of trying to get a handle on who Allison really was than for anything else, and froze when she uncovered a manila folder.

Hardly daring to blink for fear it would vanish like a mirage, she snatched it up and opened it.

Benedict Westbrook's bronzed, smiling face looked up at her.

The information! It was here, all of it, the papers that Rayburn had given her, the photographs, the addresses, the times and places!

A wave of dizziness went through her head and she had to brace herself against the wall. She clutched the folder to her chest to assure herself that it was real.

The folder was here. It had not been turned over to the police. The gun was in their hands, yes. After the shooting, it would have been taken. But not the folder. She put it in her new black purse.

The tape was gone . . . did that mean the police had the tape? Or did that mean the tape *had* been hidden?

And what about the money? If anything, *that* was what the shooting had been about. Probably the reason behind the lumpy purple mess of the girl's face, too. No attempted rape, but a disagreement over the cash. Twenty-five thousand would be a tempting pie, with everyone wanting the bigger slice.

Except . . . damn it, that didn't make sense either, if Allison was a rich

girl. Unless she was disowned. Did people still do that? She had no idea.

A sudden voice made her twitch to a state of wary, catlike alertness. It wasn't in the apartment, which was a single room with a puny bathroom, but it was close. A moment later she realized it was coming from the other side of a sliding door, and was accompanied by the sounds of running water and sliding drawers.

"– a mistake to have anything to do with him," the voice said. It was a woman, textured with a slight Spanish accent. She sounded tired and irritated.

Distantly, a male voice responded, but Jeanette couldn't make out the words. She thought one might have been 'brother.'

The woman with the Spanish accent said, "But I am your sister, Hector, doesn't that mean anything to you?"

Hector!

Pots and pans clattered. "I would think after last night you would know better," the woman said. "You could have gone to jail. Why did you have to shoot him? There must have been some other way."

Jeanette drew her gun and held it against her thigh as she approached the door. She saw that it would be easy to open – throw the bolt, slide the door, and she'd be in. She'd get some actual-damn-answers, instead of just more questions.

Cupboards opened and closed. Ice clinked into a glass. There was the unmistakable hiss-pop of a soda can, and a fizzy gurgle. "I just don't know what all that business was that he was saying," the woman said. "Purse-snatchings and women with guns –"

The sound of the pouring soda had covered the metallic rasp of the bolt, and Jeanette flung the door aside at the word "guns."

Chapter 32

She burst through into a kitchen smaller than her own walk-in closet, where the makings of spinach salad sat on the counter and fresh fish rested on a cutting board over the sink.

The woman with the Spanish accent had Spanish looks to go with it, dark and shapely with a lot of black hair up in a bun. She was barefoot in paisley shorts and a halter top, and Jeanette had the barrel of the gun at her temple before she'd begun to turn.

"What was that about women with guns?" Jade inquired.

Beyond the little kitchen was another sliding door, standing open to reveal an apartment identical in size and shape to Allison's, but much neater. A dusky-skinned young man had been sitting at a desk in there. He leapt to his feet in alarm.

"Hector, look out!" the woman cried.

"Move and I'll shoot her," Jeanette told him. "Then you."

He went as motionless as a kid playing statue-tag. His face was a mask of distress. "Eva . . ."

"It's all right," the woman said with a steadiness of tone that Jeanette would have admired under other circumstances. At the moment, she found it annoying. Steadiness was not going to serve her purpose. Terrified would have been better. Easier. People talked when they were terrified.

But something was still wrong here. Getting more wrong all the time.

"Who are you?" Hector asked. "What is this? Let go of my sister!"

"Hector, calm down," Eva said. Her voice was still steady, but Jeanette

had her by the scruff of the neck and could feel her trembling.

Eva was taller than Jeanette and outweighed her by at least forty pounds, but guns had been the great equalizer since the time of the Musketeers. Presumably, antiques expert Benedict Westbrook could have told her the exact year that power had shifted from the steel edge of a sword to the deadly potential of gunpowder.

Something, though . . . something was *very* wrong here.

There was no recognition in Hector's eyes, that was one thing wrong.

And Hector, too, was wrong.

She remembered a tall, lanky figure on a skateboard. Fair skinned, long-limbed. Hector was short, almost as short as Jeanette herself. He was stocky with muscle. His skin, like his sister's, was dark.

"Please," Eva said. "Tell us what you want. We don't have much, but —"

"Shut up," Jeanette said. She stared at Hector.

He wasn't Scoot. Not even close.

"What the hell *is* this?" she hissed. "Where's Scoot?"

"I don't know what you mean," Eva said. "Who is Scoot?"

"Don't play with me. You, Hector, come here."

"No," Eva whispered, and now there was terror. Not for herself. "No, please, whatever this is, leave him out of it. He's my little brother."

"If he cares about you, he'll step right there into the doorway but not one inch further," Jeanette said. "And he'll tell me what went on here last night."

"What's it to you?" Hector's brows drew together.

Jeanette did not let the gun waver from Eva's head. "I'm waiting."

Hector looked to his sister, and Eva nodded almost imperceptibly. He looked then to the gun, and to Jeanette's cold eyes, and she saw his throat move as he swallowed hard and took a deep breath.

"It was very late," he said. "We were sleeping, and woke up hearing shouts and crashes from Allison's apartment. So I broke through the door — you can see, there, the new bolt was attached. Someone was attacking her. A man, big and red-haired, on top of her, trying to strangle her."

"Where did you get the gun?"

"They had knocked everything over and there was a gun on the floor," Hector said. "An old gun, like something from a cowboy movie. I picked it up and yelled for him to get off her. When he did, he came for me. I had to shoot him. I didn't even know if the gun was loaded, but it was, and I shot him in the chest."

"The gun was in there?" She jerked a thumb over her shoulder. "In Allison's apartment? You didn't have it?"

193

"No," Hector said. "It was on the floor, with other things, like it had fallen from her purse."

A light was going on in her head, but it stuttered and winked like a strobe, and what it revealed in its flashes was so outrageous that she couldn't believe it.

"The man," she said. "Did you know him?"

"I never saw him before in my life," Hector said.

"He was a stranger to us," Eva said. "Allison said he had been following her, that she had only seen him around but did not know him either."

"Do you know anyone called Steffi?"

Blank looks from them both.

"Or Stephanie? Is that Allison's middle name, maybe?"

"Her middle name starts with a D.," Eva said, more puzzled than ever. "Please, what is it that you are trying to learn? We do not understand."

"Neither do I," muttered Jeanette. Except that she was beginning to. Or, really, she *did* understand but her mind kept rejecting it. "What else can you tell me? What else happened last night?"

"The police came, and the paramedics," Eva said. "I had performed the first aid on the man, and I went with them to answer their questions."

"What about Allison?"

"She went to stay with her uncle," Hector said. "We have not seen her since then, but Eva was working and I was visiting our family."

"All right," Jeanette said.

She curled her lip, and Hector blanched. He probably thought that she had gotten what she wanted and was now going to kill them both. And the thought *had* crossed her mind, no mistake about it. When she had believed Hector to be Scoot, the one who had caused her all this trouble. But she couldn't bring herself to gun down innocent, decent people, even if Hector had done her a disservice by shooting Bigfoot.

That did leave her in a sticky situation, though. They had seen her. Hector more than Eva; Eva had only gotten a fleeting glimpse if that before Jeanette had whirled her around with the gun pressed to her skull.

She didn't like walking away and leaving more witnesses, not with Bigfoot in the hospital running his mouth and spilling his guts to the police. But, in the end and though she knew she should, she couldn't just shoot them.

"All right," she said again. "Listen, I don't want to have to hurt you. I'd like to walk out of here with no more trouble. What you did last night was brave, neighborly, and noble. But if you decide to play the hero again, Hector, you won't come off so lucky. Understand?"

"Yes," he said.

"Neither will your sister."

"I understand."

"Same goes for you, Eva," she said. "No coming after me. No calling the police. Because I *will* get away, and if I have to do that, I'll come back."

"We understand," Eva said. "Believe me. We both do."

Jeanette eased the gun away from her head and stepped back. Eva did not move or turn around. She stayed stock-still in the middle of the kitchen with her hands fisted at her sides. Hector was similarly immobile in the doorway. The space was so confined, and full of weapons — there was a wicked-sharp little knife right on the cutting board — that if they wanted to make her life more difficult, they could. But she would be able to shoot at least one of them, and neither of them wanted to risk it.

Leaving the kitchen door open so she could hear if they moved, she went quickly through the apartment and out into the hall. The kid was still there, playing with his Matchbox cars. Jeanette put her gun in her purse but kept her hand on it, ready to shoot through the side of the purse if Hector changed his mind about being heroic.

No other doors opened, and Jeanette didn't linger. She shed her sweater as she went down the stairs, wadding it up and stuffing it into a trash can in the lobby. Then, slinging her purse crosswise once more, she did what they wouldn't expect her to do — she stayed in the neighborhood instead of booking it as far and as fast as she could go.

There was a bar on the other side of 6th, a bar that seemed to exist solely to cater to the crowd from the upstairs pool hall. It was called the Eight Ball, and the Sunday evening crowd consisted of two men playing darts in the back, a trio of women who looked like they'd just gotten off-shift at a grocery store, and four men ranged along the bar munching peanuts and watching ESPN.

She ordered a Bloody Mary and took a small table by the front windows, which offered her a view of the apartment building's entrance. A couple of the men at the bar turned to give her a hopeful once-over, but she frostily ignored their looks.

Stirring her drink with the celery stalk, she watched the apartments and waited. No police cars came screaming up. Nor did Hector and Eva leave in a hurry with all their personal possessions. It was business as usual over there. She was a little disappointed. She hadn't expected a S.W.A.T. team or a mass exodus of panicked senior citizens, but the lack of any activity whatsoever came as something of a letdown.

It didn't matter, though.

What mattered was what she'd finally figured out.

Chagrin at her many mistakes brought heat to her face. She had leaped from one erroneous conclusion to the next, and made the entire mess more complicated than it really was. She'd blown it up into a conspiracy, given her adversaries far more credit than they deserved, and been entirely on the wrong track all along.

Ten minutes passed. It was six-forty.

A wheelchair rolled into the intersection. Walking beside it was a tall girl with a chestnut-brown ponytail and a bruised face.

Jeanette's teeth crunched crisply through the celery stalk. She spat the green stub into a napkin without taking her gaze from the window.

Hello, Scoot.

So, she was heading for home, was she? With her dashing bookstore boyfriend. Surprising. Jeanette would have thought that she'd be miles away by now.

A cool smile played about her lips. She watched the pair go inside. Let them try to manage that clunky old elevator with his wheelchair. That was a task she didn't envy.

Six-forty-five. Any minute now, Allison would be getting quite the earful from her neighbors. She'd discover that the folder was gone.

"Pardon me, miss." One of the men from the bar had decided to try his luck after all, frosty demeanor or no frosty demeanor. "That blouse looks nice . . . but do you know what would be better on you?"

He was pushing forty, on the chunky side, wearing dark brown slacks, a yellow shirt with the sleeves rolled up and the collar unbuttoned, and a loosened red-yellow-tan striped tie. A fancy watch showing the time in three different cities, the tide, and the phase of the moon took up most of his wrist, and a gold varsity ring sparkled on one finger in a desperate effort to cling to long-gone youth and fitness. His hair was medium-brown and worn in a curly Michael Bolton mullet that made Jeanette flinch. She wondered if he had escaped from the used car lot over on Prewett.

"What?" she asked, meaning 'what did you say?' and not 'what would be better on me?' because she didn't think she had fully understood him.

The mullet-man took it as 'what would be better on me?' and beamed. He had a glass of beer in his hand, half-full. "Me."

It took her a few moments to figure out this exchange, and when she did, she thinned her lips and gave him the subzero glare.

"Bad line, huh?" He dropped into a chair at her table without an invitation. "Yeah, I know. Cornball. I thought about trying 'did it hurt when you fell

from Heaven?' or maybe 'does your face hurt —'"

"I'm not interested," she said, using the same aural liquid nitrogen she used on telephone solicitors and petition signature gatherers.

"Come on, cut me some slack."

"Why in the world should I?"

"It's hard meeting people these days," he said. "I figure, why not take a chance? By the way, I'm Larry. And you are . . .?"

"Not interested," she said, inwardly fuming. Of all the times for some loser to try picking her up . . .

Six-fifty. By now, Allison would have heard about Hector and Eva's visitor, would know that Jade had been in her apartment. Would she notice that the folder was gone?

"Hey, it's not easy for us guys, you know," Larry said, putting on the wounded-puppy act. "Try to get to know someone, and —"

He *must* be a car salesman, because he could not give up. And she was supposed to place a call in a few minutes . . . she couldn't very well do that with him hanging over her shoulder the whole time.

She got up.

"Oh, don't go away mad," Larry said.

Just like that, she wanted to shoot him. To haul out her gun and drill him right between the eyes. Public service. Maybe not as worthy of a key to the city . . .

What had happened to her? Where was the cool, calculating, emotionless Jade?

Instead of plugging him, instead of even throwing the contents of her drink in his face and leaving him sputtering with tomato juice and vodka dripping from his mullet, she stalked out of the Eight Ball and into the twilight.

Six-fifty-five.

"I'm sorry. I'm a jerk."

Dear holy God, he was *following* her!

She felt his hand fall on her shoulder. Shaking it off, she tried to continue on her way without a word.

"I'm trying to apologize here!" Now he was getting all indignant, like it was *her* fault. Like she was the rude one.

"Get away from me," she said, biting off each word.

Across the street, a man who looked uncannily like Johnny Depp had paused on porch steps beside a sign reading "Palms – Cards – Dreams – Past Lives" to watch the drama unfolding. He even had Depp's bemused little smile. A couple of teenage girls on the sidewalk had been sneaking surreptitious

glances at him, but now turned to see what he was looking at. A beefy older man loitering at the foot of the stairs leading up to the pool hall stubbed out his cigarette and snorted a smoky laugh, maybe at Larry the mullet-man, maybe at Jade.

Great. Now she was attracting all sorts of attention.

"Can't a guy get some credit for apologizing?" Larry the mullet-man whined.

Six-fifty-eight.

The age of chivalry truly was over. Here she was, attractive woman being hounded by an asshole on a busy street, and nobody intervened.

She walked faster. Not saying anything. Because if she spoke, she'd start to swear, and once she started swearing, she feared she'd lose her tenuous hold on her temper.

"Stuck-up bitch!" Larry shouted after her. "I said I was sorry!"

Six-fifty-nine. The low heels of her suede boots clacked on the concrete. She was passing the Greenview Apartments, which were much nicer than the dive where Allison lived. On the corner up ahead was a karate school with wide windows. As she came up even with it, seeing a bunch of mommies and a few daddies looking on with indulgent smiles while their kindergarteners pranced about in cunning little white outfits, her watch beeped the hour.

Seven o'clock.

Chapter 33

"She was here? Right *here*?"

Eva Cesare was pale and shaking. Hector was shaking, too, but his face was flushed dark with anger. They had just finished telling Allison about their sudden visitor.

"Did you call the police?" Jamie asked.

Allison felt like she was hooked to a helium balloon, drifting up away from the earth, away from conventional reality. This all kept getting weirder and weirder. It was like she had stumbled into someone else's life.

"No," Hector said. "I wanted to, but Eva told me not to call."

"Why?" Jamie asked her, incredulous. "Why not, Eva?"

"I did not think it would be a good idea," Eva said. "What would we tell them? Why would they believe us? It is crazy . . . this woman going around threatening people. Who is she? What does she want? Allison, what is all of this?"

"It's my fault," Allison said.

She looked around her single room, feeling violated and heartsick all over again. Her gaze fell on the magazine basket, and she caught her breath. She dashed to it and pulled out magazines in clumps. *People* with Jude Law on the cover. *Entertainment Weekly* with the cast of *Big Bang Theory*. *People* with the Kardashians. *Entertainment Weekly* with a montage of characters from upcoming children's movies. *Cosmopolitan* with a model in a slinky dress and "Ten Tips To Drive Him Wild In Bed." *People* with Will Smith, cute-as-a-bug.

No folder.

"It's gone!"

"What's gone?" Jamie wheeled closer.

"The folder. The one with the pictures."

"Allison, what is all of this?" repeated Eva. "What was in that envelope you had me hold for you? Who is that woman? You have to tell me!"

"God, she was *here*!" Allison wrapped her arms around herself.

"It's almost seven," Jamie said. "If we're going to call the police, we'd better hurry."

"What envelope?" Hector asked.

"I don't know what to do," Allison said.

"Please, tell me what is going on," Eva said.

"Everyone, be quiet," Jamie said.

For a moment, they were, and they could all clearly hear Mr. Kaminski's television through the back wall. It was tuned to *Wheel of Fortune* . . . whirr-clicky-click and the dismal down-spiraling noise of someone landing on Bankrupt. That sound summed up Allison's mood.

"I can't do this," Allison said, looking helplessly at Jamie.

"You know you can," he said. "You're tough."

"I'm not. I'm a wimp."

"I could never love a wimp."

Flustered as much by what he'd said as by the matter-of-fact tone in which he'd said it, she dropped magazines all over the place. Love? Had he really dropped the L-bomb on her? Just like that, out of the blue and in front of Eva and Hector and God and everybody?

She stared at him, momentarily robbed of the power of speech. His eyes were dark and deep and full of trust. That warm curve of patented Jamie Tremayne smile melted her like so much gooey chocolate on a summer day.

"Okay," she said. She went to the phone.

She would call the police. She would dump all of this on them and deal with the consequences as best she could. Then, maybe, if she got through it in one piece, she could see if there was still a chance for something to develop between the two of them.

Before she could pick it up and dial, another phone rang. This one was in her pocket, the chirping ring of the pre-paid cell phone. Her sunburst clock pointed to a minute past seven.

"It's her!" she said in a foolish stage whisper.

Jamie swore silently, looking grim. "You'd better answer, Allison, and see what she has to say."

"What is —" Eva began, but stopped at a stern gesture from Jamie.

200

The cell phone chirped again. Allison answered. "Hello."

"Hello, Allison."

"Look, I know you wanted to talk to Scoot –"

"Oh, enough of that," snapped Jade. "Did you think I wouldn't figure it out? Did you think you'd fooled me?"

"Um . . ."

"Now, Scoot, or Allison, or whatever you're going by, we have a problem here. Don't you agree?"

"What do you want?"

"I want this never to have happened, but unless you can turn back time, we'll have to make do somehow. We'll have to improvise. Where's my money?"

"I . . ."

"And don't lie to me, Scoot. Don't think you can get away from me. Even if *you* could, other people would pay."

"How can you –"

"Like your boyfriend in the wheelchair. Or those neighbors of yours, who seem like such decent people." Jade paused, while icy worms of horror burrowed into Allison's stomach. "Or your uncle . . . or even little Missy, your precious baby sister who writes you such adorable letters."

"No!" The word, blurted louder than she intended, drove a sharp jab of pain into her throat.

"The money?"

"I have it. I have it right here."

"And what were you going to do? Keep it? Turn it over to the police?"

"I hadn't decided," Allison said, then went ahead and admitted the truth. What did she have to lose at this point? "But I was leaning toward keeping it."

She had turned away from the open gawking curiosity of Hector and Eva, away from Jamie's steady and encouraging eyes. She saw the letter from Missy, the envelope with her family's address on it. Of course, she'd known from Jade's tone that it hadn't been a bluff. This was only conformation. The icy worms slithered and knotted.

"At least you're a criminal too," Jade said. "There's that we have in common. You know that if you go to the police, they'll have some very serious questions about your own habits and activities. Right, Scoot?"

"Right," she said, downcast, head hanging. She wanted to protest that she was nothing like Jade, nothing at all, but didn't want to anger the woman on the other end. "I have the tape, too."

"The tape." Jade let out a breath that sounded strained between clenched teeth. "I can't take your word for it that you haven't copied it, and there'd be

no way I could know."

"I haven't!"

"I'd like to believe you, but like I said, I can't. And it doesn't matter, really."

"I just want this to be over," Allison said.

"There's another thing we have in common. You've caused me a lot of trouble."

"I'll give back the money."

"You certainly will. But what else am I going to do about you?"

"Oh, stop it! Don't play with me!" Allison surprised herself by raising her voice. It was coarse as a file scraped over metal. "If you're going to kill me, just go ahead and say so and quit dicking around!"

There was a long, thoughtful silence after this outburst. A long, thoughtful silence in which Allison could see her life slipping away like the last few grains of sand in an hourglass running empty.

"I'd really prefer not to have to do that," Jade said at last. "Despite what you might think, I am not some murderous maniac. It's all business, Scoot. Always business. What would I gain from killing you? I admit, you've been a pain in the butt and I've had my moments of revenge fantasies, but I can't afford to risk indulging them. Nobody would pay me for getting rid of you. There's no profit in it, even if it would be a measurable public service. So I'm prepared to leave you alone."

Her words hung in an expectant way.

"If . . . ?" Allison prompted, not really wanting to hear the rest but knowing that she had to.

"If it goes both ways. If you're prepared to leave me alone."

"What's that mean?"

"That means, I get my money back, and you destroy that tape, and you don't go to the police. You forget that this ever happened."

"Boy, would I love that," Allison said, and she meant every word.

"Wouldn't we both," remarked Jade dryly. "That's my deal. You keep your end, and convince your neighbors to do the same. I'll keep mine. We'll never have to deal with each other again."

"What if I can't convince them?"

"Try," Jade said. "Try really hard."

"But what if I can't?"

"Like I said, if I'm unable to get at you, I'll start with your friends and your family. I won't enjoy it, I won't profit from it, but business is business and I'll do what I have to in order to keep my career afloat. You got that?"

A tear trickled down Allison's face and she wiped it away, thinking of

Missy, and Jamie, and Uncle Bob, and everyone else whose lives were hanging on a thread thanks to her. "All right. But there's one other thing I want."

"Oh, and you're the one calling the shots?" Jade asked with bitter humor.

"Don't do it," Allison pleaded. "The guy . . . the guy with the sailboat . . . leave him alone, too."

"What's he to you?"

"Nobody. I just can't stand to see anyone else hurt."

"How many times do I have to say it? It's business."

"*Please!*"

Through the phone, she heard muffled traffic and street noises. She heard a gusty sound that might have been a sigh, and might have been Jade snorting in disgust at this display of soft-heartedness.

"Jade?" Allison ventured. "Are you still there?"

"I'm here."

"Can't you let this one go?"

"It's a moot point, you know," Jade said. "By now, the police will have tracked him down as the owner of that gun. It's evidence, so they might not give it back to him right away, but they'll have informed him where it came from and he will be suspicious. What did you tell them about where you got it? Not the truth, I know."

"No," Allison admitted. "I told them I bought it from a street vendor."

Jade laughed. "Clever. Lying to the police to save your own skin. Good job."

She said nothing, writhing inwardly with shame.

"But anyway, it *is* a moot point," Jade went on. "I couldn't get at him now. He'll be alert. The police might even be watching him, thinking that *he* had something to do with all of this. If we're lucky, maybe they'll even find a way to pin Weasel on him."

The admission, made so casually, sent a shudder twisting through Allison.

"So, I'll agree," Jade went on. "I won't kill him. I'll just have to repay my up-front fee and deal with some disappointed clients. This has put a serious blot on my record."

"You'll really leave him alone?"

"Yes."

"And me? And my friends, my family, my neighbors?"

"Yes to all of the above."

"So I just give the money back, and destroy the tape, and it's done?"

"It's done. Not that I expect you to trust my word, unless there *is* honor amongst thieves. Which is what we both are when you scrape away the veneer. You steal purses, I steal lives. Well? What do you say? Is it a deal?"

"It's a deal," Allison said. She didn't dare look at Jamie, Eva, or Hector, sure that they would be staring at her in contempt, not understanding that she was only trying to look out for and protect the people she cared about. "When and where do you want me to bring the envelope?"

Again, Jade laughed, and this time it was mirthless. "So that you can set a trap, and have the police there to catch me?"

"No!" Allison hadn't thought that far ahead, and once more felt hopelessly out of her depth.

"Let's not even give you the chance," Jade said. "Step outside on your balcony, why don't you?"

The slithering icy worms inside her froze into a solid tangled mass, which then plummeted as the bottom dropped out of her stomach. Her throat contracted into a pinhole again, and fine hairs stood up all along her arms and the nape of her neck.

She could easily picture herself drawing back the draperies and finding Jade there on the balcony. Phone in one hand, gun in the other. The last sight she'd see would be Jade's green eyes and cruel smile, and maybe a muzzle flash.

"Are you going to shoot me?"

"We've been through this already," Jade said impatiently. "If I'm going to shoot you, wouldn't you rather get it over with?"

Strangely, that relaxed her. She covered the mouthpiece while she dug around in her duffel bag for the envelope. "You guys go into Eva's apartment, okay? Stay there until I come back, no matter what."

"Allison—"

"Please, Jamie. Don't argue."

"You are making a deal with the devil," Eva said, shaking her head.

"I know, but I have to. Go on. I'll be right there."

"I don't want to leave you," Jamie said.

"Trust me," Allison said. "I know I don't deserve anybody's trust, but . . . please. This once."

"I do trust you," he said. "I'll go, but, Allison, I don't like it."

They went into the next apartment. Jamie looked back at her like she was on her way to the gallows or the guillotine. Maybe she was. If so, the last thing she wanted was for any of them to be hurt as well.

"You're too good for me, Jamie," she said.

Once the kitchen door was shut, Allison bolted it from her side. She went to the drapes. Steeling herself, she pulled them back.

The balcony was empty. Allison slid the glass door open and stepped out. She looked over the rail. There, in the alley where she'd been only a few

hours ago, was Jade. She was wearing different clothes, but it was her, all right. Phone in one hand . . . gun in the other. But the gun was held low against her leg, not pointing up at Allison.

"Toss it down," Jade said.

"You promised, remember."

"I know."

Allison held the fat envelope of cash over the rail. Twenty-five thousand dollars. Enough money to help a lot of people. She found that her fingers didn't want to let go. She forced them to open.

The envelope fell straight down and slapped into the alley. Jade, still keeping an eye on her, bent and picked it up. She tore away the tape, riffled the bills, nodded. "It's all here?"

"Yes."

"And the tape?"

She tossed it down. The tiny cassette did not crack when it hit the ground. Jade picked it up, examined it, and pocketed it. "Good. One more thing."

Somehow, Allison managed not to flinch. This was when it would come, the sudden raising of the gun, the whipcrack of the report, the flash, the impact.

But the shot didn't come. Instead, Jade cocked her head and surveyed her like she was a germ under a microscope.

"Why, Allison? Why do you live in a dump like this? Your family's got more money than I'll ever make and you threw all that away to live like . . . like *these* people. *Why?*"

The questions hit her almost as hard as bullets. "What does that have to do with anything? You got what you wanted. Now go!"

"Call me crazy, but I'm interested," Jade said. Her tone was grudgingly admiring. "You've caused me no end of trouble, dressing as a boy, riding around on that damned skateboard . . . you've got guts, I'll say that much. You're quick, too. The way you lied on the phone when you must've realized it was me . . . that whole 'Steffi' thing . . . pretty slick."

"Not so slick." Allison didn't know what to say. She didn't *feel* like she had guts . . . she felt like her guts running down her legs into her shoes. And she did not want this woman, of all people, to admire her.

"Maybe we're not so different after all," Jade said. "Maybe that's why I don't really want to kill you. Inside, we're the same. So, answer my question. Why?"

"If I stayed with them I'd never have my own life," she was astonished to hear herself say. "That's all I want. My own life."

"Yeah," Jade said. She put her gun away. "Me, too. Goodbye, Scoot. Steer clear of Century Plaza from now on."

"Count on it."

Jade headed for the mouth of the alley. At the end, she paused and looked back. "I'd tell you to stay out of trouble," she said. "But I don't think it would do any good."

Chapter 34

A different crowd from the business-suited lunch-lemmings filled the Stag and Hound on Friday nights. Younger. Louder. Boisterous. Music thumped and throbbed from the speakers. In a vague attempt at keeping with the ersatz Olde English pub atmosphere, the songs were all by British artists. The waitresses wove their way among packed tables, carrying trays laden down with pint mugs of a dozen kinds of beer, and more baskets of the fish and chips.

In the same corner booth under the same print of riders in a foggy meadow, Jeanette sat drinking amber ale and munching on pretzels. She, however, was not quite the same.

Even if the place had been filled with the exact same people who'd been here that afternoon a week ago, they wouldn't have recognized her. The platinum pixie-cut bob was gone, replaced by a shorter, sassier strawberry blonde hairdo. Large gold spiral earrings hung from her lobes, and she wore a knee-length black skirt with a sexy slit up the side, a silky black off-the-shoulder blouse, smoke-colored nylons and strappy black high heels. The gold chain with the jade dragon pendant had been replaced by a choker of onyx beads.

"I like the new look," said a voice like rough velvet.

She arched an eyebrow at Rayburn. "Likewise."

He came to the table, scruffy with a week's worth of unshaven beard and a shorter haircut that really showed the silver . . . more George Clooney

than Pierce Brosnan. A plain white shirt open at the throat showed a hint of chest hair, and he was wearing snug, faded jeans and a well-scuffed leather jacket.

"What are you going by these days?" he asked, sitting opposite her and signaling for a waitress. One appeared with such alacrity that she might have been a genie summoned from a lamp. He ordered his usual Guinness.

"Jade will still be fine," she said when they were alone again.

"No tape recorder?" He indicated her purse, a black faux-snakeskin number on a long gold chain-strap, too small to hold more than a wallet, keys and the barest essentials.

"Didn't think I'd need one." Jeanette passed him a thick envelope she'd been carrying folded inside a newspaper. "Here."

"So you're sure? You're turning down the offer?"

She narrowed her eyes at him. "What's that supposed to mean?"

"Only that the job is still open, if you want it."

"I thought my run of bad luck put an end to that particular assignment. Are you telling me the Company is willing to give me a second chance after all?"

"Well . . ." He shot her a roguish smile that could have – and probably *had* – melted the resolve of sterner women than she. "Maybe they don't know about that."

"What are you saying, Rayburn?"

"Do you want complete honesty?"

"In our line of work?"

He turned serious. "My employers aren't involved this time."

"What?"

"Well, Jeanette . . . can I call you Jeanette?"

"Why?" She tried not to show the effect it had, hearing him purr her own given name in that smoky voice. It was almost enough to make her slither under the table in a boneless puddle.

"This is personal."

"Rayburn, you'd better start making sense pretty soon here."

"Michael."

"What?"

"My name. It's Michael."

"This is getting too strange even for me," she said. An uneasy feeling was creeping over her. This was not the way their game was supposed to be played. This was not in the rules. She didn't know how to react.

"My employers didn't arrange that last job. They never even knew about it. *I* hired you."

"You?"

"Just me," he said. "I'll understand if you're angry with me."

She was too stunned to be angry, at least not yet. "Let me make sure I've got this straight . . . you approached me just like always, through the usual channels you've used all those times before. But you were acting on your own this time?"

"That's right."

"Why?"

"I told you it was personal."

"Yes . . .?" She lifted her voice at the end, querying.

"I put it all together just like any of the other assignments we've given you, but the money was mine and the target was of my choosing. I hired you. Fletcher, Christopher, the others . . . none of them knew. Which means they don't know it went wrong."

Now she did feel a twinge of anger. "You set me up."

"No. No, nothing like that."

"If Fletcher had found out I was working independently for *you* . . ."

"But he didn't. They don't know. They never will. This was, and is, between the two of us. Just you and me, Jeanette."

Jeanette rubbed her temples with her thumbs. "God, Rayburn! What were you thinking?"

"Michael."

"Whatever! But what were you thinking?"

"I wanted him out of the way." He folded his hands on the table and sighed, looking down at them. "It was the only thing I could think of to do. I never dreamed it'd turn out like this. I know I shouldn't have involved you, but you are the best. I didn't trust anyone else to get it done."

"Maybe you should have," she said. The anger was rising now. Duped by a skateboard kid, and now to find out she'd been tricked by Rayburn right from the very outset? "Or maybe it's just as well that I failed. This is not the way I work. I never should have accepted it in the first place. I don't take personal cases. How many times have I said that? Now I find out that you were using me?"

"You *are* angry."

"Damned right I'm angry. I came closer than I ever have to being caught, and I didn't even get paid. Double my usual fee, my foot . . . you were going to cheat me, too, weren't you?"

He pushed the envelope back toward her. "Keep it. I'll see that you get the rest."

"No. I don't want it, and if you think I'm still going to *take* this assignment,

you're out of your mind."

"Then keep the twenty-five. For your trouble. It's the least I can do."

"The least you can do is tell me exactly why you jeopardized everything like this. You owe me that much at least. Who is he? What's he to you?"

He bowed his head for a moment, then looked up at her with those striking cobalt eyes. They were darker somehow, darkened by pain, to the indigo of midnight sapphires. "I knew his reputation. A stud. A playboy. One girl after another, and when he was done he'd throw them aside like yesterday's news. I didn't want to see her hurt."

"Who?"

"Sophia."

An image of the gorgeous brunette in the red dress came to her . . . the brunette with the deep blue eyes . . .

"Oh, my God," she said. "I *thought* there was something about her, something that looked familiar. She's your daughter."

Rayburn nodded.

"And she's dating Westbrook."

"I've tried to talk her out of it. Tried to talk sense to her. But she wouldn't listen to me. She thinks it'll be different with her. She thinks that he'll treat her right, and won't abandon her like he has all the others. Jeanette, she's my little girl. She's all I have left. What kind of father would I be if I didn't try to do something?"

"So you decided to have him 'dealt with'?" She made little finger-quotes as she said the last two words. "Jesus, Rayburn . . . you've been in this field for too long when that becomes your first solution to every problem!"

"What else could I do?"

"Talk to her!"

"I tried –"

"Talk to him!"

"And tell him what? That he'd better not hurt my baby?"

"It could work. And really, didn't you think it would hurt her to have him end up dead? Murdered? Shot by his own gun?"

"Better that than have him ruin her!" he said with a sudden fierce passion that rocked Jeanette back in her seat.

"You idiot," she said. "My God."

"Am I an idiot for wanting to protect my child?"

"What if they suspected *her*?" she shot back. "Did you even consider that? What if they decided she did it, and put her away? Is that your idea of protecting her? Sending her to jail for murder?"

210

He blinked several times, mouth unhinged. "I . . ."

"You didn't consider it, did you? Or what about the possibility she could have been hurt? What if she'd been with him when I made my move? I didn't know who she was. She might have ended up collateral damage."

"No," he said firmly. "No, I know you. You're precise. Like a surgical laser."

"Accidents happen."

Groaning, he propped his elbows on the table and buried his face in his hands. "I only want what's best for her. My Sophia. I never want her to go through what I did."

"You told me you were a widower," Jeanette said.

"I am."

"Then how in the hell would killing Westbrook keep your daughter from going through what you did? It sounds to me like you'd be putting her through the exact same thing!"

"Angela had an affair," he said. "It was brief. It ended. She came back to me repentant, remorseful, swearing that it had been a one-time fling, a momentary aberration. I should have known better, but I loved her so much . . . needed her so much. Sophia was still a child then, and needed her mother. So, God help me, I took Angela back."

Jeanette had a chill, knowing what was coming next.

"For a while, it was all right," Rayburn said. He spoke like someone finally unburdening something that had been weighing on him for years, which it probably had been. "Better than ever. But then, a few years later, she met someone else. It wasn't just a fling that time. She wanted a divorce so that she could marry him. She wanted to take Sophia away from me, too. I couldn't let that happen."

"Does Sophia know that you had her mother killed?"

"To this day she thinks it was an accident. She grieved. But she never had to know that her own mother would have abandoned her. I protected her from that, and I'll protect her from Westbrook the same way. I'll do it myself, if I have to."

"You can't protect her from ever being hurt by anything or anyone in her entire life," Jeanette said. "Rayburn, you can't. It's impossible. She's a person, not an exhibit you can keep under glass."

Even as she spoke, she caught herself wondering what it would have been like to have a father – or a lover, or *anyone* – willing to go to such lengths for her. Willing to kill for her. Not for profit, not for gain, but solely because it was personal.

"I can't sit back and do nothing."

"You can. You will. You have to."

"What you're saying is that you won't take the job. All right. I'll find another way."

"What I'm saying is that you aren't going to do this, Michael."

He raised his head, startled by her use of the name.

"You're going to leave him alone," she said.

"But Sophia —"

"Needs to handle this on her own. You have to let her lead her own life. That's all any of us want." She wasn't about to tell him that she'd just learned that herself, and from a damned skateboard kid, no less.

A terrible wrenching spasm of grief twisted his expression. Somehow, it didn't make him any less handsome. "She's all I have left."

"Does she know you love her, and that you're there for her no matter what?"

"Always."

"Then she'll be fine. Better than the rest of us." She rose smoothly from her seat, shaking her sassy new hairdo around her face.

"I don't blame you," he said. "Not many women would accept a dinner invitation from a man who'd just confessed to murder."

"Well," Jeanette said, sliding into the booth beside him, "luckily for you, I'm not like many women."

Chapter 35

"I will miss being next door to you," Eva said

It was a nice sentiment, but Allison thought it wasn't completely truthful. Things hadn't been the same between them in the past few weeks. The casual camaraderie and the shared meals in the kitchen had turned stilted and uncomfortable, then come to an end. Allison couldn't shake the feeling that Eva kept waiting for the moment when someone *else* would break into the apartment with a gun.

"Me, too," Allison said. "Without you right next door, I'm going to have to learn how to cook."

"No," Eva said. "You will have a fine cook. Perhaps you will learn something."

"And you'll still have Hector to mooch meals off of you. I'm glad he's going to live here. I'll miss the place, and it feels better knowing someone I like is moving in."

Hector had tried moving back home after the oldest living Cesare brother had gotten out of jail. He'd thought that Juan the Rattlesnake would be able to handle their drunken, abusive stepfather. As it turned out, Juan had handled him so thoroughly that the stepfather was dead. Juan was back in jail, having done one of the quickest turnarounds in parole history.

"Thank you for talking Teddi into it," Eva said. "And for helping him get the job at the bowling alley."

"That was Uncle Bob more than me. Uncle Bob's got connections." Allison looked around the room. It had a vacant, cavernous feel although she

had left most of the furniture for Hector. Without her books, trinket boxes, clothes and other assorted personal effects, the place no longer felt homey or familiar.

She and Eva hugged, though it was the stiff and awkward hug of distant relations or old friends who had subsequently fallen far out of touch.

Allison picked up her trusty old duffel bag in one hand and her skateboard in the other. She headed out of the Dunley Apartments and onto the street.

Outside, the day was hot and sunny and the Dog Haus was giving off fragrant clouds of barbecue-smelling goodness. She saw Martha coming back from another successful Dumpster dive behind the craft store, Jake Oberdorfer and his friends throwing a football in the street, the Beekers on their way to the diner, Tina Wendmeyer headed for work up at the 7-Eleven. All well and good and as it should be.

No one even looked at her like she was the neighborhood pariah. Though Jon Wharton had eventually caved in under pressure from his mother and the detectives, the story he had spun was so bizarre that no one had given it any credence. They all thought that he was trying to muddy the waters, cover his tracks, pick-your-metaphor.

Allison hopped onto her board. She wasn't wearing the baggy jeans, the hat, and the windbreaker. She sped down 6th Street in white denim cut-offs and a snug cotton-candy-pink tee shirt, ponytail flying.

Her bruises had faded, her voice was back to normal, and she felt wonderfully alive and free. No more purses since Jade's, and no urge for them either. As for Jade, she was evidently keeping her end of the bargain.

She jumped off the curb, veered across the street, and flipped the board up into her hand as she made a running stop in front of the Greenview Apartments.

Jamie Tremayne, in his chair, met her at the door. She leaned down and kissed him, not caring that the people on the sidewalks had stopped to grin bemusedly at them.

"This is it, then?" he asked when she straightened up.

"This is it. I'm officially moved out. Too late to change your mind."

"Wasn't planning on it." He gave her a once-over as he backed into the apartment. "I like the new look."

"New look?"

"Without the disguise."

"Ah. Yep, I'm off the hook," Allison said. "I don't have to be Scoot anymore."

"That's kind of a shame. You were pretty cute dressed as a boy."

214

"Is there something you're not telling me? You prefer boys, is that it?"

"I prefer girls, thank you very much. Didn't I just tell you that I liked the new look?"

"You keep saying that, but I'm not seeing the proof."

"And what would you consider adequate proof?" he asked.

"Come here and I'll show you," she said, yanking the rubber band out of her hair and letting it spill over her shoulders.

*　　*　　*

THE END

ABOUT THE AUTHOR

Christine Morgan divides her writing time among many genres, from horror to historical, from superheroes to smut, anything in between and combinations thereof. She's a wife, a mom, a future crazy-cat-lady and a longtime gamer, who enjoys British television, cheesy action/disaster movies, cooking and crafts.

Her stories have appeared in several publications, including: *The Book of All Flesh, The Book of Final Flesh, The Best of All Flesh, History is Dead, The World is Dead, Strange Stories of Sand and Sea, Fear of the Unknown, Hell Hath No Fury, Dreaded Pall, Path of the Bold, Cthulhu Sex Magazine* and its best-of volume *Horror Between the Sheets, Closet Desire IV*, and *Leather, Lace and Lust.*

She's also a contributor to The Horror Fiction Review, a former member of the HWA, a regular at local conventions, and an ambitious self-publisher (six fantasy novels, four horror novels, six children's fantasy books, and two roleplaying supplements). Her work has appeared in Pyramid Magazine, *GURPS Villains*, been nominated for Origins Awards, and given Honorable Mention in two volumes of *Year's Best Fantasy and Horror.*

Her suspense thriller, *The Widows Walk*, was recently released from Lachesis Publishing, and her horror novel, *The Horned Ones*, is due out from Belfire in 2012. She's currently delving into steampunk, making progress on an urban paranormal series, and on a bloodthirsty Viking kick.

She can be found online at:
> http://christine-morgan.com and
> http://facebook.com/ChristineMorganAuthor
> http://www.smashwords.com/profile/view/christinemorgan

www.ingramcontent.com/pod-product-compliance
Lightning Source LLC
Chambersburg PA
CBHW070020120726
47909CB00003B/1009